Praise for the story of us

☆ "Caletti's latest Pacific Northwest romance is a stunner, with depth and ambiguity that respects and challenges the reader. . . . One of Caletti's best, this is a title to reread and savor."

—*Booklist*, starred review

"Thoughtful and poetic . . . quite moving . . . a rewarding story of a girl's struggle to live and love in a world of constant change."

—*Publishers Weekly*

"Caletti tosses readers into a story that is fast-paced from the get-go. Cricket is very appealing. Her concerns about life's changes feel real; her relationships with her mom and brother are loving and honest. . . . A thoughtful and enjoyable book."

—*School Library Journal*

Also by Deb Caletti

The Queen of Everything

Honey, Baby, Sweetheart

Wild Roses

The Nature of Jade

The Fortunes of Indigo Skye

The Secret Life of Prince Charming

The Six Rules of Maybe

Stay

the story of us

DEB CALETTI

Simon Pulse

NEW YORK LONDON TORONTO SYDNEY NEW DELHI

SIMON PULSE

An imprint of Simon & Schuster Children's Publishing Division

1230 Avenue of the Americas, New York, NY 10020

First Simon Pulse paperback edition March 2013

Copyright © 2012 by Deb Caletti

All rights reserved, including the right of reproduction in whole or in part in any form.

SIMON PULSE and colophon are registered trademarks of Simon & Schuster, Inc.

Also available in a Simon Pulse hardcover edition.

For information about special discounts for bulk purchases, please contact Simon & Schuster Special Sales at 1-866-506-1949 or business@simonandschuster.com.

The Simon & Schuster Speakers Bureau can bring authors to your live event. For more information or to book an event contact the Simon & Schuster Speakers Bureau at 1-866-248-3049 or visit our website at www.simonspeakers.com.

Designed by Karina Granda

The text of this book was set in Adobe Caslon.

Manufactured in the United States of America

2 4 6 8 10 9 7 5 3 1

The Library of Congress has cataloged the hardcover edition as follows:

Caletti, Deb.

The story of us / Deb Caletti.

p. cm.

Summary: After jilting two previous fiancés, Cricket's mother is finally marrying the right man, but as wedding attendees arrive for a week of festivities, complications arise for Cricket involving her own love life, her beloved dog Jupiter, and her mother's reluctance to marry.

ISBN 978-1-4424-2346-6 (hc)

[1. Weddings—Fiction. 2. Remarriage—Fiction. 3. Dogs—Fiction. 4. Love—Fiction.] I. Title.

PZ7.C127437Su 2012

[Fic]—dc23

2012002734

ISBN 978-1-4424-2347-3 (pbk)

ISBN 978-1-4424-2348-0 (eBook)

To my daughter, Sam, and to my son, Nick,
with endless gratitude for your love, generosity,
good hearts, and just plain great company throughout
our own life-adventure. I love you guys so much.

And in memory of Jupiter, our beloved pal.

ACKNOWLEDGMENTS

Thank you to my two dear, steadfast partners: my agent, Ben Camardi, and my editor, Jen Klonsky. I'm counting my blessings just thinking about you guys. Thank you as well to all of Harold Matson Company, most especially Jonathan Matson. They've been supporting me and my books for a good long time now, and I am grateful. Simon & Schuster, too, has always been my publishing family, and all of these folks work their tails off in the name of book love. Thank you for bringing your talent and energy to our books: Jon Anderson, Bethany Buck, Mara Anastas, Paul Crichton, Lucille Rettino, Michelle Fadlalla, Laura Antonacci, Venessa Williams, Jessica Handelman, Dayna Evans, Katherine Devendorf, Julie Doebler, Carolyn Swerdloff, Dawn Ryan, and the entire sales force, with an extra hug of appreciation to Leah Hays and Victor Iannone.

On every acknowledgment page so far I have thanked my family, and if you knew them, you'd understand why. So, to my funny, giving, and always-supportive clan, thank you for being there. And for letting me steal your stories. And for a million other things. Evie Caletti, Paul Caletti, Jan Caletti, Sue Rath, Mitch Rath, Tyler Rath, Hunter Rath, and the entire, extended clan—you are the best.

And to John Yurich, my husband, who, I swear to you, is sun and goodness every single day—thank you for the story of us. Steve and Audrey Yurich raised a fine man, and I am ever so thankful for that.

chapter
one

I found out something about myself as all those boxes piled up: I hated change. Hated it, and was bad at it. I suppose I got my feelings about change through some genetic line, because my mother, Daisy Shine, had left two husbands-to-be at the Sea-Tac Airport in order to avoid it. Imagine the spinning baggage carousel going round and round, the roaring liftoff of planes. The landings. The comings and goings. And some guy with his dreams in a suitcase, and my mother nowhere in sight.

Far as I knew, there were no airports on Bishop Rock, which was a lucky thing for Dan Jax. For all of us. I loved Dan, and this was one wedding that I . . . Well, I hoped she married the guy, I really did. The other ones were assholes, and she was right to leave them. But you got to wondering. You know, if she could do it. Maybe some people just had trouble with forever.

Outside, Ben beeped the horn of his truck. My brother was always on time. And, change? Whatever. He was fine with it. Jupiter—her, too. She'd see her leash and your car keys in hand, and her little butt would start swiveling in circles of joy. She didn't know if she was going to Gram's or to Taco Time, or if she'd land at the vet getting shots, but still there was the hopping around and the *yay, yay, yay* dog dance. She loved the ride anyway, no matter where she ended up.

But not me. What's to love about uncertainty? Nothing. It's scary—a big black hole of possible outcomes. Change requires bravery, and I don't even like to walk into creepy basements alone. Sometimes I've even wished there was a human pause button, where you could choose some point in your life where you could stay always. Here's the time I'd pick: my sophomore year of high school, when Janssen and I were crazy in love and my stupid brother still lived at home, and we'd all have those breakfasts on Sunday. Janssen would walk down the road and knock on the door, and Mom would be up early, and we'd have bacon and French toast, and Jupiter would sit by the table being her best self for a dropped crust. Sure, maybe things could get better than that, but things could get worse, too. I'd take it because I knew where I was then. I knew where home was. Things were sure.

Obviously I have my own troubles with forever, and what I did to Janssen proved that.

I heard my mother breathing hard, her suitcase bashing and banging into the walls as she brought it down the stairs. I could just see it—my mother, tripping and tumbling, broken leg, broken arm, no wedding. I listened for the crash. Janssen once said I was *always* listening for the crash.

"Be careful!" I called, but she was already safe. The bag thudded to the floor, and she sighed. She must not have heard me because a second later she was yelling up the stairwell.

"Cricket! Ready?"

Ready? I guess that was the question. Were *either* of us ready? For the last few weeks our house was a maze of cardboard cartons and mixed emotions. You could barely walk in there, and every stupid thing was a memory. Boxes were stacked up wherever you looked; stacked up and labeled in fat, black pen (or crayon or eyeliner or whatever was closest). KITCHEN. ATTIC. BEN'S STUFF. FRAGILE! Clumps of newspaper were strewn around, and so were the odd piles of things no one knew what to do with. A CD that belonged to one of Mom's friends and needed returning, manuals to varied appliances, mystery keys.

What do you keep hold of? What is meant to go? One thing was clear—I'd had a childhood marked by Disney movies. *Cricket, you want to keep your and Ben's old* Lion King *game? How about these Princess Jasmine slippers? Cricket, look what I found in the garage. Remember this?* Beauty and the Beast *magic-mirror-slash-squirt-gun Happy Meal toy. You loved this.*

When you were moving, every little object was a decision.

3

That seventh-grade report on the Industrial Revolution—keep or toss? Christmas sweater knit by Great-Grandma Shine? On one hand—obviously I'd never wear it. On the other—she was dead, and putting it in the Goodwill bag made me feel like she'd be looking down, getting her feelings hurt. I couldn't break hearts in heaven, I just couldn't. Here on earth was bad enough.

My mother was worse than I was about all that stuff. Of course, she was happy, too. Really happy. Whenever Dan Jax would call or come over with a homemade something (Dan Jax was a great cook), she was *giddy*. I'd never seen her like that. But then came the sorting and the packing of our old baby clothes, tiny shirts yellowed with spit-up, miniature sweatshirts with trains and bears that she was supposed to be getting rid of, but that she only solemnly folded back up and returned to the box. She did better with our baby toys, but she was still weepy and sullen with each teething ring and stack of plastic doughnuts (largest to smallest, in rainbow colors) that she decided to part with.

"You can be happy and sad, too," I had told her, which was a joke between all of us, because that was a line in *Monkey M. Monkey Goes on Vacation*, one of her most popular kiddie books. *"Monkey M. Monkey was happy to go, but sad, too. He knew he would miss Otto and Willa and the others."*

"Do you want this for college?" she had answered, holding up a plastic yellow toy telephone. When I was four, I'd swung that at Ben once and gave him a bloody nose.

"Ha," I'd said. "If I ever need to call home . . ."

Finally she found a solution—she kept a few of the toys and then spread the rest out on the floor and took photos of them. She even crouched for close-ups. My crib-side Busy Box got more poses than I did for my senior pictures. Hopefully she'd order wallet sizes so it could pass some to its friends, the shape sorter and the Fisher-Price garage.

Was that what I should have done with everything that was mine and Janssen's too? Taken pictures, so that I could leave it all behind, if leaving it behind was what I was going to do? Hundreds of pictures, it would be. Dried flowers and stacks of sweet notes and the scarf he tried to knit me once but which ended up about two inches long. Pictures of pictures, too, I'd have to take. That one of him on Moon Point, where his hair is catching the sun and it's a curly mess, and he's grinning like mad, his arms out, as if he's trying to hug the moment. He's the cutest, he is. God. That's a great picture of him.

Mom was down there with her bag, and in the driveway outside Ben leaned on the horn. He was ready a long time ago. He had this enviable ability not to linger over feelings. Get a move on, let's go. I loved that. Maybe it was a guy thing. I wished I had it.

"Bus is leaving!" Mom yelled.

"Coming!" I yelled back.

"Jupiter!" Mom called.

From the doorway of my room, I could see Jupiter get up from her pillow. She stretched one thin beagle leg out behind her and then the other—oh, the old girl had to get the kinks out lately, before she could get the whole body moving. She clomped down the stairs, front paws and then back end, in a little hop. She'd already had a big day. A bath that morning, where she'd sat, miserable, in the tub with flat, drenched hair, until she was finally out and free to roll around on the carpet, smelling like strawberry shampoo and wet dog. Now she was fluffy as she made her way down. Some dogs—they're just sweet; you can feel their kindness in their soulful eyes, and that was Jupiter. I snagged her bed and her favorite ragged blankie, too, and Rabbit, that flat stuffed-animal roadkill she loved.

"Don't forget these," I said to Mom.

"Thanks. Stinky dog bed . . . check. Deflated old Easter bunny."

"This was one of ours?" We used to get a stuffed rabbit every year in our baskets.

"Yours, I think. Didn't you give it to her?"

I felt a pang of something sad and bittersweet as I looked at that dreary, matted used-to-be fur. Even a stupid smelly dog toy had its stories. Stuffed toy glory days, long gone, but still, Jupiter kept on loving that flat old rabbit. It kind of choked me up. God! That, right there—*that* was evidence of the mess, the knotted, impossible, stuck mess I was in. Sentimental feelings about something that disgusting . . . I don't know. That thing *stank*.

We hauled the gathered luggage to the porch. Ben hopped

out of his truck, headed over to help with the bags. Jupiter had already tangled herself on her leash around the front hedge. Mom shut the front door and then locked it. The door seemed huge all of a sudden. Years and years huge. We'd moved to that house when I was ten years old and Ben was twelve, after our parents got divorced.

"Well," my mom said. Her voice was wavery.

"I know," I said.

"It's not the last time. We'll be back. We'll have to check to see if the movers left anything behind . . . ," Ben said.

"Still," I said. "Let's hurry."

"Good idea," Mom said. "I hate good-byes."

But we didn't exactly hurry. Even Ben didn't. He set down the bags he held. We all stood on that wide, wide lawn in front of our old Victorian house in Nine Mile Falls, my mother's arm around our waists, mine and Ben's. Behind that door—no, wait, on that lawn and up that drive *and* behind that door and everywhere else on that property—there was what felt like a lifetime full of memories. Middle school angst and Christmases, the huge blanket of maple leaves every fall, our creek out back, the sound of it—soft and trickling, or rushing with too much rain as the boulders tumbled underneath. My father with his car idling out front, picking us up for the weekend; Jon Jakes and his rotten kids who lived under our roof for two years; Ben and me—fighting and laughing and more laughing. Ben and me and Mom and Jupiter.

Home.

And Janssen, of course. My very own Janssen Tucker. Who right then did not belong either to my past or my future, which was all my stupid doing. I'd put him in some waiting place of in-between, and he'd just made it clear he wasn't going to stay there much longer. Could you blame him? Me and my Janssen, our clock was ticking. *You gotta figure this one out on your own,* he told me. *You gotta decide.* I loved, *love*, that boy. That's the first part of this story that you need to know.

"Smell," Mom said.

"What?" Ben said.

"Blackberries ripening. Along the creek. Smells like summer."

"It does," I said.

"Summer was great here," Ben said. "Except for cutting this goddamn lawn."

"How many lawn mowers did this lawn kill?" I asked. The lawn was huge. The first cut of the spring—the grass was ankle high and so thick and hard to mow that it took a couple of days to do the job. *I fought the lawn, and the . . . lawn won,* Mom would sing, after taking a long drink of water out of the hose.

"Three," Mom said.

"Two Weedwackers," Ben said.

"And what about winter," Mom said.

"Yeah," I said. The wind would blow so hard that tree branches would crack loose, and the power would go out for days.

"Here . . . ," she said. Her voice was soft.

8

"What?" I asked.

"So much of our story is here."

I didn't want to cry. I hated to cry. All three of us were the same that way. She kissed the tops of our heads. Ben cleared his throat.

"Look at that crazy dog," Mom said.

We did. She had about four inches of leash left and was now bound tight to the lilac bush. She had given up. Lain down right there and set her chin on her paws. She sighed through her nose.

It was great comic timing. That's part of what made them so great, right? The mess, the barking, the trouble—one reason you put up with it all was for the relief of ridiculous dogs during big moments. Ben laughed. "Oh, poor you," Mom said to her. "Poor defeated baby."

I went to untangle her leash. Ben picked the bags back up, and Mom put her house key in the pocket of her jeans. All this past and all this future and all this unknowing, and there was only one thing we could do about it. One choice, and so we did it. We got into Ben's truck to see what would happen next.

chapter two

Dear Janssen—

That sounds so formal. I was trying to think how
many letters we've written to each other over the
years. Not many, really. Notes, yeah. But we've
never actually been apart that long to write regular
e-mails, have we? Well, when you went to Spain
with your parents after graduation. That was only
two weeks, and I remember it seemed like *forever*.

Anyway, I got your letter. When you said that it
might be a good idea for me to write things down
to help me sort out my feelings . . . Maybe you

didn't mean I should write to *you*. But how can I *not* write to you? You've been in my life for *eight years*. Eight of eighteen. Let's subtract that first year of being a preverbal baby vegetable and say you've been there for almost half my life. You're like my *arm*, or something.

I can hear your voice now. Don't even say it. *I don't want to be your arm.* I know, I know. *Decide, Cricket,* you say. *Stay, or leave.* I hate when you say that. I hate when you say "leave." It hurts. You don't leave an arm, Janssen. You just don't. I love that arm.

The house is packed up. Of course you know that. You'll be driving by and seeing it empty except for all those boxes until we're out for good and strangers move in. I don't like the thought of other people in our house. That'll be really weird for you too, I guess. But worse, Janssen—the new place in Seattle feels so *new*. My room, the kitchen . . . Even though it's an old, old house, we're all new there. No memories in it yet to make it feel lived in.

If I go away . . . Janssen, where will I go to find home then? This is my really big worry.

I'll look around some stupid dorm room in an
unknown city, and there won't be the usual things
we do and there won't be my familiar people,
and that's like living without your favorite stuff
around. Like your favorite stuff was wiped
out in a tornado. I have no idea where home
will be.

I've decided to write down our story, okay? That
way we won't lose it. All this newness—I worry
it might barge in and shove our stories away until
they disappear. I'd hate that. What does my
mother always say? Each story, good and bad,
short or long—from that trip to the mall when you
saw Santa, to a long, bad illness—they are all a line
or a paragraph in our own life manuscript. Two
thirds of the way through, even, and it all won't
necessarily make sense, but at the end there'll be
a beautiful whole, where every sentence of every
chapter fits. I like that idea, but who knows. Some
books are lousy or boring or pointless, even if there
are those rare ones that leave you feeling forever
changed.

Anyway. I don't want to forget.

All right, then. Day one of us.

It was winter. You know how I love this story. I
still get happy when I tell it, even when I just tell it
to myself. Wait—does this hurt you? I don't want
to hurt you more than I have. I hope it doesn't.
Tell me if it does.

So. Mom and Ben and me and Jupiter had just
moved out to our Victorian house in the country
from the place we'd lived with Dad in the suburbs,
the Highlands. You know *that* neighborhood.
What did your mom used to call it? Stepford
Land? Looking down the street, it might have
been one of those mirrors with the images that
go on and on, because every house was the same
and the same, and the same with only a slight
variation. I could go to friend's house to play and
always know where the bathroom was. In that
place everything was clean and new and orderly,
and the closets were huge and each bathroom had
two sinks. You could feel the creeping, multiplying
bacteria of competition there, though. It was
baaad. It meant you had mean boys on bikes and
kiddie cell phones. Moms with manicures and
Dads with BMWs. Everyone had those TVs as
big as walls, and huge Costco cookies, and garages
full of toys with wheels. We didn't fit. We had
a wooden swing set with a tire swing. They had

"play structures" with slides and rubber chips if you fell. Other kids thought our house was quiet because the TV was never on. They thought it was weird. We had books. Art supplies. No video games (until Dad bribe-bought them for us later, after Mom and Dad got divorced).

I don't know what we were doing in that neighborhood. Dad liked it, I guess. He hung out with the neighbors and mowed when they mowed, all that crap, but Mom, she was never the Fourth of July block party type, right? Can you see it? Some cake that looked like the American flag done in strawberries and blueberries—ha. Ben and I, we liked the pool. We liked riding our bikes around the cul-de-sacs. But most of the time we just ran around trying to stay away from the Washelli twins, those little pervs.

No one knew the real reason we left. They thought it was all about Jon Jakes, when it had nothing to do with Jon Jakes. I remember those women standing in a circle by the school when my mother drove us there in the morning. They'd look her way (our way) and snip, snip, snip, gossip, gossip. I felt ashamed, but mad, too. Even in Mrs. Ferber's fifth-grade class, the kids knew my parents were

getting a DIVORCE. Mrs. Ferber was extra
nice to me, like I had a terminal illness. Like my
childhood had a terminal illness. And then, shit.
Remember the Bermuda Honda? Named after the
Bermuda Triangle because bad, mysterious things
always happened in it? Well, the muffler fell out
of it right in front of those same women that time.
Right in the school parking lot. You should have
heard the noise. I was *humiliated*. I wasn't too
young to feel relief, you know, when we moved.
We packed up our secrets and got out of there, is
what it felt like.

Now, five miles out, and there we were in another
world. Well, *you* know. You lived there your whole
life. Acres between the houses, when before we
could always hear Mrs. Washelli yelling at Nathan
and Malcolm through our bedroom windows.
Here we were, down a dirt road speckled with
splashy, rain-filled potholes, out in the middle
of nowhere, with neighbors that kept *goats, and
horses, too. Goats!* Not an American Girl doll in
sight! Minivans—gone! Just off that dirt road
was our long gravel driveway, lined with five fruit
trees (apple, peach, pear, plum, and cherry), and
that electric gate swinging across the entrance.
THE MIGHTY MULE, a sticker on it read, which

we thought was hilarious. What was that gate supposed to keep out, that's what I wanted to know. We'd been told that no one should bother having cats there, because of the occasional mountain lion. Jesus! We didn't have *those* in the suburbs.

Mom kept saying *It's an adventure!* but she didn't always seem so sure. Not when she was driving that U-Haul over there, with bad brakes and our whole life sliding around in the back. Not when the kitchen sink pipe broke on our first night, or when the coyotes began to howl and you realized how dark it got out there. Not when our new fridge hadn't come from Home Depot yet and we had to keep our milk out in the creek so it would stay cold. Not when she was paying bills, for sure. Or when Dad would come pick us up, his face tight and his hand gripping those stupid bags we had to pack every other weekend, to go to that apartment of his with all our familiar furniture. Our old armoire, our dining room set—they all stood around in there looking kind of awkward, as if they were at the wrong party.

Ben and me, we were *definitely* not sure it was "an adventure." Can I say again how dark it got

out there? Dark-dark. The suburbs were maybe
milk-chocolate dark. But this was definitely
semisweet dark. With the sound of restless wild
animals coming down from Moon Point to find
prey . . . *Creepy!* One night I heard a rabbit scream
as a hawk found its dinner. I was so scared, I went
to get Jupiter so I wouldn't be alone, but Mom
had gotten her first. We stayed up awhile together
until the shivers wore off, as Ben snored away in
his room. He could sleep through anything.

Were we more safe or more vulnerable now? My
father could drive down that road with rage and
revenge on his mind, and who would hear?

But finally maybe it *was* an adventure when that
snow fell, and that huge lawn was this pure,
untouched blanket of possibilities. Our own
footprints on it, no one else's. We all bundled up
and ran outside. Those snowy mornings—so many
clothes and the only thing sticking out was your
face, and you felt the sting of cold on it. You don't
even need all those layers, but that's part of the
ritual—scarves and mittens and boots and a hat
that you eventually toss off because it's too hot and
scratchy. Mom flung open the front door, and we
all ran out, even Jupiter, a puppy then, snow up

to her tummy. We rolled in it, and threw snow at each other, and Ben started rolling up a snowball.

"Remember that time," Mom said. Her cheeks were red.

"Yeah," Ben said.

I knew too. We told the story every time it snowed. It happened at our old house. We were going to walk a snowball all the way home from the school yard, but it had gotten so big, we had to abandon it in the middle of the street.

"Look," Ben said.

And it was you. You, a boy, Ben's age. On a horse. You were, what, twelve? But, goddamn, you looked . . . grand. It's a strange word to use for a boy, but it was true. We'd seen that horse. We'd seen two horses, actually. In the pasture across the road from us. We'd given them names—Chocolate and Vanilla. But we'd never seen a boy. And now here he was, riding Vanilla down our snow-covered road. Talk about a princely image. White steed, ha. Head of messy brown hair (I've always loved your hair). One hand holding those reins. We were too far away to see your sweet eyes, but you had them, even then.

Jupiter started to howl, remember? She didn't just *bark*, she *ow-ooo'd!* with her head up, same as a cartoon dog howling at a cartoon moon. You—we didn't know it was you yet, but it was—smiled. You smiled, and I think you waved or something. Ben looked so glad to see a boy his age out there, and when you rode on, I think he was crushed. We kept on playing. Tried to get snow down Mom's back. She got tired. Unwrapped her scarf. Sat down on the now slushy porch in her once-a-year snow pants.

"I'm out," she said.

But right then, at the top of the hill across the road, here you came. With three big pieces of cardboard. In our old neighborhood they'd have had fancy snow saucers bought at Costco, but you could give a shit about fancy. You knew what worked.

"Hey," you yelled, and it began.

If my father drove down that road with rage and revenge on his mind, who would hear? I didn't know it then, but you would. So would your father,

Gene Tucker, with his huge shoulders and sense of right and wrong, and your mother, Danie Tucker, with her warmth and kindness and no-nonsense air. But mostly you, who had all their best traits combined. You would hear fathers or coyotes or wild animals. You would know what to do.

I liked your list, Janssen. You wrote it to cheer me up, and it did. Dogs—yeah, we love those stupid creatures (especially Jupiter), don't we? So, thank you. Please be patient with me as I figure myself out. (See how I snuck that in?) I'm adding to your list, because I'm guessing you might need some cheering up too.

Things to Love About Dogs (Part 2):

6. Their furry chins
7. Eyes that seem to know important things
8. The way they keep your secrets
9. Velvet heads
10. The way they can always find their way back home

Love always,

Cricket

chapter
three

Well, if there was actually going to be a wedding, Bluff House on Bishop Rock was a beautiful place for one. Set up on the edge of the cliff, the house was all white, with three levels of wraparound decks, and a rambling boardwalk leading to the beach. It had a green lawn with white Adirondack chairs, and it all could be something from a movie, except that it was a little beat up by wind and salt air. Dan Jax was old friends with the owners, Ted and Rebecca Rose. We stepped inside the entryway, Ben holding Jupiter under his arm. Through the doorway I could see a sliver of the living room beyond—a huge fireplace, two-story windows, a deck overlooking the sea.

"Hello?" Mom called.

"Here, I'm here!" a woman shouted, and then Rebecca Rose appeared, hurrying down the curved stairwell, nearly tripping on a cat, who dashed out of her way. Rebecca Rose was in her early fifties, I'd guess, with a long gray braid, aging-hippie patchwork skirts, and sandaled feet. A whiff of pot smoke made it down the stairs just before she did.

Ben sniffed dramatically beside me. Caught my eye.

"I know," I said.

"Guys . . . ," Mom whispered. "Stop." Ha, she smelled it too. Jupiter was squirming her fat little sausage self under Ben's arm. She would have loved to go after that cat, who was now weaving around Rebecca Rose's ankles.

"Welcome, welcome. Oh, it's a celebration. Come in, fine people." Rebecca Rose leaned in to hug us. Pot, all right. Her hair reeked of it. Believe me, I knew the smell. I sat next to Jesse Shilo in practically every class in the ninth grade. "You must be Daisy. I hope you're Daisy, or else I'm hugging strangers! Let's see." She squinched her eyes at us. "Dan and . . . insect name. Beetle?" Great, Ben would love that.

"This is *Ben*. And *Cricket*. Catherine, but we call her—"

"You look just alike," she said. "All of you." Maybe it was a pot thing. Ben and Mom were the ones that looked alike, with their gold hair and blue eyes. People always said I looked more like my father—brown hair, brown eyes. "Especially when you smile." She waggled her finger at me.

"*She* probably looks like us too," Mom joked, nodding toward Jupiter. Jupiter looked like herself. She was mostly black with bits of white—that small spot on her back, her tummy, the tip of her tail. There was a little brown thrown in too, around the edges of her ears. That cat was making her crazy.

"Oh, exactly. Exactly. One of the family," Rebecca Rose said. "Anyone hungry?"

Ben snickered.

Jupiter twisted herself free. There was a midair moment before she landed on the floor. Ben kept hold of her leash, but she was pulling and straining, making that yelp-howl of panic-excitement. The cat dashed around the corner.

"Jupiter!" Mom lunged for the dog, and her purse slid off her shoulder. Stuff fell out—a brush, a tampon. She looked a little panicked herself. "Maybe we should just—"

Rebecca Rose clapped her hands. "Your rooms! I'll take you. You can get settled in. Explore, before your lover man gets here? I remember that Ben. Hands like a beefsteak. Mmm."

"*Dan*," my mother corrected.

Rebecca patted her hips. "Keys. Let me find some."

She hustled out, skirts swirling again around wide hips. "*The High Innkeeper*, scene one," Ben said as I handed Mom her purse. "How'd you say you knew her again?"

"Dan knew them in college or something." Jupiter was coughing now, like she did when she strained at the leash too hard—an alarming hack/honk that involved a frightening display of lurching. "Jesus," Mom said.

Rebecca Rose reappeared. She didn't even seem to notice the noise. I picked Jupiter up, and tried to soothe her. "You're okay," I whispered.

"It feels insane, bringing the dogs on top of all this." Mom said. "But Jupiter's never stayed in a kennel . . . and Dan thought, you know, these two have got to finally *meet*, so let's just do it. Get the whole family together. I keep thinking, *chaos . . .*"

"Oh no, no, no." Rebecca waved away the problem. "The more the merrier." She had already moved toward the stairs, and we followed her up dutifully, carrying bags and one now quiet dog who was enjoying the ride. I felt like an overloaded duckling, following the stoned and muddled mama duck, who abruptly stopped in the hall. She flung open three doors. "King bed here," she said to Mom. "Shared bathroom, right? Ted told you? Down the way. You might see our son, Ash, around."

"Great," Mom said.

"He's in and out. I'll let you . . ." She swirled her hands around.

"Thank you so much," Mom said.

"You'll all be at dinner tonight? We're totally organic."

"I bet," Ben whispered to me. I snickered now.

"Wonderful," Mom said. She shot us a look. "Dan will be here by then. He's just picking up his girls at the airport. Everyone else will be straggling in . . ."

"Beautiful!" Rebecca Rose said. She grasped Mom and kissed her cheek. It was a wet one too. I could see the little bit of shine her lips had left. Rebecca Rose hurried back down the stairwell. Mom wiped her cheek with the back of her hand. We heard Rebecca stumble and then her voice. "Shit!" The cat yowled.

Mom sighed. I set Jupiter down. I could feel it, the familiar crawl of things going sideways. The sense that the nice little path you'd been walking on was suddenly getting steep and twisty. I hoped Mom wasn't feeling it too. I looked over at her. Her face seemed frozen. She had her purse and her travel bag draped over her arm, but she wasn't moving either forward or backward.

"This . . . ," she said.

"Don't say it," I said.

"Is a bad sign."

Ben had already disappeared into his room. He was walking around in there. "High innkeeper, okay," he said. "But this room is amazing."

"See?" I said.

"All right," Mom said.

"It'll be fine." I imagined a forgotten joint catching some couch cushion on fire. Smoke pouring from windows, animals and people running everywhere. No wedding, and only the cat manages to escape unharmed.

"It will."

And then we both looked down at the same time. Jupiter was squatting on her shaky little back legs right there in the hall. A puddle was spreading out from under her.

"Oh no," I said.

"We weren't paying attention," Mom said to her. "It was our fault."

Mom was right. You could tell Jupiter couldn't help it. She looked embarrassed. She never peed inside.

"Shared bathroom, down the hall. I'll get the paper towels," I said.

When I returned, Ben was back out again. "It's okay, Jupe." He scruffed her little black head. "Cricket used to puke after long car rides."

"Oh, God, you did," Mom said. She took the paper towels from me, started cleaning up.

"You guys obviously have memory failure," I said.

"Crystal clear," Mom said. "Kinda hard to forget."

"So? *You* used to suck on rocks," I said to Ben.

Mom chuckled. "That *was* kind of strange."

"You called us by the dog's name," Ben said to Mom.

"Still do," I said.

"Old age," she said.

Ben tossed our bags into our rooms.

"Rock sucking in early childhood leads to success in later life, huh, Beetle? *I* got the best room."

"Shut up, you idiot," I said.

He was right, I saw, but I didn't mind. Things could get off track, but there we still were, the three and a half of us. We'd been through a lot. And we'd always been okay so far.

Rebecca Rose might not have been able to deal directly with life without a protective barrier of marijuana haze, but the rooms of her inn were beautiful. Ben's was bigger, sure, but mine had a sloped ceiling and a side dormer window that made it feel like a snug attic space. There were white plank floors, soft throw

rugs, linen drapes blowing gently from the ocean breeze coming in. And the view—the windows opened out to the wide,
wide sea. I could have stayed in that room for a long while.

Score a point for Dan Jax. Score *another* point for Dan Jax.
He'd already made plenty of points with us, because he was a
good guy. Maybe even a great guy. Probably Mom's first one.
I love my father, but it's a complicated love. He can be great,
really great, and then he's suddenly a storm slowly building,
a storm that finally tosses lawn furniture and garbage cans,
knocks trees down onto roofs. Dan was a regular, calm sky.
You kept looking up there, and, yeah, it was still blue and still
blue. I said a silent prayer to whoever was in charge of these
things, love things, that nothing bad would happen and that
my mother would actually marry Dan Jax. There was no reason, really, that she wouldn't, right? I mean, the other guys
were assholes. Still, past assholes could make a person feel
skittish. You had to be careful. It could all suddenly be different than you thought it was. A big possible mistake could be
hidden anywhere, ready to blow up everything, same as stepping on a land mine.

I was the dog-loving girl, so I had Jupiter and her bowls
and stuff in my room, which I didn't mind, even though her
bed smelled and she snored like an old man. She was lying on
her bed right then, her small chin on Rabbit. I lay on my bed
for a while too, and then I got up. Jupiter only lifted her head,
I noticed. Used to be, you'd make a move and so would she. If
you went downstairs, she went too. If you went outside, she'd

be right behind you. She followed you as dutifully as a Secret Service agent. But lately she didn't mind just waiting until you got back.

"Anyone want to go to the beach?" I called down the hall. I knocked on the bedroom doors on either side of me.

"Shut up. Jesus," Ben said. His voice was groggy, muffled by a pillow. Taking a nap already, I guess, and he hated to be woken up.

Mom poked her head out. "Wanna be here when Dan and his daughters arrive."

"Okay. Jupiter? You and me. Want to go for a walk?" She thumped her tail on her pillow. I grabbed her leash, and she rose, stretched, wagged her tail.

"They should be here soon," Mom said. "Did I tell you Grandpa was coming tonight? He's bringing a friend." I raised my eyebrows. "No, a friend-friend. Golfing guy or something. Gram's coming too, later, with Aunt Bailey. I told them they'd better behave."

"Good," I said.

"When those two get together . . ."

"Watch out," I said. Maybe I shouldn't have opened my stupid mouth, but I couldn't help it. "Hey, Mom?"

"Yeah?"

"You can't like them better than us," I said. She knew who I meant. I was only half joking.

"Impossible," she said.

• • •

Something tomato-saucey was cooking downstairs, but I didn't see Rebecca Rose or anyone else. Jupiter wasn't great on her leash, and she was twisting and pulling toward the dining room, smelling that cat, probably. In one of my dog books, I once read that a beagle is something like one hundred million times better at smelling than we are. A *hundred million* times. They can track human feet even when the trail is four days old and the person was wearing *shoes*. They can smell forty feet *below ground*. Jupiter's whole world was smell. A hundred million smells of information. She didn't just smell cat. She smelled **CAT**. She could probably smell what that cat was *thinking*.

We headed down the boardwalk to the beach. The board-walk was steeply sloped and looked like it could be rickety (image: me breaking my neck; no wedding), so I held the railing with one hand until I realized it was pretty sturdy. The sun was out, but it was windy down there, and the beach grass was whipping around. I was really giving Jupiter a treat, because before us was an endless ocean of smell—seaweed and salt air, deep water and dead things on the beach. Her nose was down to the ground. She was pulling to the right. There was probably a decaying beached sea lion two towns over. I took my shoes off, let her lead. We picked our way over the driftwood and the layer of creepy stuff and broken shells to the hard sand where it was easy to walk. Oh, that beach felt great, peaceful, and I hadn't felt peaceful in months. We walked a long ways—when I looked back, the Bluff House was tiny.

"Look how far we've gone," I said to Jupiter.

I suppose even if you were computer geeks like Gavin and Oscar, who were not prone to dreaming or philosophizing (unless it was about the release date of some video game, Horizon Gate Six, say), a walk on the beach would still get you wondering about the direction of your life, your purpose, the big questions. Beaches, music, and car rides—they could all bring on a sudden bout of deep, dreamy thoughts. See, I was seeing the beach and the houses, and I was thinking about how to describe it all to Janssen. I was talking to him in my head. I realized it, and then my heart clutched up. My chest had this aching pain, thinking what it might mean not to talk to him anymore. Because that's what breaking up meant.

The realization hit me with all its power and simplicity. You couldn't break up and still stay together, could you? You couldn't break up and still call each other every night and tell each other how the day went. He would go on with his own life, and I wouldn't even know what *happened*. How could you not know the way the story would end up, when it was a story you'd been following for so many years? I wouldn't know if Janssen was happy, or miserable, or if he needed me. Or if he still loved Taco Time (beef soft taco meal, number three, with a root beer). I wouldn't know about his friends, or how he managed that economics class he was dreading next quarter. His mom had had breast cancer last year. It could return. She could *die*, and I wouldn't even know.

What was I doing? Crashing and burning my own life. I

wasn't leaving Janssen at the Sea-Tac Airport, but what was the difference?

If I left Janssen, I wouldn't know what was going on with him, but someone else *would* know. That was the other piece, wasn't it? Maybe he'd do the *Godfather* film fest again with that person. Maybe he'd teach her how to swim the butterfly too. It could be one of those ideas you play with in your head, to see how it feels. You'd imagine his hands on her under the water. . . . You could pretend that you, too, were alone and free. But you could take it too far, let it scroll out a day or a week past someone's tolerance and you'd mess it up forever. Especially when your mother was maybe finally getting married, and you were moving, and home as you knew it would be gone. It was an avalanche of change, so much snow barreling down right at you that parts of you were saying, *Screw it. Go ahead and bury me.*

Maybe I'd messed it up forever already, after what I'd done. Maybe it was already too late.

Why would you leave someone you love? Natalie had said to me. Even *she* was getting frustrated. *What is wrong with you? You usually have it so together.* I counted on her to understand me, but she couldn't understand this. She poked me with the straw from her drink. *You're going to lose Janssen, and it's going to be your own stupid fault.*

And I would say to her, *How do I know what love really is?* And she would say back, *You're nuts, you know that? It's been right there in front of you all these years.*

Oscar and Gavin were getting tired of my questions too. I could tell. They'd change the subject. *You'll figure it out, Crick. Hey, did I tell you about this clock I got? All the numbers are replaced with equivalent equations.* . . . Other people's confusion could get old. I guess it was a little like the time Janssen broke his leg skiing. You're caring and giving, but sometimes you just want the person to *walk* already.

Jupiter and I were tromping along, when I guess she just had enough. At least, she plopped right down and decided to go no farther.

"Okay," I said. "Can we at least sit by those rocks?"

Nothing doing. You could tell when she had her mind made up.

"Well, fine, then." I picked her up, carried her over, and sat down on the sand with my back against a large flat boulder. Jupiter sat next to me. She liked to sit real close. I put my arm around her.

"Good dog," I said. "How'd you get to be so sweet, huh?"

She looked straight out to the ocean. She looked like she was thinking important things. The direction of her life, maybe.

"When you're old, you know things," I said to her. But she didn't turn to look at me. She kept looking ahead, sitting still with her own weighty thoughts, or else keeping watch for a seagull or a far-off boat or an unfamiliar one of her kind that might wish to do me harm.

• • •

The Bluff House got larger and larger again as we walked back, and when we were almost there, I could see people on the grass on the bluff, a bunch of people, and a dog running around. Cruiser, Dan Jax's dog. I'd played with him a few times when we'd gone to Dan's for dinner, but so far he and Jupiter had only watched each other through car windows. The idea of getting them together—it scared me. Cruiser was young and physical, with boisterous big-dog energy. He was strong. Three times Jupiter's size, easy, with a thick neck and meaty haunches. His fur was a golden tan, with a splotch of white on his chest in the exact shape of the shield on Superman's suit.

Cruiser was a little out of control. He sort of reminded me of Kenny Yakimoro, our old next-door neighbor. Ben and I used to spy on him through our fence because he was always doing thrilling things we'd never be allowed to do. Shooting cap guns or playing war with Nathan Washelli, using real-looking plastic rifles. Kenny wasn't a bad kid, but he was always in trouble for running in the halls, or for getting carried away and knocking someone's lunch tray over. The kind of guy you wanted on your kickball team because he gave it everything he had. That was Cruiser.

This—them, us, the families coming in over the week before the wedding—it was all Dan Jax's idea. I guess I could see his thinking: If you want to introduce two dogs who are going to live together, you bring them to neutral territory first. You have them meet. You let them participate in mutual activities—a walk, say. A Frisbee toss. You let them hash it out, and before you know it, they've figured out how to deal with each other.

Maybe I should just say right here that Jupiter wouldn't fetch a Frisbee to save her life.

Maybe I should also say that Cruiser wouldn't be my choice for Jupiter if I was playing dog matchmaker. I'd choose another old girl that might want to lie in a shady spot when it got warm. Not a big guy who'd tear up that lawn with his strong black toenails, sending bits of grass and dirt flying as he covered the places where he'd lifted his leg to mark his territory.

I could see two girls up on that grass too. We'd never met them before either. Dan Jax's daughters, Hailey and Amy, eighteen and fifteen, lived in Vancouver, Canada. When our parents married each other (*if* our parents married each other), only I would be moving into the new house in Seattle. Ben would be away at school, and I'd be home until college started in the fall, or maybe later, depending on where I finally decided to go. Up in Vancouver, Amy and Hailey would be in the relationship sphere of distant cousins, I thought. Children of your parents' friends, maybe. Those people you mostly just heard about, listening with one ear until some jealousy-inducing words flew past. *Harvard, fabulous job, moving into your old room.*

I could feel, right there, my attitude edge into something craggy and unwelcoming. I'd had bad experiences with steps. The word "step"—it's perfect, isn't it, for those people linked to us through remarriage? You step toward, you step away, but if you are "stepping," you have never, will never, arrive. Thanks to Jon Jakes's kids, Olivia and Scotty, who lived with us part-time at our old house, I didn't believe families were meant to blend. Blend—it makes you think of smoothness and order, when it's all more like that closet in Olivia's room, with all the shit stuffed in and falling out. Blending was a great idea, yeah, but Olivia and Scotty didn't care about school and ate junk food for breakfast, and on the weekends they'd stay in their pajamas in front of the TV until the day got dark again. We *did* care about school; we ate Cheerios, not Skittles, in the morning; and on the weekends we'd go to a baseball game of Ben's and come home only to find them in the same place as when we'd left. You can use whatever words you want, but I knew they weren't my brother and sister. I felt more connection to my cousins Zach and Kristina on my Dad's side. We'd only met them once, but they had our same noses. You know your people. You recognize your tribe, same as a dog knows a dog is different than a cat.

Anyway, here's what happened: Jon Jakes's kids kept try-ing to *Parent Trap* their mom and dad back together, until my mother finally lost patience. She handed back her engagement ring at the Sea-Tac Airport, just before a romantic pre-wedding trip for two to Cabo San Lucas. After the Jakes trio was finally gone, Gram brought over these small bound packages of sage we were supposed to burn to get rid of the bad feelings in our house. She went around our rooms waving the smoking bundle in the air as Ben and I cracked jokes. *Put some juju smoke in the laundry hamper, Gram. Ah-ha-ha-ha!* We didn't need the sage, though. A week after they'd left, my mother was already back to singing loudly in the kitchen as she made her morning coffee, with Jupiter dancing happily around her feet. *Good morning, sunshines! You brighten my daaaay!* The bad feelings had taken their Skittles and gone home.

Amy and Hailey, though. They were Dan Jax's daughters, and it was a new start for Mom, for all of us, or so went the talk I gave myself as I made my way up the boardwalk. My mother deserved my good attitude, and so did Dan Jax, and Amy and Hailey were probably great people who were nothing like Olivia and Scotty. Maybe I would even like them. They were Dan's kids, so why not? I had a brief fantasy—Amy and Hailey and Natalie and me, having coffee someplace in Seattle, going to the film festival. Amy making us laugh so hard. Hailey staying over in my dorm room. The thing was—it could be great. A big family. It was a possibility. Even if my experience in these things told me that their alien planet was likely on a collision course with our alien planet.

"Well, Jupe, here we go." She definitely noticed that dog up there. "Let's do it, huh?"

I could see them up on the bluff standing on the grass too, my mother with her wavy gold hair falling below her shoulders, in her pastel sundress and bare feet, and Dan Jax, with his black hair combed back into a pony tail, wearing his jeans and denim shirt, and yeah, with those strong hands that came from his work as a contractor. The two of them looked like salt and pepper, day and night, but they were so similar, it could get annoying. Still, I could see it even from there. She was being herself, something she never was with Jon Jakes, or Vic Dennis, or even my father. I wondered if that's what love looked like. Is that what I felt with Janssen, those summer days when we lay on a blanket on the grass, just reading, toes entangled with toes? Or was being with Janssen something else? Like that time we'd driven out to see the hot-air balloons in Woodinville, maybe. When we'd stood on the ground and held hands and we watched one take off, lifting to join all the others up above. I was glad I wasn't on that crazy thing. But I thought something else then too. What if you never felt what it was like to rise and rise into the sky?

Mom saw me and waved. Even from there, I could see how bright her smile was.

"My mother thinks two dogs is too many," Amy said. Amy had long, shiny black hair parted in the middle, and so did her sister. They were both thin, with hungry hip bones jutting from tight clothes. Amy smiled, sugar-cereal sweet. She wore a pink T-shirt, and I had no reason to think it, but I did—pink could be cruel too. Hailey looked off into the distance as if even the ocean itself was irritating. One corner of her mouth curled up, as if she'd just stepped in something disgusting.

I was smiling, but inside my stupid head a siren started to blare, a mental fire truck rounding an internal corner. You were supposed to pull over when you heard that. I wondered if Mom heard it too. I looked her way, but she was just laughing at something Dan said.

"He's soooo cute," Amy said. She was stroking Jupiter's black head, but she was looking at Ben, whose hair was shoved up in the back from his nap. He'd straggled down to join us outside, and he'd greeted everyone and joked around, still wearing a pillow wrinkle on his face.

"She," I said.

"He's got the cutest ears," Amy said.

"It's *free*-zing out here," Hailey said.

"Well, they're doing okay so far," Dan Jax said, gazing at the dogs. Cruiser was sniffing Jupiter's butt, and she was handling it with a great deal of dignity.

"She's not really used to other dogs," Mom said. She was hovering a little, standing close enough to rescue Jupiter if she needed it. Cruiser was only three years old, and Jupiter was ready for retirement. He looked like he could snap her up in one rambunctious bite. Now he wanted to play. He got down on his front paws, barked loudly. But she was playing it cool. Or else, that beach walk tired her out.

"You guys want to walk them around a little together?" Dan said.

Ben took the leashes from Dan. "If they kill each other, it's not my fault," he said.

"They'll do fine," Dan said. He kissed the back of Mom's neck. He was likely right—Cruiser was now busy investigating an old cigarette butt, and Jupiter didn't look capable of killing anyone, with her graying muzzle and that friendly white spot on her back.

"Come on," Ben said to me.

We headed away from the group. The dogs ignored each other, doing their own thing at the end of their own leashes. I wouldn't exactly call it bonding. Jupiter sat down, watched that big dog out of the corner of her eye, just in case. Cruiser kept his distance, but lifted his leg on every blade of grass. We were on the far slope of the lawn. The view up there was great. "It's beautiful here," I said. "Oh, wow. Hey, look—that house has a helicopter on the roof."

Ben saw it too. "Cool," he said.

"Well? What do you think?"

"I wouldn't want a helicopter pad on my roof."

I socked him. He knew what I meant. "High mainte-nance," Ben said.

"We've got to give them a chance."

"Yeah, we do. We *will*. Still, it is what it is," he said. And it was true. You knew more often than you didn't right away about people. One butt sniff, like Cruiser and Jupiter, and you understood pretty much what you needed to. Sometimes dogs didn't even need a butt sniff to form an opinion. A certain guy could walk down our road, and Jupiter would bark her head off. Not everyone got that reaction. She just distrusted certain people for her own reasons, same as us.

"We can't expect to love some strangers we're thrown

together with," I said. "Gavin and Oscar irritate the hell out of me, and I actually *chose* them."

"I know. What can you expect? It's like going into Starbucks and coming out with two new relatives."

"Dan, though," I said.

"Good guy." There was efficiency to male language. Those two words were what guys said about other guys that they really respected. Guys they could count on, that were solid, whose word you trusted, who your mother better marry or you'd really question her sanity. The language for the other kind of men—even more efficient. Cut down to a single word they deserved. Asshole.

"Janssen?"

Ben looked at me like *my* sanity was in question. "Janssen *is* family."

chapter four

Gram and Aunt Bailey had arrived, and so there were ten of us having dinner in the dining room of Bluff House. Cruiser lay under the table near Dan, and Jupiter sat by my mother's chair, staring at her with love eyes. Ted Rose had come home too. He was a large man, with gray curly hair and a gray beard, and with stories from their college days that were making Dan Jax slide his finger across his throat in a *Cut!* motion.

"Tell us the sordid details," Gram said. She was twirling spaghetti around her fork. Some exuberant sauce had already speckled her blouse.

"We love sordid," Aunt Bailey said. She was Gram's younger sister. The two of them and a twenty-dollar bill could cause enough trouble to shut down a Target. They got kicked out of one once, trying on bathing suits.

"Nothing I'm proud of now," Dan Jax said.

"Those twins . . ." Ted Rose chuckled.

"Daddy!" Hailey gasped.

"I thought you met Mom when you were eighteen," Amy said.

"Who were those twins *we* knew?" Aunt Bailey elbowed Gram.

"Oh, baby," Gram said. "Jerry was one."

Aunt Bailey chuckled. "I remember Jerry. He had that belt buckle. . . ."

"Those twins were hot, hot, hot!" Ted Rose sang, snapping his fingers, and Rebecca swatted him with a pot holder. I liked Ted Rose. He spoke with a large, warm voice, the way a bear would talk, if bears could talk. I noticed the friendly wrinkles around Rebecca's eyes now too. Or maybe it was just that candlelight softened things.

"There's one I haven't heard," Mom said. She was smiling.

Hailey sat on the other side of her father. She put her hand over Dan's. "There's probably a lot you don't know about Daddy. You can ask us if you want to know."

Gram kicked me under the table. Ben nudged my side. Mom's smile got stuck there in position, same as the Bermuda Honda in second gear. I could tell what she was thinking, and I knew Ben could too, and he could tell what I was thinking, and Gram could tell what we all were thinking. All our thoughts were having their own conversation.

"Thank you," my mother said through her frozen smile. "I

may have to take you up on that." She slipped Jupiter a bit of carrot under the table, and Jupiter rolled it around her mouth and then spit it out on the rug. Apparently it wasn't to her liking.

"So tell us. How'd you two meet?" Ted Rose asked.

Dan and Mom laughed. Looked at each other. "A horse . . . ," Mom said.

"Cricket's boyfriend, Janssen . . . ," Dan said.

"You have a boyfriend?" Hailey asked. I nodded, and she raised her eyebrows in interest, but Mom and Dan Jax were on a roll. They loved their story of how they met.

"They live up the road," Mom said.

"They needed new stables. A *pregnant* horse."

"It was a big, complicated job. He had to keep coming back."

"Not as complicated as I made it once I saw her out there mowing this huge lawn."

"Ben usually cut it, but he was away at school."

"Every time I passed, another piece of it was finished, like a damn quilt."

They were laughing. Everyone was, because they looked so happy, and because candles were flickering in the large glass windows that faced out to the sea, and because there was good food and garlic bread and the sweet, warm smells of melting wax, and probably a wedding.

"All I want to know—" Rebecca Rose said.

"Is what happened to the horse!" Ted Rose shouted and

everyone laughed more as Rebecca Rose refilled the wine-glasses.

"We love that horse!" Gram said. "We should send that goddamn horse a present." Gram felt the same as I did. She loved Dan. She wanted this to go right.

"Never look a gift horse in the mouth," Dan said.

"Ha," Mom said, and ruffled his hair.

Amy pushed back her chair. She got up, whispered something to Dan. Her chin was down, eyes up. His eyebrows lowered in concern. He pushed back his own chair. Put his hand on Amy's cheek.

"You're not warm," he said.

"Da-deee," she whined.

"Not feeling well," Dan told the group, and there were mumbles of concern.

"Attention deficit?" Gram whispered to me. I gave her leg a pinch under the table.

"We're just going to go upstairs," Dan said. His eyes met Mom's. Now *they* both had a silent conversation that I'm sure we all heard. Her eyes said, *What's this?* His seemed to say, *I know, but what am I supposed to do?* He took Amy's arm. Ben looked at me, rolled his eyes.

Hailey got up next. "I'd better go too."

One thing about Cruiser—if something was happening, he wanted to be a part of it. Sometimes maybe his manners weren't so great, but his enthusiasm was 100 percent. He didn't want to be a bad dog; he was just wholehearted. People were getting up; he got up. People were moving; he was moving. He raced over to Gram, put his huge paws on her lap, knocking her knife off the table.

"Whoa. Big boy," she said. His head was suddenly even with hers. For a second they looked like odd dinner companions.

"Cruiser, down!" Dan Jax said.

But Cruiser was sniffing Gram's neck, and his tail was thwacking Aunt Bailey's chair. "He likes my Jean Naté," Gram said as she tried to put her hand to his chest and shove. Aunt Bailey grabbed his collar and yanked, and now Jupiter was up and barking and heading his way. Cruiser was back on four legs, but Jupiter's hair had risen up along her back in an alarming ridge, like some angry dog Mohawk. She growled. Then she snapped at Cruiser and nipped him sharply on his huge butt.

Cruiser yelped, and so did Mom. "Oh, my God!"

"Jupiter!" I said. I'd *never* seen her do anything like that before. I told you, Jupiter was sweet down to her bones. But she seemed to mean business now, boy. Cruiser was backing off. He was actually, literally, *walking backward* from the crazy old lady who just bit him.

"Poor thing!" Amy said. "Dad, did you see that? Cruiser, come here, baby."

"I'm so sorry," Mom said. "She's *never . . .*" She was up now. She was dragging Jupiter over to her side of the table. Jupiter's toenails were sliding on the floor, but her expression was calm. *We took care of that nonsense,* she seemed to say.

"It's okay. They're working it out," Dan said. "That's what dogs do." He didn't look so sure, though.

"Let's *go*," Amy said.

"I'll be right back," Dan said.

The three and a half of them left. Mom sat down again. "What a terrible idea, bringing the dogs." She looked like she might cry. The table had gotten quiet. You could hear the ice clink against Aunt Bailey's water glass when she dared to take a sip. Ted Rose cleared his throat.

"Too much excitement, maybe," Aunt Bailey said.

"They'll get used to living together," Gram said.

The possibility of a great lie, a huge lie, settled over us all. The awkwardness in the room snuck into my body and sat cruelly in the pit of my stomach. Ben tore off bits of his white paper napkin and made a napkin snow pile. I studied the wine bottle near my plate. *Lockwood Vineyard, 2007 Monterey Merlot. Our location in warm southern Monterey County is ideal for producing rich and flavorful merlot with remarkable balance . . .*

Finally Rebecca Rose clapped her hands. "Dessert!" She disappeared into the kitchen. A few seconds later a drift of burning weed snuck into the dining room.

"I smell pot," Gram said loudly.

Rebecca Rose came back a while later, with homemade pie and a container of ice cream. She talked to Ben about his design classes, and Aunt Bailey showed me murky pictures on her cell phone, from her trip to the Oregon Caves with her reading group. Ted asked Mom questions about her books. We were pretending the bad moment had passed, but I could see Mom looking toward the doorway hoping for Dan Jax's return, and I could see Rebecca Rose watching her. Even Rebecca Rose understood she should be worried about what might happen here, and she likely didn't even know about Jon Jakes getting ditched at Sea-Tac, or Vic Dennis, fiancé number two, that rich loudmouth that Mom left standing by the baggage claim, waiting for her to pick him up after his business trip to Chicago. I always wondered how long he stood there, how long it took for him to realize she was never coming, the baggage carousel going round and round with only one lost bag, maybe, or some stupid set of golf clubs that should have been in Florida.

Now it looked like Dan Jax was the one not coming back. We ate our dessert, and Aunt Bailey had another glass of wine and started laughing too loud. There was a pounding on the front door then. A rush of activity brought in Grandpa Shine, overloaded with bags. A young Japanese man stood at his side, smiling shyly.

"Look who the cat dragged in," Gram said.

Suitcases were dropped, and introductions made. The young guy was Keiji Takagi, *Goes by George!* Grandpa Shine's golf caddy, or something. I didn't get the full story. Grandpa Shine wore his white cowboy hat and his red golf shirt. He pointed both fingers at me, gun-style. "You!" he said. "Goddamn it, Munchkin, look at you!" You had to love Grandpa Shine. We hugged, and then the hugs started all around. Ted Rose brought more chairs in.

"That boy is better than another bimbo," Gram said, and sniffed.

"Rise above it, Marian," Aunt Bailey said.

"You planning on playing *golf* while you're here?" Gram said. It was said in the same tone as one might say, *You planning on watching pornography while you're here?* Or, *You plan on visiting a handful of prostitutes while you're here?* Then again, twenty-five years ago Grandpa Shine ran off with the petite blond golf pro who'd been giving him lessons. Lurid sex and golf would likely be forever linked in Gram's mind.

"Whenever I can, whenever I can."

"You look great, Dad," Mom said.

"Damn it, I feel great," he said. He slapped one hand on the table and made the silverware jump. "And look at this." He gestured around the table. "*Look* at this. All my favorite people in one place. Here to celebrate *the future*."

Were his eyes actually getting misty? He'd been in the insurance business for years, now retired. He'd grown up on a ranch, and he could lift a chair with one hand. Grandpa Arthur Shine was not the type to cry, and definitely not the type to get poetic about life. Gram opened her mouth and shut it again. She narrowed her eyes.

"It's a beautiful thing," Grandpa Shine said.

"Indeed," Ted Rose said.

"Bet you anything he's getting some," Gram whispered.

• • •

I could hear Dan Jax and Mom murmuring in the next room. Not an argument exactly—they never argued, far as I knew. Intensity. Urgency. Mom's words felt fast, insistent.

There was a knock at my door.

"Cricket!"

Ben. His own voice was urgent. I scrambled out of bed. Jupiter was exhausted after all of the day's events; she didn't move from her little comma-curled self on her bed. Her chin was tucked in snug, and her snoring sounded the way our vacuum did before it finally burned out.

"I think they're fighting," I told him. "Not *fighting*, but sort of fighting."

"You'll never believe what I saw."

"What?"

"He was hugging him."

"Who was hugging who?"

We were standing there in the hall. Everyone's door was closed. I could hear Mom and Dan's murmuring even better from out there. If Ben would shut up, I might be able to hear their actual words.

"Grandpa Shine."

"What?" I was having trouble taking it all in. Ben's hair was all crazy, and he was in his boxers and a T-shirt. He looked like he'd just fled from a burning building.

"I got up to pee. I saw them going up the stairs to their rooms. Grandpa Shine was hugging that guy. . . . It was weird. Really, really weird."

"Big deal. Grandpa Shine hugs a lot of people. So what," I said.

"It was a different kind of hug."

"A different kind of hug?" I snickered.

"Yeah. It was *meaningful*. Stop laughing! I know what I saw."

"Jeez, Ben. Meaningful? It was nothing."

"It didn't seem like nothing. It seemed like something."

We heard footsteps on the stairs. That's when I first saw him. A guy, appearing on the landing. A guy Ben's age, I'd guess. It had to be Ash, Ted and Rebecca's son. Somehow I hadn't pictured *this*. Black hair buzzed short, full mouth, and dark, dark eyes. He was wearing jeans and a white T-shirt with the sleeves cut off, a vest. These arms—large, built muscles. Some ad for jeans—that kind of sexy.

Ash paused. He looked straight at me.

"Well," he said.

That was all. Just, *Well*. I might have said something. I thought . . . *Yeah*. I don't know if I said it out loud. He kept walking up to the next floor. I watched the back of him. Oh, man. God. I think my heart must have escaped my chest. At least, it felt like it was pounding madly enough to leap out, rebelling, becoming the sort of heart it had never been before, a sorority girl heart, say, set loose in Daytona Beach during spring break. Not my heart, not the devoted and steady one I knew.

"Cricket," Ben said. He was watching me. "I can't believe you."

"What?"

"Jesus."

I could hear my mother's voice from behind the shut door. It sounded almost as if she were pleading. And then two clear words from Dan Jax—*Daisy, wait.*

Ben looked from me to my mother's door to the stairs.

He shook his head, exasperated. A hint of disgust too. "You guys are all losing it," he said.

chapter
five

Janssen—

I like this game. Famous Dogs—ha. Your list was
great. But you forgot Scooby-Doo! We love him!
Okay. Now my turn.

Five Amazing Dog Facts:

1. One in three Americans lives with dogs.
   Best guess is that there are fifty-five
   million dogs in our country. We have
   more dogs than babies.
2. 81 percent of people give birthday or

holiday presents to their dogs.

3. 33 percent talk to their dogs on the phone or on the answering machine when they are away.

4. 70 percent sign their dog's name on greeting cards.

5. 33 percent have confided a deep secret to a dog.

Aren't you glad I brought my laptop, so that I could find out these things for you? Think about it. Fifty-five million dogs. Less people than that live in Spain, and just a few more live in Italy. (I looked that up too.) Dogs could have their own country. Instead of all those little separate selves we used to like to watch at Green Lake—the Cocos and Sophies and Butches and Mollies and Bos; the short, narrow dogs; the tall, thin ones; the dogs with tiny legs trotting so fast to keep up with some woman in a jogging suit—they could all be together with their own kind, ruling their own land. I think I love that idea. They could have a monarchy. Pedigrees and all that—plus, monarchies have the wacky hats-with-feathers vibe that would mesh well with goofy dog personalities. If they ruled themselves, poodles wouldn't have to get those haircuts.

But more to the point, the presents, the phone calls . . . It's amazing when you think about it. Here we are, two different *species*, but we have this deep connection, one that's been going on for centuries, ever since the first wolf and the first man decided to hang out together. It's kind of beautiful: not-furry and furry, one who talks and one who doesn't, two-legged and four-legged. But relying on each other. They are devoted, but we return that devotion. We look at their funny, sweet ears and the little leash dance they do, and our hearts swell.

One time I went with Mom and Jupiter to the vet. . . . Did I tell you? I'm sure I did. She was just getting her regular shots. But there was this man sitting in his car in the parking lot. A big man, in army fatigues, his hair in that military buzz. His palms were pressed to his eyes, and he was sobbing. His shoulders were heaving. He held a blanket on his lap. Just the blanket. Mom looked at me, and I looked at her, and we both looked at our own girl down there on the ground, sniffing the sidewalk, getting the day's dog news. Mom said, *Oh, honey,* and I just shook my head, nothing we could even speak aloud. But I never forgot it, that raw grief.

We are so vulnerable, giving out our love like that. Still, it's strong, that bond. Us and our good pals.

And, thank you for your suggestion, but as you can see (dying dog story, above), I could never be a vet like you. You'll make a great one, but I couldn't handle it. I love dogs, I always have, but I'm not wild about *all* animals. Hello, *birds*? Yeah, sorry about all the screaming I did whenever one got too close. When you're a vet, will you have to fix creepy bird legs? Oh, God. Shiver.

I'm not really one of those crazy dog people either. I wouldn't have ten of them. I don't love each and every one in some sort of dogs-are-better-than-people way. I mostly just like the ones with sweet eyes. I do try to smile at every poor, patient guy tied to a streetlamp outside a store, no matter what they look like. I feel so bad for them. But face it, there are the leg humpers and the mean ones, the bullies, the opportunists, the overly anxiety-ridden, same as us. I guess my love is more of the everyday kind. Where you shout at them to stop doing some annoying thing and then carry them around on your shoulder, watching how pleased they are to be up high. You admire their beautiful ears and serene expression and then get mad when they pretend they can't hear you when you call them to come. And it's all forgiven; the ways both of you are imperfect. A devoted relationship, with the regular, daily togetherness of rawhide and slow stop-and-sniff walks. One girl and her own one dog.

Same as you and me. One girl and her own one boy.

After we met, the next big moment in our story was The Day Things Changed Between Us, right? You know when *that* was. You *better* know, butt head. You said in your last letter that I shouldn't worry about writing things down, that the important stuff will stay with us. Probably. But it's worth it to take a little extra care, isn't it? I do believe this: Stories are what you have when the place is gone and the dried-up roses have crumbled and the ring is lost and that old car is finally junked. Stories are where the meaning ends up.

So, here. The story of that day.

My parents—their divorce was finally over. You weren't there when they were together, but you know what the deal was. You know how I hate to

talk about it. My father's dark moods, the holes
punched in the walls, the rest of it. I remember a
few times, seeing things, I told you. It wasn't all
bad, though, right? We weren't some TV movie
drama. We went to Disneyland. We drew chalk
pictures on the sidewalk, and Ben had a basketball
hoop. We got bikes for Christmas. My dad had a
briefcase, and my mom packed our lunches. He
never lifted a hand to Ben or me.

She'd say it herself, years later—the worst way
to leave an angry man is the way she did it, but I
guess she was scared, and she thought Jon Jakes
would save her. Us. He would put a big, strong
cloak around us all, and guide us out of the evil
forest with the grasping trees that came alive
at night. Of course, Jon Jakes was also chosen
because he wouldn't hurt a fly. Opposite of my
father. A good thing, ordinarily. But not in
someone who was supposed to fight dragons.

You remember what my father did to Jon Jakes that
time. I don't even like to admit my father could do
those things. And I have to give Jon Jakes some
credit because he didn't run from my mother then,
when most people would have. *I* would have. He
was good to Ben and me, really. But he felt he

deserved what my father did to him, because you don't go off with another man's wife. He didn't understand that for my father the rules didn't work quite that logically. There wasn't a rule for what he did to my mother all those years, was there? Some rule that supposedly made violence okay? Or some rule for what my father did to his sisters growing up. Or even to other men in some neighborhood football game on a Saturday morning—hitting too hard on purpose. Digging into some guy's heels with the toe of your shoe because you hated his superior attitude. We used to sit on the sidelines of those games with our mother, counting the swear words the dads would say.

Anyway, she left him, and then there was this bad time of meeting in parking lots to exchange our bags and all that, visiting him for the weekends. Bags shoved roughly into the trunk . . . The muscle in his cheek tightening, clenching . . . He'd try to change the mood as we drove away, joking with us, though his eyes were still on her car in the rearview mirror. I saw a pack of cigarettes in his ashtray, and he'd never smoked before, that I knew of. And, oh God, when my father fought for custody and lost, the complicated pity we felt . . . Because we wanted to love him. Did love him. *Do.*

Very much. In spite of everything—what he used to do—he was the one we felt sorry for.

But finally the divorce papers were signed. My mother put some weight on again after getting so thin. After a long while Jon Jakes moved in. Mom tried to be the "good" divorced parent, but when we'd come back from seeing Dad, she'd always ask how things went with this tipped-up high pitch to her voice, and it drove us crazy. I know she worried, but jeez. It didn't help anything. We could handle it! Mostly we could.

I remember Ben and me in your rec room, telling you about all this. We *never* talked about it. Every now and then to Mom, but no one else. Even she—she knew her own story, but not our story. You listened. And then you did the best thing you knew to do. You got out your video games, and we spent some good hours destroying things.

We—ha. It was more like the two of you guys, putting up with me hanging around. Every day since that snowy one. You two became the best of friends after all those car rides to school with your mom and my mom taking turns driving. Those car rides were the best. The sunrise light on the mountains, the fog lying low in the valley, the car not warmed up yet, and Mom's coffee cup steaming in the cold. We'd take that secret shortcut and see those three old people on their morning walk. Remember? Bob, Betty, and Louise, we named them. Said the old guy had two wives.

I'd get so hurt when you two would kick me out of Ben's room! But mostly you let me come along, and I was happy. We'd all go to the baseball field and run Jupiter around the bases. She could run so fast then. I think she'd have a heart attack if she ran like that now. We'd ride our bikes down to that small, weedy lake in the woods, which was choked with lily pads and surrounded by cattails. We brought our sketch pads that one time. Bike freedom. The only freedom we had until we could drive!

But this day just you and me walked down to the church grass. I don't know why. I don't even remember where Ben was. We had Jupiter on her leash, and we were lying on the lawn, drinking out of water bottles we'd brought. We were practically spread out right by the church sign (sort of sacrilegious, come to think of it), the one that always had those corny and inspiring messages.

God Serves Soul Food, whatever. Your head was back, looking at the sky. Cloud shapes. I watched them too. Jupiter was scratching her back on the grass, upside down, paws in the air.

"Clown head," you said, and pointed.

I didn't see it. Then I did. "Ha, clown head," I said. My turn. I pointed now. "Cow."

"Yeah. His ears there," you said. Changing white forms on a blue magic slate. What was I, thirteen? I don't even know. You propped on one elbow to look at me. I propped on one elbow to look at you. Our bodies were lined up, our toes almost touching. And all at once you looked different to me. Not different—the same. The same but *more*. You held my eyes. You seemed surprised. There was this *girl* lying next to you. A girl, not just Ben's sister. And you reached out—you tucked a lock of hair behind my ear. That's all. You had the tenderness of a good guy already. How did you have that right then? How is that possible? You grew up around horses. You knew how to be gentle, and how to set a firm hand on something skittish. Though, maybe it was just the way you came. Who you are.

"So, Cricket," you said. "How'd you get your name?"
Of course you already knew. Nowhere special. Just
something that came from me trying to say my own
name when I was small. But you asked like we were
first meeting. Teasing me. And you grinned.

And I grinned back. There was this strange energy
between us. I felt it. I could almost *see* it.

At that moment Jupiter righted herself to dig
madly with her front paws at something she
smelled underground. It ruined the mood (*and* the
lawn), and I was so embarrassed. You'd seen her
do bad stuff a hundred times, but it was something
embarrassing all of a sudden.

Later I thought about it over and over, that finger
tucking my hair back. Yeah, I must have been
thirteen or so, because I remember thinking about
it in Senora Becker's Spanish. Middle school.
¿Dondé está el baño? Senorita Catherine! That
finger, my hair, that finger, my hair. Your own
crazy hair, swooped down over your forehead.
Looking at me intently with those eyes.

I still think about it, that finger. And of course all
that happened later.

I will definitely tell Gram and everyone you said hi. Yeah, I'll tell her you said to behave herself too. And I will give Jupiter a pat hello. Right now she's looking at me patiently, but like, *Cricket, are we done yet, please? Can we turn out the light? I can barely keep my eyes open.* Your new boss sounds like an asshole. Really? He made you serve him coffee? And it wasn't black enough for his taste? He doesn't deserve you.

I guess after what happened, after what I did, neither do I.

Love always,

Cricket

chapter
six

"Sleepyhead," Mom said to me as she let me into the shared bathroom the next morning. She was brushing her teeth, and her mouth was all white froth. *Sheepyhahd*, it sounded like, the mix of words and Ultrabrite with foaming action. She spit, wiped her mouth with her robe sleeve. I hoped Dan Jax knew all her disgusting habits.

"Have you heard of a towel?" I asked.

"Why look for a towel when your sleeve is conveniently located right on your arm?"

"You better not drink from the milk carton when you live with Dan," I said. "Or the Coke bottle." I hated when she did that. I went into the tiny adjoining room where the toilet was, shut the door between us.

"I'm *supposed* to irritate you right now," she called through the door. "It'll help us separate when you go away to school."

"Doing a great job," I said.

"You could irritate me more, okay, honey? Because I'll miss you like crazy."

"Don't worry. You'll still have Jupiter."

"Thank God dogs don't go away to college. It's going to be pretty quiet."

"Can we not talk about this right now?"

The school question. God, the school question, where I'd been stuck all my senior year and still was stuck, one of those annoying squares on a board game where you sit and sit until you finally roll the magic number that frees you.

I could hear Mom unzip her makeup bag. "I know you hate it when people point out that you're cranky, but are you cranky?"

I flushed, came back out. My mother moved over so that I could wash my hands. She was putting on her mascara, and she had that mascara face people get—chin dropped down, mouth open. It looked silly, but then, honestly, I had the same face when I put on mascara. I guess I *was* cranky.

"Did you hear those stupid mating raccoons last night?" I asked.

"Is this a joke?" she said.

"No, they were on the roof or something. Then when I finally got to sleep, I had a dream about Janssen. One of those dreams that go on and on the whole night. You know those dreams within a dream? Where you say, 'That's just like that dream I always have and now it's actually happening,' but *that's* happening in a dream?"

"I hate those," she said.

"I have this same one, over and over. He's lost, and I can't find him. I look for him behind the doors of this big house. I try to call him, but I can't dial the numbers right. How can I think about going away without him if I miss him like this after two days?"

"You've known him so long. He's a part of you. Like your *arm*, practically."

There are downsides to divorced mothers who date and have relationships. First, the obvious—your *mother* is *dating. You're* the one that's supposed to be dating. And *I* wasn't even dating. I'd been with the same person for forever. Mothers dating, there's just something wrong about it, against nature, like those sixty-year-olds who have quintuplets. Oh, she'll borrow your clothes, too. The dating, the clothes, and the excitement and nerves she shows as she's getting ready—it's all your territory, you know? It's bad enough when they listen to your kind of music, something they have no right to have even *heard* of, and then this. A mother, your mother especially, should be in those mother jeans with wide ass pockets and high waists, and she should maybe be, I don't know, clipping coupons and making dinner and not having men wanting to touch her. Jesus, you've seen him touch her, and it honestly gives you the creeps. *Sex* and *mother.* See? Just reading those words in the same sentence made you feel that way. Imagine the truth of it in your own house.

But on the good side? All the relationship stuff—the excitement and the nerves but also the deep feelings and confusion and crushing blows to the self-esteem and the sense of getting it right, of *flying*—she could understand. It wasn't some distant memory from a long-ago part of her life. It was fresh enough that she got it. She tossed and turned with it in her own bed late at night, same as I did when I fought with Janssen. She hurt over it, she screwed up, didn't know if she should call or not, called, wished she hadn't called. When we talked, it wasn't all shoulder patting and stupid expressions like "There are plenty of fish in the sea." She knew how stupid that expression was. Because it was about a particular fish, *that* fish. See, a person in your territory—they might be a trespasser, but they might also be a friend.

"He's like my other half. I hate that expression. Not *half.* He's like my other whole."

Mom hugged me. I decided to try and relax. Maybe I just needed to go downstairs and have whatever smelled so great down there. "I love you," Mom said. "You are my own sweet nut head, aren't you?"

"My nut head is a mess," I said.

"Your head has never been a mess. You have a case of human nature, that's all. Change is a messy business. Maybe you need to go downstairs and have some of those great blueberry pancakes Rebecca made."

"That's what smells so good."

I suddenly remembered: that boy on the stairs. The dogs and the daughters. Mom and Dan, arguing but not arguing.

"You doing okay, Mom?"

"Two cups of coffee, never been better."

Yeah, well, looking on the bright side was one of my mother's worst habits. No matter what she was going through, all she needed was the easiest invitation to optimism—coffee, say—and she was in. She gave too much optimism to Jon Jakes and Vic Dennis. But once she ran out of it? It was gone for good, forever gone, and they were left wandering the wide, crowded halls of Sea-Tac, stepping over the carry-on bags of weary businessmen.

Mom was back to her makeup now. Come to think of it, there was also a lipstick face.

"The wedding?" It was a test.

"Planning out the logistics today with Rebecca. Who will do what, where. Some cake guy Rebecca knows is coming tomorrow. "

Relief. But then I had a nightmare vision—dogs, cake, some bad romantic comedy movie where the two inevitably merge in disaster.

"Can you see it?" she said. "The dogs destroying some huge, fancy cake, like in the movies?"

My mother had this creepy way of reading my mind, I swear. I decided to test her. *You have a creepy way of reading my mind,* I thought.

But she only looked at me and smiled.

"See you downstairs," she said.

Jupiter must have strolled out from my open door, hopped downstairs, and found Ben to let her out. I knew because Rabbit was in the middle of the hall, dragged like a carcass and then abandoned for smells of sausages. I was surprised to find her and Cruiser in the dining room, sitting stiffly next to each other there, looking formal and attentive as if they were at a job interview. Yeah, Ben had treats. He sat on the floor in front of them as Dan and Hailey and Amy watched. Everyone else was standing around in the living room talking, their syrup- and blueberry-streaked plates abandoned on that huge wood table. The ocean was all morning newness and sparkly beginnings outside those large windows.

Ben opened his mouth dramatically, stretched his arms. "Aww." He yawned. "Aww, awwww!" He yawned and yawned again, and I knew what he was trying to do. It was something I discovered one day. I don't know why I thought of it, but it occurred to me to wonder if maybe you could make dogs yawn, same as you do people. So I tried it. I was on the old leather couch in our living room, and Jupiter was on the chair she wasn't supposed to be on but was always on, and she was watching me while pretending to sleep. I saw her peeking. She always kept one eye on us; that was her job. I knelt up close to her. I yawned, and then she did too. I was so happy. I was *thrilled*. It was like a scientific discovery. I went and got Ben, and we both tried it again to make sure it wasn't a coincidence. It took some doing, but sure enough she yawned again, though maybe she was just bored with us people and our weird games. *Sometimes my humans are very puzzling,* she seemed to say. Still, the yawning discovery felt important. It said something significant about animals and humans, though who knew what.

I lifted the foil from the plates on the table. Sausages. There they were. Pancakes. I sat in a chair, which was still warm from someone's recently vacated butt. I *hate* that. My crankiness, there and then not there, was back again. More than just *back*—it was the nun on the *Sound of Music* hilltop, singing with cruel volume, its little arms flung out wide. It was childish, I know, but dog yawning was *our* thing.

"They're not going to do it," Amy said. She sat on Dan's knee, arms around his neck. She looked miraculously cured of her illness from the night before.

"Tell 'em, Cricket. They don't believe me," Ben said.

"Cruiser does all kinds of tricks," Amy said.

"He rules the total house," Hailey said. Her lip was curled up again in disgust. It was possible this was a permanent condition, same as Mom's tipped-up nose, say, or Janssen's eyes that always looked a little sleepy.

"Jupiter doesn't do tricks," I said. Jupiter was an independent thinker. We'd tried to teach her to shake a few times, but she just stared at us in firm refusal, as if she simply preferred not to. Throw a ball for her, and she'd look at you as if to say,

Plan on getting that yourself. I respected this. Still, I don't know why I was being such a bitch, engaging in some stupid dog contest. Cruiser was a great guy with sweet folded-down ears, even if he was a little wild. If we did get to choose family, as Ben said, I'd probably even pick him.

Right then, though, Jupiter had had enough of sitting beside that tall dog. She walked away, came over to me, and put her front paws up on my legs. I petted her soft black head. Neither of them had yawned on cue, and I was glad. Maybe sometimes you just feel like everything can be taken from you all at once.

"They'll never believe me now about the yawning. Tell 'em, Crick," Ben said.

"It's true," I said. Jupiter sat upright by my chair, showing me her straightest self for pancake bits. Her eyes followed every move of my fork. I gave her a bit of sausage, and she trotted off to eat it on the rug.

"I'm taking you at your word," Dan said.

"Are we just going to *sit around* all day?" Hailey said.

"I thought we could all go for a beach walk," Dan said. "Something like that? What would you guys like?" He stood, displacing Amy, who put an arm around his waist. She reminded me of those spider monkey babies. The ones who clung to their mothers as they swung from tree to tree.

"Morning, all!" Aunt Bailey said. She was wearing a yellow Windbreaker with her jeans and tennis shoes.

Gram appeared beside her a moment later. "Moped rental

in town, if anyone wants to join us." She was wearing a yellow Windbreaker too.

"Twins," I said to them.

"I bought mine first," Gram said. "She always has to copy me."

"Who ran down to Ross and bought my very same rain boots?" Aunt Bailey said.

"Do we have to wear a yellow coat if we want to go?" Dan Jax asked.

"Comedians," Gram said. "A bunch of comedians." Aunt Bailey held her purse tight to her side as if anticipating muggers.

"Humiliating tourist activity on two wheels—" Ben said.

"A couple of old broads leading the way," Gram said.

"I'm in," Ben said. "How fast those things go? Sixty, seventy?"

"I'm not exactly in the mood to break my arm," Hailey said.

There was the sound of heavy footsteps on the stairs. Grandpa Shine appeared with a big smile, wearing his cowboy hat, and with his golf shoes hooked over his fingers. George was beside him, looking crisp and handsome in khaki shorts and a polo shirt. Ben looked at me, and I looked at him and shook my head. Ben shrugged. As close as he'd get to admitting a mistake.

"Found a nine-hole in Anacortes. Want to join us, Dan?"

"Can't leave us *alone*," Amy said.

"I am not riding a moped," Hailey said.

"Come on, guys," Dan said, shooting a flare of impatience.

"Dad . . . ," Hailey whined.

Dan weighed his options, which didn't take long. I guess there weren't many. "Thanks, Art. But I guess we're going to find something to do here." Dan's face was tight. "I'm a terrible golfer anyway."

"Munchkin? Hit a few balls?"

"Mopeds," I said. I'd suddenly decided. Embarrassing myself on one of those things with Ben and two old ladies dressed like daffodils sounded better than my other options.

"Better put some fuel in the fire, then, kiddo," Gram said. "We got a full day's rental and want our money's worth."

"You ladies know how to get around," Grandpa Shine said.

"You're one to talk," Gram said.

"I can give you lessons, if you would like it," George said to Dan. It was the first time we'd heard him speak a full sentence, though I couldn't blame him for feeling shy around all of us.

"This guy's a *player*," Grandpa Shine said. "Let me tell you—"

"Takes one to know one," Gram said.

"Marian," Aunt Bailey said.

"I thought Mom told you to behave," I said.

"What? Grandpa's a great golfer," Gram said, and winked.

"Nothing like this guy." Grandpa Shine grinned, jingled some spare change in his pocket.

Ben looked at me, raised his eyebrows.

Aunt Bailey grabbed Gram and shoved her toward the

front door before she could say anything else. "We'll wait for you two outside," she said.

There was the ring of a cell phone song, playing in the dark depths of someone's purse. Hailey's. She retrieved the phone, walked a few steps away, flipped it open, and plugged her other ear for better hearing. She laughed loudly. I finished my pancakes. Hailey handed her phone to her father.

"Mom needs to speak with you," she said.

Amy smiled. Dan shut his eyes briefly as if hoping to find strength behind his eyelids.

This was going to be the longest week of my life.

chapter
seven

We rented mopeds at the Bishop Rock Moped Shack, and followed behind Gram and Aunt Bailey, who were ticking along at five miles an hour. I couldn't really concentrate on the scenery because I was too worried about the way Aunt Bailey was screaming and then swerving toward the edge of the road whenever a car came. The edge, too—it went straight down a sheer rocky cliff toward the sea, and I had visions of a happy trip turned film noir. The twisted metal of a pink moped, splayed daffodil limbs on the rocks. Jesus.

I scooted up next to Ben. At five miles an hour, you could carry on an entire conversation on one of those things, as if you were sitting comfortably in a living room.

"Reminds me of you learning to drive," I said. I went along once when Mom was teaching him, and I wore the old 49ers football costume that Great-Grandma Shine had given him, helmet, pads, and all, which made Mom laugh and pissed him off.

"And who ripped the side mirror off the Bermuda Honda?" he said.

I shut up. Gram was getting too far ahead, and Ben was shouting at her to wait up, so obviously we were both worrying like parents whose toddler was walking too far ahead in a crowd. In town Gram put her turn signal on and then waited several weeks before pulling over. We all followed and parked behind her.

Gray hair curled under Gram's helmet. Her face was rosy. She unstrapped that helmet like a pro, held it under one arm, same as a NASCAR driver.

"I stopped feeling my butt cheeks three miles back," she said. "Who wants a Coca-Cola?"

"Sounds good," I said.

"Fine," Ben said.

"I can't hear what you guys are saying," Aunt Bailey said. She was struggling with the clasp of her helmet.

"We were saying how our parents always liked me better," Gram said.

Ben helped Aunt Bailey with the clasp. She finally got that helmet off, and shook her hair loose. She'd been watching too many shampoo commercials. "My keister is still vibrating," she said.

We got Cokes in red plastic glasses at Butch's Harbor

Bar, one of those cool places with the groovy beer signs of waterfalls that look like they're moving. That had to have been Butch behind the bar. He winked at Aunt Bailey, which made her blush. Ben ate fried clam strips and french fries, proving for the millionth time that he was always hungry. He and Janssen were both like that, I swear. They'd eat a big breakfast, and a half hour later they'd be scarfing cold pizza from the fridge. Still, both of them were lean. Janssen had those great strong shoulders, but he was trim from all those hours in the pool, practicing with the swim team. I remember the first time I watched him, racing against some team whose name I forget. The way he got out of the pool. The way he leaped out, with water dripping off of him, standing there with confidence, no thought at all to the crowd's eyes on him. Me, I could watch him forever, he was so beautiful. My heart was so full then, it hurt. His wet skin. As slick as a seal. *My* seal.

Gram and Aunt Bailey wanted to hit the shops, those cramped places with ceramic seagulls on rocks and glass floats held in nets. Ben and I were set free, and so we hit our respective gas pedals and headed out. For the first time you could see how beautiful the island was. Blue, twinkling sea set around the jagged curves; a lighthouse perched on one tip like a postcard picture. I breathed deep, salt air and sun, and I passed Ben just to be an ass, and he passed me to be a bigger one, and I started having a great time. We parked our mopeds by the lighthouse and sat out there on the grass, admiring the view.

He handed me his phone to take his picture. He wanted to send it to Taylor, a girl he was seeing back at home.

"Your ugly face is going to make her miss you?" I said. He actually looked great in the picture—blond hair, wavy, like Mom's. He was starting to get tan.

"You're just jealous because I got all the looks *and* the brains," he said. "Want me to do your picture?"

"I don't think Janssen would appreciate that." I wrapped a piece of beach grass around one finger.

"Yeah, he would. I'm sure he's going crazy not being here."

"He tell you that?"

Ben held up both hands. "Don't know the details, not my business. Just know how he feels about you. All of us. Mom getting *married*, and not being here. You know how he loves her."

"Great. I feel like crap now."

"Look, I don't even know what's going on. I don't care. As long as you two are happy. Together, not together, fine with me."

"Did he tell you what happened? What I did? God. I am truly a fuck-up. A mess."

"You were born that way. Hey, I don't know anything. I don't want to know. I'm just saying, it's strange not having him here."

It was tricky when your best friend was going out with your sister. But Ben walked this great line. He loved us both and didn't discuss us with each other. He had lots of practice keeping people separate, I guess. We'd both done the same with Mom and Dad. It was a skill. You had to have the firm tones and the patience of a recess teacher. If one veered too close to the other with questions or opinions—*Is your Mom still with that guy?* or *Fathers need to show up emotionally* and *financially,* you shut down the conversation as efficiently as Mrs. Johnson with her whistle on the Challenger Elementary School playground, separating Jason and Jared, who couldn't play together without someone getting hurt.

"Well, you're right about that," I said. "It is strange not having him here."

Ben got up, held out his hand to help me up too. "Let's go buy some stupid T-shirts," he said.

We went into the cool, musty lighthouse gift store, bought two BISHOP ROCK ROCKS! shirts from the girl that worked there. I went into the bathroom to put mine on. Ben took his shirt off outside and wore his. We thought we were hilarious.

I looked at Ben, straddling that moped, flinging up the kickstand with one foot. It made me think of him on his bike and me on mine. At our old-old house, even, the times we rode with Dad and Mom. And with just Mom, around the wooded trails. That time she screamed when she almost drove over a snake on the path.

"What?" he said.

"Nothing," I said.

"Come on, what?"

I thought. "Not everything changes," I said to him.

I expected some smart-ass remark. But he just looked at me calmly. "Some things never will," he said.

When we got back, Gram and Aunt Bailey went to their rooms to clean up, and Ben went to his to take a nap. He slept as much as he ate, I swear. From my own windows I could see Dan Jax down there on the beach with Hailey and Amy. He was running back and forth, trying to get a kite to fly. He had his shorts and a T-shirt on, and his black hair was pulled back but was coming loose in frazzled strands. The kite would lift a foot or two above his head and then nose-dive into the sand. He was working so hard. I felt something I couldn't name, maybe sadness, but not just sadness. The feeling you get, anyway, when you see good people trying and trying. Same as hearing Mom in the old days, too cheerful on the phone with the gas company, bill past due, or watching Janssen trying to change that tire when I got a flat one time, his face red and puzzled and the jack and hub cap and three of the four bolts lying on the street in the mocking way objects have after two hours of frustration.

Of course, now I needed to go out there. Goddamn it. I had always preferred the peace that came with doing the right thing, like it or not. My attitude had been bad, and probably needed changing. Hailey and Amy were the ones who lived away from their father, and I saw more of him than they did. Maybe that's what made them seem clinging and unhappy. They were thrown together with us too, and my old T-shirt and jeans were as foreign to them as their pink, tight clothes were to me. I hadn't done much to help them feel welcome either, had I? Likely they were good people trying to adjust to something they didn't ask for. The attitude I was feeling from them—well, what about mine? It could get complicated, maybe, to figure out who was rejecting who.

I trotted down the boardwalk. "Hey, guys!" I shouted.

"Cricket!" Dan's face lit up. "We're trying—"

Hailey's hands were stuck deep inside her sweatshirt. "*He's* trying."

"No wind?"

"Too much, not enough," he said.

Amy was throwing sticks down the beach for Cruiser, but when she saw me, she came running. She came up behind her father, stuck her fingers in his belt loops. "Dad!" she said, breathless. O-kay, I got the idea. He was hers. Might have been simpler to just urinate in a circle around him, same as the dogs. Her legs had sand on them, which she brushed off. She swatted at her ankles. "Something's *biting* me."

Cruiser ran up from behind us, full speed. He was dragging a rope of seaweed in his teeth.

"Eyuw, gross!" Hailey screamed, and dodged him.

"Drop it, Cruiser," Dan said. His voice was husky. He sounded exhausted.

Cruiser dropped it. Then he started to roll in it. Dogs, they love their stinky stuff. We'd want to roll around in a summer day or new love or clover. But they want to roll around in glorious, smelly dead things.

"Sick," Hailey said.

"You guys want to go to town or something? They've got the required beach town taffy shop," I said.

"That's a great idea!" Dan said. He patted me on the back. "You can take my car!" He was suddenly talking in exclamation points. Dan wasn't usually an exclamation point kind of guy, but now he was throwing them like spears at the approaching enemy. He was someone who always tried hard. You got the feeling he was always trying to make a kite fly in no wind if it made other people happy. It made you wish he'd wake up one day, open his window, and see a hundred kites flying all on their own.

"We want to stay here," Amy said.

"My phone's about to die," Hailey said.

"I can show you guys this rock cave I found yesterday," I said. "Up the way from here. Very Hardy Boys. Totally cool."

Nothing. I tried a different approach.

"A long walk in the sand is great for leg toning."

"All I've been doing is sitting around, eating," Hailey said.

"Great!" Dan said. "I can see how your mom and Rebecca are coming along." He clapped his hands for Cruiser. "Come on, boy!" Cruiser ran full speed forward, had a little trouble stopping. Man, he looked happy. He loved it out there.

"We'll be fine." Hailey sighed.

Amy carefully brushed sand from her legs but didn't say a word. "Come on!" I said. Awkward silences could bring out my inner camp counselor. It was Mom's optimism coming down the genetic line, taking a left turn and becoming some twisted belief that you could cover up most shit with enthusiastic effort. Or maybe I'd learned this from Jupiter. She did the same thing every morning in the front yard.

I watched Dan Jax walk up the boardwalk to the big white house. His head was down. His shoulders sloped like lonely desert hills. His ponytail, usually buoyant and cheerful, was riding as low as a dragging tailpipe. If a ponytail could be defeated, it was. All that kite flying had tired him out. He had one hand on the boardwalk railing to aid the climb up. I had always thought of Dan Jax as being a man of total commitment. Solid. He would stand by my mother's side and never waiver, and if she herself did, he would hold her elbow firmly and guide the way. I guess I thought she had room to falter, because he never would. Same as me and Janssen, yeah. Same thing.

But Dan Jax's bent shoulders reminded me of something. Something that made me feel suddenly unsettled. He was only a man, wasn't he? He could fall too, if enough weight were loaded upon him. I realized it then: anyone, *anyone*, could buy a ticket and get on the next plane out. We don't like to think it. No, better not to. But it came to me. I could be left standing there by myself. I could be the one holding a suitcase full of hope and ten days of clean underwear.

I used the trick I'd accidentally discovered when I got stuck being partners with Zoe Hammell for a junior year project on the Middle East. Zoe was a golden wall of inapproachability; she'd never talk to me unless she had to, and her friends wouldn't either. She smelled like nail polish and self-tanner, and her hair glowed. No matter what situation you're in, just like dogs, there's a hierarchy. You don't understand the reasons for it, but it's there, and I was somewhere in the middle, too average for Zoe Hammell and her friends, too boring. I'd had the same steady boyfriend for forever, and my friends liked their parents and we thought getting high was stupid. But we weren't Shawna Jarredy and her group either. We didn't wear creepy black felt fedoras and black vests and discuss fantasy books in odd but arrogant detail. We took AP classes and got grades that were good enough to get us into college but not so perfect that we'd become like that *other* group (which, let's see, fell below us but above the Shawna Jarredys)—the isolated slaves of parental expectations.

If Zoe Hammell was disappointed at getting paired up with me, I was just as disappointed ending up with her. There's some teen movie cliché that says that I (lower level, see above) would be thrilled and fawning at her possible attention, which was stupid. It's a strange but cherished myth that everyone wants to be in the "popular group." I'd always been someone who could see pretty clearly (then, anyway), someone who knew my own mind. My mind knew this: Zoe Hammell wore those sweatpants with words written on the ass, and I hated those. I ended up looking at her ass, when I didn't want to look at her ass. In her tight shirts and short skirts, she was a walking advertisement for her own body. It was shallow, but also kind of sad. Kind of desperate. Behind any ad—even the cool, hip ones—they're still trying hard to sell you something.

So I had to get through my time with Zoe Hammell as much as she had to get through her time with me. But I accidentally figured out something: Zoe opened up with a few compliments. (Something, no doubt, that Trevor Woods figured out too, ha, if you believed what you heard.) I once told her I liked her shirt, and she beamed and told me where she bought it and for how much and what her friends thought of it. Man, compliments worked like magic on some people—I wish I'd known that trick before. I'd tell Zoe I liked her handwriting, and she'd tell me about her second-grade teacher and about her best friend that year who moved away and left her heartbroken. The project was over and she didn't know a thing about me, not a single thing, except what pen I used. But once, she'd even cried after I'd complimented her haircut. She broke down about the fight she'd gotten into with Trevor Woods, who preferred it long, that jackass.

I tried the trick again on the beach, and there it went, working like a charm again. First, awkward silence. And then I complimented Hailey's sweatshirt. Wow, it was like using the secret key on the golden door. The door swung open, and I heard about Hailey's boyfriend, Brad; it was his terrific sweatshirt Hailey was wearing, given to her on a cold night, how sweet, but then she'd kept it and it was like having his big, warm arms around her all the time, even though he wanted it

back. Her great ring was a gift from her mother, after Hailey
got in to UBC, where she was studying environmental science
because her mother thought alternative resources would be
the wave of the future. She didn't mind, though, because the
building was near the gym where the football players worked
out, and Brad would have to understand: You could *look*, but
not *touch*. Brad could be so *insecure*.

Amy ran track (*You're lucky you're so tall*, I'd said), because
all the cutest guys ran track, and she played the clarinet too,
even if the band kids were geeks. She used to dance until she
quit, which caused a big fight with her mother, who thought
she had a real future with ballet. *You're really mature for your
age* ticked off her sister, but opened the secret door behind
the secret door, just like in those adventure movies, where the
right stone is touched and the cave wall swivels and there is a
shimmering treasure, but a forbidden one, riddled with skulls
and bones of those who came before. Her mother didn't think
she was mature, obviously, Amy said. She hadn't even wanted
them to come on this trip. She didn't even *know* this woman
their father would be marrying, who would now be spending time with *her* children. What if their father had chosen
another one like that Denise, with the kid who took drugs?
What's his name, with the tattoo? Amy said. *Freak Job Junior,*
Hailey answered. Amy rolled her eyes. *Still, Mom wanted to
come on this trip with us! I'm not* six.

By the time we got back, Hailey had let me try on her ring
and Amy was teaching me dance moves on the sand, which I

hope no one saw. I felt a little ashamed, manipulative—you could press on other people's egos for your own reasons, and it worked too well. It felt wrong, even if it helped things between us. I also felt tired. Egos were hungry things. Like Ben and Janssen, you could feed it breakfast, and a half hour later it would want pizza. You could start out using and end up being used, and by the time I got back up to the house, Amy and Hailey seemed full and happy, and I felt nothing but empty and exhausted.

I needed a nap now too, and so I headed upstairs to my own room. In the stairwell I could hear music coming from the floor above mine. A guitar. My feet had a plan of their own, or so I told myself. At his half-open door I glanced in. He saw me. He was sitting on his bed, playing that guitar, but he stopped strumming then and met my eyes.

"You wanna come in?" he asked. Ash. His dark hair, his olive skin—so different than Janssen's. His long fingers rested flat on the strings to still their hum.

"That's okay," I said.

"I'll play you something," he said.

No words came. Here I was, almost eighteen. Supposedly going away to college next year. Supposedly a smart, confident person. But I fled, like I was a child who'd just come across a Stranger, capital S, offering candy. That dangerous man your mother warned you about.

It was embarrassing, God, but I quickly turned away. I went back downstairs like I was being chased. I shut my door;

my heart was pounding as if I'd been running. I actually put my hand to my chest, the way people do in the movies when they're having a heart attack.

I tried to lie down. But of course I couldn't sleep. Suddenly, I was completely awake.

I don't know why we do it. But sometimes we just swim straight for the net.

chapter
eight

Dear Janssen—

I miss you. I miss you so, so much. I shouldn't
be telling you this, but it's true. I wish you were
here right now. This minute. But I know you can't
come. You said you wouldn't, until I got clear, and
you're right not to. So don't. Even though I wish
you would. Don't.

Wait. I almost forgot. I loved your dog list. Okay,
here goes. Try this.

Ways Jupiter Embarrassed Us and Ways We
Embarrassed Her.

Jupiter:
1. When we brought her to the dog park,
   she just stood there and barked at
   everyone.
2. She ran away, and Mom had to chase
   her through people's yards wearing her
   nightgown.
3. She farts a lot, even when we have
   company.
4. We took her for a walk that time, and
   she got so upset at one guy and his dog
   that she got frothy-mouthed, like she had
   rabies.

Us:
1. We fold down her ears over her head so
   that she looks like the Little Dutch Girl.
2. We lift up her lips to show her pointy
   teeth to pretend she's vicious.
3. We called her Juniper to see if she would
   still come, and she did. (I still feel bad
   about that.)
4. We dressed her in that dog angel costume
   with the halo for Halloween.

You know, Janssen, aside from the angel
costume, I realize how much our dogs have
patience with us. They put up with almost
anything. We sing bad, stupid songs to them.
We make them dance with us. Sometimes we're
really not nice, calling them names, or being
short with them and hurting their feelings. We
ignore them. A whole day goes by sometimes, and
then I remember I've hardly paid any attention to
Jupiter at all, like she was a piece of furniture. But
then I look and see that she's still there, alive and
breathing and standing by, with her watchful,
loving eyes.

But it goes both ways, because they get into the
garbage, they eat your good underwear, and
you've got to pick up their crap, but still you're
crazy about them. They mope around sometimes,
looking like you're not giving them something
they deeply desire, but you don't think, "Jesus,
she's moody! I'm outta here!" They lie where it's
most inconvenient, and we just step over them. I
guess it's a different relationship. When someone
has to turn three circles before lying down,
maybe you feel they really need looking after. But
I'm sure they look at what we do and think the
same thing.

We hurt each other, is the point. Hurt, annoy, embarrass, but move on. People, it just doesn't work that way. Your own feelings get so complicated that you forget the ways another human being can be vulnerable. You spend a lot of energy protecting yourself. All those layers and motivations and feelings. You get hurt, you stay hurt sometimes. The hurt affects your ability to go forward. And words. All the words between us. Words can be permanent. Certain ones are impossible to forgive.

We don't have long, intense conversations with our dogs either (except those one-sided ones), so you don't get distracted by who said what. No one says things they permanently regret. It makes forgiveness pretty easy to hand over. You focus on the fact that the next day comes and there you are, still loving each other. They are a good friend to you, and you try to be a good friend back. They look after you and care for you, and you look after them and care for them. It's so simple. Pure. That's what's so great. That's what you treasure. You'll never get that anywhere else. It's a unique, wordless relationship.

And you know what else? You can totally relax and be yourself with them too. You can burp or leave the bathroom door open. You can look like shit.

You can fail. You can make so many mistakes—
they don't care. They don't judge. They love you,
no matter what. And *they* are themselves too.
Always. You don't lie on your back like that with
your feet hanging in the air if you're not content
just to be who you are. They look goofy, they bark
when the doorbell rings on TV, they *wuf, wuf* in
their sleep, chasing dream bad guys. They're just
their honest selves.

Not that they don't tell you plenty with their
eyes, and not that it's so lovey-dovey that your
relationship isn't real. When I take some piece
of garbage away from Jupiter that she's cleverly
snitched, it's not exactly love she looks at me with.
You wouldn't respect them or believe them if they
thought you were fabulous every second.

I'm not saying anything here, I hope you know.
About forgiveness. About your forgiveness. About
acceptance. And patience. People, it's different, is
my point.

Okay, maybe I am saying something.

Of course, with Jupiter, though, we started out
with this sort of traumatic bonding, and isn't

there something about that? Where you meet in traumatic circumstances and it strengthens the tie? Did I read that somewhere, or did I hear it in that psychology elective with Mr. Shriver? Hostages, or something? Some experiment where a man and a woman meet on a rope bridge and it's dangerous and they fall forever in love.

You've heard this story before, but it's an important one. It's a before-you story, but still it's about us, all of us. So.

My father—well, this was back at our old-old house, before we moved up by you. He had finally left, and it was this crazy time—fear, relief. Mostly an unsettling feeling of who-knows-what-might-happen-next. I was scared a lot. We all were. He was so angry. I don't remember what the situation was, but I remember one night Mom actually hung bells on the downstairs doorknobs. Bells from this musical instrument box we got for Christmas when we were little. She was afraid he'd break in and she wouldn't hear him downstairs. He'd called, like, fifteen times that night, and the feeling in the house . . . I don't like to remember it. Fear, is all.

But there was also this sense of . . . I don't know.
That we were starting something new together.
The three of us. I think my mother decided to sort
of celebrate that idea by getting a dog. Or maybe
she just felt guilty after everything and decided to
finally give in to me, ha! I wanted a dog so bad! I
don't know, but the decision felt more like triumph
than guilt. Exciting, you know? We were *all* so
excited. I'd been doing research about what kind
of dog would be best for us. I was such a nerd—I
read *Dog Fancy* magazine. I did. I got it from the
library. But I woke up one night and found Mom
on the couch reading it too. She was looking at the
pictures and smiling, her robe tucked around her
knees.

I guess you know what I'm like when I set my
mind to something. I was looking at the puppy
ads for weeks on the *Little Nickel* want-ad site
online. Waiting for my baby beagle. And then
one Saturday, there she was. One purebred
beagle puppy, all the way over the mountains in
Wenatchee.

We can drive out there, no problem, my mother
said. It was a three-hour drive, and we could be
back before dinner if we left right then. *It's an*

adventure! Mom said. (This should have been our first warning.) She called the breeder, some old guy, and claimed our puppy. We hopped into the car and headed over to the pet store to get what we needed. And then we set out over the Cascades. We were high with the thrill of unlimited possibilities. It felt like a new beginning.

It was late February, a beautiful day, and we were piled into the Bermuda Honda, listening to music. We were so happy with puppy excitement, and our mother was singing along with the radio and Ben was eating Red Vines. I don't think my mother had ever even taken a trip like this by herself before. She had to keep looking at the map. It was a prove-something-to-yourself trip, and the radio was up and we were flying high.

Everything was going fine—we were on the other side of the pass, pulling off onto the Wenatchee Highway, about to head toward the breeder's house, when suddenly there was a bad smell. A really bad burning smell and then smoke—huge barreling plumes of smoke—rising from the hood of the Bermuda Honda.

Mom pulled over. *Oh shit, oh shit, oh shit,* she said.
Her face had gone as white as an egg.

Mom? I said. Ben had turned silent. We were
sitting on a dirt road next to a gas station and
endless orchards of apples, miles from home. No
cell phone—this was before Mom could afford
one. And what would these car repairs cost? Add
that to the list of worries. The smoke kept
pouring out, and Mom's stunned face watched
as the Bermuda Honda died one of its nine
lives.

Mom put her head down on her arms on the
steering wheel. I was scared. Again. I thought she
might cry. Every bit of new-life joy was gone, and
there was only fear once more. And defeat. Utter
defeat. In the car, before it broke down, there had
been this feeling. I wouldn't repeat this to anyone
but you, because it's disloyal to my father, who is
still my father. But there was this glee that maybe
in the end the good guys could win, this rising
feeling in the heart. And then the smoke, and the
defeat, and the sense that *anything* could happen,
bad things that my mother couldn't handle
after all, and suddenly I realized that the simple,
naïve ideas of good guys and bad guys and

things turning out the way they should was probably over for me forever.

Mom? I said again. I was really getting scared. No one knew where we were. No one even knew we'd left.

I looked at Ben, and he looked at me.

But Mom lifted her head. *Okay,* she said. *Okay.* It sounded like a plan, or at least like a plan was on its way.

The gas station right there, right off that exit, it sat there like a 76 station gift from God dropped down from the heavens. But a gift without the needed batteries—it was closed. But, yeah, there was a phone booth, and Mom got out and walked toward it, but before she'd even gotten five paces, a Wenatchee County Water and Sewer truck pulled up. A kind-eyed young guy was driving, a guy who used the word "Ma'am" and who had a radio in his car. If God is up there directing this great big human play, I guess sometimes I don't understand him. I want to love him, but he makes it hard, honestly. Sure, there is beauty and love and planets, but as a father he can shove you down from behind

one minute and then pick you up the next minute
and dust off your knees. It's hard to keep up with
what you're supposed to be learning, is all I'm saying.

So we were on the ground and then back up, and
the kind man called a tow truck. He delivered
us to the only person we "knew" in the area, the
breeder, who my mother had talked to on the
phone for all of five minutes back home.

The breeder and his wife were expecting us. He
was a gruff man in a plaid wool shirt who had a
barrel chest and smelled like cigarettes. Our road
angel in his tan county uniform made sure we were
all right and then drove off. I was worried again,
really, to see him go. He seemed like safety. At
that house, with its smell of something cat and the
sound of a football game playing in another room,
Mom made another call. She shut her eyes for a
moment before she dialed. A prayer, I'm guessing.
She's not a churchgoing sort, as you know, but she
believes there are reasons for things. I said a prayer
of my own. Jon Jakes hadn't moved in yet; he was
out of the picture then, out, in, in, out, dealing
with his own divorce. My prayer—I was hoping it
wasn't my father's number she was calling. Please.
Anything, but not that.

Then the breeder went out to his barn, came back, and set a tiny puppy on their green shag rug. A tiny, trembling black puppy with a white spot on her back and a tail with its tip dipped in white. The last of the litter, a puppy who slept outside. A vulnerable little someone who tried to hide under their television stand. *We would've made her into a hunting dog if no one wanted her,* the breeder said.

I'd expected to feel bad, taking a puppy from the family she knew. I'd readied myself for some sort of guilt. But the living room had paneling and a TV tray set up with an ashtray and a *TV Guide* on it, and the last of someone's sandwich. A hunting dog. A puppy who had to sleep in the cold. We picked her up, our Jupiter. We took her from that strange home and the strange family she knew, to become one of us.

Our mother decided not to wait in that place. We got a ride from the breeder's wife into town. We waited at a restaurant with a lawn in front. We had a leash and a water bowl, and we tried to get the tiny, shaking dog to drink.

And then the sky turned dark. It did. It began to snow. Yes, *snow.* It was a beautiful blue-skies day

back at home, with no chance of bad weather, and
now this. White flakes coming down, down—
some sign that things indeed could get worse,
and then worse again. We stood in the restaurant
looking out the windows. Tiny Jupiter was zipped
up into Ben's sweatshirt.

And then the truck arrived.

"I have never been so glad to see anyone in my
whole life," Mom said.

"Get in, munchkins," Grandpa Shine said, opening
the truck door. "Who's the new member of the
Shine family?"

The last thing you want when you're trying to be
big and brave is to be rescued. But thank God we
are rescued when we need it. And that day was
a whole entire day of rescue. We thought about
Jupiter living outside, the snow, that strange
smoky house, that gruff breeder. That small baby,
a hunting dog. We thought we'd rescued her. But
when we finally got home, the three of us plus
one more, it felt like something huge had shifted.
We'd created a new family, moved on from the
old one by bringing in a little somebody, who was

scampering around our wood floors and cracking us up, biting our fingers with sharp teeth, looking so small beside her huge bowls now set on a colorful place mat on our kitchen floor.

Tell me, who was rescuing who?

And you, too, Janssen. I guess we had some traumatic bonding of our own. You arrived in our life when we were still shaky. Yeah, you say I was always strong, but inside I was small and trembling on green shag. But after that incident with my dad . . . Well, you put your arms around me, didn't you? And then you kept them there. We still had to figure out how to walk the bridge over from kid sister to something else. Our future hadn't really even arrived yet. But there you were. And I felt safe. And I've never stopped feeling safe, thanks to you.

Love always,

Cricket

chapter
nine

After seeing that guy and that guitar, I gave up trying to rest. I went downstairs, where I found Mom and Dan sitting snug and close together on one of those plush couches. The living room was as inviting as the rest of the rooms—stone fireplace; those two-story-high windows; polished floors and thick rugs; those big, soft gray couches the color of the sea on a moody day. My mother and Dan had their bare feet up on the wood plank table, and Dan had his arm draped around her shoulder. Two glasses of red wine relaxed on the tabletop; it was a quiet moment, and I didn't want to interrupt. But Dan spotted me, waved his arm for me to come over, and Mom patted the spot beside her.

"What's this?" I said. I crooked my head toward Jupiter and Cruiser. Jupiter was lying on the big pillow that was Cruiser's bed, gazing serenely toward the windows and the sea, her chin on her paws. Cruiser was stretched out on the hard floor. His ears twitched with nerves and awareness. You had the feeling he'd be sleeping with one eye open tonight.

"The little old girl is the dominant one," Mom said.

"Oh no. Look at him. Should we chase her off?"

"No," Dan said. "Leave it. They've got their own rules. Man, if only people-rules were that straightforward."

"Poor guy," I said.

"But she's telling him what she'll tolerate, I guess," Mom said. "She's drawing the line."

I leaned over Cruiser, scruffed his head. He leaned on his side passively. "Are you the big dog?" I said. "Are you a giant woof? You're not just a dog, you're an adventure, right?" Oh, it was pathetic.

"But I gotta say," Dan said, "that boy will take on the biggest, nastiest dog at the dog park. And look at him. Scared of the old lady. She's whipping the big guy into shape."

She did seem to have things handled. *There*, she seemed to say. No more of that crazy running around and jumping of the night before. No large dogs getting on Grandmas.

I sat down, sunk into that couch, which soaked me right up. "Rebecca sure can cook," I said. I smelled something right then. Wine and mushrooms. Garlic. "You guys figure out all the wedding details?"

"We thought we'd take care of business right here in this room," Mom said.

"Great," I said.

Still. *Take care of business.* Didn't it lack romance? Maybe in a worrying way? Then again, romance required throwing caution to the wind, and after Dad, after Jon Jakes and Vic Dennis, Mom clutched her caution like a mace can in a creepy parking lot. And why not? I mean, Dan Jax meant she'd gotten to her car safely, but what about something hiding in your own backseat? What about sudden ambush from ruthless bad guys hiding behind cement pillars? What about careening Audis or jealous bystanders waiting to key your perfect paint job?

"We were just thinking about those movies where there's the last race to the church to stop the wedding before someone makes a mistake," Mom said.

Wait. Had I heard that right? "What?" I said.

"Those movies," she said. "The interrupted wedding scene. Someone always has to run to the church."

"Stupid movies," I said. *"Stupid."*

"I swear, how many films end like that?" Dan said. "I'm curious about the whole history of the thing. Like, what was the first movie that showed that scene? And then, why did it seem like such a great idea that now it's a romantic comedy requirement? Do you need more wine, sweetie?"

"No, thanks," Mom said.

Dan—his hair was out of his ponytail, so it was wild all over the place, and I noticed that his watch had stopped at ten fifteen. He was such an innocent. A puppy. When Mom left Jon Jakes and Vic Dennis, we—Ben and me—we wanted to clap and cheer. Balloons should have fallen from the sky. I'm sure even Jupiter celebrated with us. She never liked either of them. *She* wasn't herself with them either. But this time, with Dan Jax? If it turned out there *were* jealous bystanders wishing to wreck this, or, even worse, something in her own backseat, I think my heart would break.

Mom spun the stem of her glass in thought. "The scene resonates, that's why. Too many people watch those and wish *they'd* had someone run in and save them."

"But think of all the other bad choices people make that would resonate," Dan said. "All kinds of scenes where people should get stopped at the last minute from making a huge mistake. Someone runs in right before you're signing papers on some disaster house . . ."

"Packing up to leave for the wrong college . . . ," I said.

"Buying a used car," Mom said.

"Picture it," Dan said. "Used car lot. Flags blowing. Piece of shit car with the keys dangling from the ignition."

"Our heroine, about to shake hands with the used-car guy with the receding hairline and gaudy college ring . . . ," Mom said.

"The hero runs in . . ."

Mom took a last sip of wine. "But it's always the weddings," she said.

I heard the front door open and then Grandpa Shine's booming voice.

"Anybody home?"

"We're in here," Mom called.

"You hit a typhoon out there?" Dan asked. George's once-crisp shirt was crinkled and shoved in at an angle into his pants. Grandpa Shine's forehead glistened with sweat, and the underarms of his polo were ringed with wet circles.

"Typhoon?" Grandpa Shine said. "Oh, we were working hard. Wanted to see every inch of that course."

"Your hat!" Mom said.

Grandpa Shine punched it back out again from the inside, where it had been dented in. "Right!" he said. "Look at that! Tossed the clubs right on it. Got carried away."

"Hot day," George said. He took a pinch of his shirt and waved it in and out.

"Golf is a rougher game than I thought," Dan said.

"Oh, it's a physical game, done right," Grandpa Shine said. "The old farts with heart conditions need to respect that." George smoothed down the back of his hair.

"Well, you be careful out there," Mom said.

I had a Grandparent Moment at her words. You know the ones. Where you realize they won't live forever, and you suddenly want them to know how much they mean to you. It's a rush of guilt and goodwill. A collision of love and realization. "You know what I was just thinking about?" I said to Grandpa Shine. "The time you came and saved us when we got Jupiter."

"Oh, don't remind me," Mom said.

"That damn car. Remember Christmas Eve?" he said.

"Don't remind me of that, either," Mom said.

I groaned. "My cello," I said.

"Cello?" Dan said. "Any story with a cello ends badly."

"Christmas Eve," my mother said. "Bad time in my life. Divorce." She looked at George to explain, and he nodded an *ahh*, as if he understood. George looked too innocent to understand the ugly corners of love. Valentine boxes in second grade, maybe, a crush on some little golfer girl.

"We were headed to Dad's house for Christmas Eve. The car was packed with presents, some food we were bringing. During a Seattle *monsoon*! Driving on the freeway at night," Mom said.

"The Bermuda Honda?" Dan said. He knew what that meant. "Oh no."

"It stopped. I swear to God, the thing just *died. Again!* There was enough forward motion to pull over, and that was it. Christmas Eve, and no star of Bethlehem. BUT, an orange glow in the sky . . . The one way God looks out for me—," Mom said.

"A 76 station," Dan and I said together.

"I drove out to pick them up, and I get out there, and everyone's drenched, and we're moving all this stuff to my truck," Grandpa said. "And I open the trunk, and on top of everything else, there's a damn cello in there."

"Cricket had just started playing, and she was going to perform for us after dinner. I swear, I'm about to lose it—that damn car *again*—but then it suddenly seemed like the most huge and ludicrous thing. A cello! I started laughing," Mom said. She was laughing now, too. "Cracking up. We laughed so hard. Jesus, I've never laughed so hard in my life."

"I almost wet my pants. That car had a curse," Grandpa Shine said.

"The cursed Bermuda Triangle, Automobile Edition, where odd and mysterious things happen," Ben said. He was suddenly there, leaning in the doorway.

"And we went home and had Christmas Eve," Grandpa said, and George smiled.

"And Cricket played that cello like an angel," Mom said.

"I wouldn't say that," Ben said.

"Okay, maybe not an angel," Mom said.

We were all laughing and smiling, and it was stupid, but I was worried. Jon Jakes and Vic Dennis and even my father were ditched the same as a professional hit man takes care of a body—with utter certainty and without hesitation. Clean. She put up with a lot of shit, but once she'd decided she'd had enough, it was over. But there'd been warnings. The final act seemed sudden, but the inner working of her mind left fingerprints and blood droplets. You'd hear music by angry chick singers playing with greater frequency in her car. She'd buy a *fuck-you* outfit, something she'd look great in and wear without him beside her. She'd sit alone and think too long. She'd spin a wineglass by the stem, and speak in double meanings.

We had dinner in the big dining room again. Gram's cheeks got red with spicy food and cabernet, and Aunt Bailey was a little tipsy too, laughing too much and flirting with George, who told us about his childhood in Chiba, Japan, and his trip here with his family. George was sweet. He made sure to hold the salad bowl for Aunt Bailey while she scooped, since it was heavy. He told her and Gram that two lovely ladies like themselves should have husbands, which was sort of an insult, but he meant well. He kept saying how beautiful everything was.

I lost all the ground that I'd gained that afternoon with Hailey and Amy, or else I was just too tired to give them the kind of attention that made our relationship work so well. They sat together near the end of the long table, twirling pasta on their forks, looking down on us like two ravens on a telephone line. Amy picked the mushrooms from her sauce and piled them up on her plate, and Hailey would whisper to her and she'd whisper back until Rebecca or Mom or Aunt Bailey would ask them a question and their heads would pop up, wearing tight, polite smiles. They were the kind of smiles that said, *I wish you'd curl up and die but I'd never, ever say so.*

Sometimes you wanted more from people. I wished Jupiter would get *them* in line.

After dinner I headed to my room. I wanted to write to Janssen and tell him everything that had happened that day, but halfway there I changed my mind. I wanted to see the beach at night, I told myself, and myself told me what a liar I was. From the dining room I had seen the small bonfire, the orange glow that looked so inviting. I saw the figure there too.

Of course, I could tell who it was even from there. The short hair, the wide shoulders. That stupid-girl hot-guy reaction wasn't me, though right then my body didn't seem to know that. It was new, that want. But it felt safe to play with. Desire could feel like a demand, but I knew it wasn't one.

It was cool outside. I should have brought a jacket. What I was doing felt wrong, but I kept stepping toward wrongness, kept picking at it, the way you pull a loose bit of yarn even though you see the sweater starting to unravel. That hot guy—well, I was stuck, and maybe he seemed like a way to shove myself in one direction or the other. You pull the bit of yarn and it unravels, and you either stop because you remember how much you love that sweater, or else you keep pulling, because it's already ruined. But at least you *do* something. I could smell burning wood, and the ashy heat lifted up into the air and sent a swarm of firefly sparks dancing down the beach. I could hear the snap and pop of the fire as I got closer. He turned when he heard me.

"Hey, Cricket," he said. He knew my name.

"Hey, Somebody with a Guitar," I said.

"Ash," he said. "Pull up a log." He sat on a blanket, his back against a large piece of driftwood. His guitar was propped beside him like a shy friend. He moved it so I'd have a spot. I sat down. It felt close. Very close, closer than I'd been to anyone except Janssen. A male, non-related anyone. Oscar and Gavin, maybe, but they didn't count.

The fire made my face burn hot. The waves slid across the sand, their foamy edges bright white in the moonlight. I felt far away from Marcy Lake, where Janssen and I would sit sometimes at night, listening to crickets and watching strange insects dip down for drinks of murky water. I might as well have been in a different country, or in a different life altogether.

"You live here," I said.

"I do." He threw a stick at the fire and missed.

I responded with several highly intelligent statements. "Oh," I said. "Wow."

"Your mother getting married, or your father?"

"Mom."

"When my father got married, they made us all go barefoot and throw pieces of paper with wishes for them into the sea." He twirled a finger by his head.

"What was your wish?"

"I was, like, five. I think I wrote, *'No fighting.'* *F-I-T-I-N-G*."

"That's a good wish. Rebecca's not your mom?" Well, obviously, if he was at the wedding. Oh, I can be an idiot when I'm nervous. Total lack of cool under pressure. It's one of the things I like least about myself. Of course, I didn't have much practice at this. You have a steady boyfriend, and whole rooms are closed off, red velvet cords across the doorway like in museums, so you can only peer in.

"Nah. See?" he said. He pointed to his skin, his chest, where it was bare under his gray sweatshirt. He was looking right in my eyes—and my heart, that traitor, pretended it was a fish flopping on land. "Brown." He crooked his thumb to the house. "White. My other family is Puerto Rican."

"Oh," I said.

"San Juan. Not the San Juan with the pools and hotels, right? The *other* one. The one tourists don't see. My mother is still there."

"Do you get to see her much?"

"I'm going down there next month. See all the crazy relatives," he said, but smiled.

"That must be hard. To be away. You must miss her."

"Yep. I do. But she's happy I'm going to school here. And Rebecca's cool. Smokes way too much. I've been high on secondhand smoke since I was six, I swear. Still, she's all right. And my dad does the usual 'You got to think about your future, son,' but he's calmed down now that I'm going to college. I took a year off, you know. All that 'What do I want to do with my life' bullshit."

"I know." I did. You could be so sure about what you wanted. All senior year, it was all about getting *out*. But then, out . . . Out was a huge place. "Where you going?" I managed to make it sound casual. But I noticed the quick skip of worry I felt. I was thinking, *Far away.*

"Seattle U. But don't ask what I'm studying, because I have no idea. You're supposed to plan your whole life right now? I don't know what I want for breakfast tomorrow."

"Same. Up until now I wanted to be an astronaut, a cowgirl, or an explorer."

"Yeah," he said. "Up until now you thought those things were *possible*."

"Exactly."

"Reality's a bitch. Wait, now you. I hate people like, 'Tell me more about myself.' You in school?"

"Just graduated. Trying to decide. I'm holding a spot at two places. USC. U-Dub," I said.

"Whoa. LA."

"Yeah. Not sure, though." I didn't want to tell him or anyone else that LA, in my secret heart of hearts, sounded a million miles from home. You weren't supposed to admit that. You were supposed to want the best school, no matter what. You were supposed to be *ready*. And you were supposed to *want* to leave. "And don't ask me what I'm studying, because I don't even know what I had for breakfast *today*."

Ash laughed. "Pancakes."

"Riiiiight," I said.

"See? I can help you."

I smiled at him, and he smiled back.

"You cold?"

"No, I'm great," I said. I didn't feel cold. I didn't feel anything close to it.

"You shivered." He unzipped his sweatshirt. Holy crap, the sudden view—just a tank top stretched across that chest, and the round, hard muscles of his arms. I mean, wow.

"Oh no, that's okay," I said. "I'm fine." But he'd already tossed it around my shoulders. It was warm from his body heat, and it smelled like he must smell—good, some musky soap. Really good.

We watched a solitary seagull taking a long walk down the beach. He looked like he had things on his mind. I stared at that leaping fire, looked into the deep, enchanting red, way down by the coals. I hated to admit it, but maybe Hailey was right about a guy's sweatshirt, the way it could make you feel.

Behind us, from far up on the hill, you could hear a door slam. An angry shudder, maybe, or just the force of the wind.

"Ouch," Ash said at the sound.

I looked at the house behind me, white in the moonlight, with the yellow glowing windows. I saw a light shut off. Nearly all my people were in one place.

"Hey, I'd better go," I said.

"Yeah? Too bad."

I tossed his sweatshirt across his lap. He stood when I did. He looked at me with those dark, intense eyes. "Hey, you can share my log anytime," he said.

"Great," I said. I don't know. The way he looked—he seemed as dangerous to me as that ocean then, with its tides and undercurrents. With its wide possibilities, stretching to other unknown continents.

"Okay," he said.

"Okay," I said back.

I turned to head home. But Ash called out.

"Hey, Cricket Girl," he said.

"Hey, Ash Boy."

"You seeing anyone?"

I didn't know what to say. Janssen and I *were* and *weren't*.

We were in some relationship waiting room, with bad maga-zines and a clock ticking too loudly.

"I'm seeing you, right this minute," I said.

He laughed. "All right. Gotcha. Playing it cool."

The moon was above me on the boardwalk. Half full, but you could see its shadow half there, too dim and waiting to be revealed. I breathed in the smells of wet sand and fire cinders and sea. A deep breath. The truth was, I was mad at myself for how I was feeling. Those shoulders—those eyes . . . That kind of desire was disloyal. True, you wanted more from people sometimes. And sometimes, you wanted more from yourself.

The screen door of the house banged shut, and my mother came out. She wore a long, white sundress down to her ankles, a mismatched dress shirt, probably one of Dan's, hastily thrown over the top. No shoes again. My mother and her bare feet . . . She was walking fast, and her hair was riding out behind her, a wave of yellow. She saw me, and held up her hand to indicate she didn't want to talk. It was a gesture of upset I remembered from her encounters with my father. I knew the feeling—when too much had suddenly gathered before you and you needed to catch up.

I let her pass. Something was sinking in my chest. We've got a special size of worry for the people we love, somewhere between a mountain range and a small planet. You could wish sometimes that you were the kind of person who didn't care. Who could see someone hurt and turn on the television or order some new shoes online, thinking only about tan or black, seven or seven and a half. But I wasn't a person like that. I guess we'd had a lot of troubles. We saw the damage one person could do to another. You got to thinking that a person could be harmed, broken, swept out to sea.

I brushed the sand off my legs, clapped my shoes together to clean them off. Inside my room Jupiter was already asleep on her pillow. But at the sound of the door, she rose and headed for the far corner in shame. Dogs remembered their guilt, even for something they'd done hours before. I'd felt the same thing, wearing that sweatshirt. I wondered what it was. Had she chewed up something she couldn't resist? Eaten the gum from my purse? I looked around. I saw the small puddle near the front door.

"Oh, honey, are you okay? Did that stupid Ben forget to take you out?"

I cleaned up as fast as I could so she wouldn't feel so bad. She stayed over there in her corner in spite of my reassurances. She didn't think she deserved forgiveness, I guess.

There was deep apology in her eyes. And although I'd seen her regret many times before, I couldn't shake the feeling that this time it seemed different. It seemed to be an apology for something bigger, even, than any simple accident on a wood floor.

chapter
ten

Dear Janssen—

Your list made me laugh. There was that other
time Jupiter was furious with us too, remember?
When we tried to make her go swimming? We
thought dogs loved that. We yanked and pulled
her toward that water. We carried her in. She
was up to her knees, frowning at us. She refused
to move. I think she was mad the rest of the
day.

Okay.

Things Dogs Do That Make You Think
You've Glimpsed Their Top Secret, Hush-Hush
Intelligence:

1. When you catch them watching TV
2. When they "accidentally" wink at you when you're talking
3. When they know the sound of your car engine and door slam versus every other car engine and door slam
4. When all the dogs bark to each other at night like in *101 Dalmatians* and you know they really are passing emergency messages
5. When they rush to sit in the driver's seat when you go inside somewhere to run an errand, as if they used to drive in a past life
6. The way they purposefully use the Power of Looking Sad to their advantage

How do we *know* they don't have great abilities we're unaware of? They can detect cancer in a human by scent, for God's sake. But, we say, they're "just" dogs, and other animals are "just" too, and for that matter, we can look at other people as "just" an awful lot of the time. It bugs me, our human displays of superiority, our single-minded, self-centered blindness. Our lack of generosity. We go about our Important People business, not even noticing their important animal business going on beside us. Dogs are trying to do the job they know to do, to demonstrate their devotion to us by doing it well, and we're so in our own heads, we don't even notice. They scratch up the kitchen cupboard trying to hunt that mouse they're supposed to find for you, or run around like crazy trying to herd two people in an apartment, and we yell at them. Some poor Chihuahua is on a leash, running like hell to keep up with her owner, a hundred steps to one, and the owner doesn't even see. They're trying to do their best keeping one foot in our world and one foot in their own dog world, craning their necks whenever they see one of their own, and we yank them hard to get a move on. We're inconsiderate.

Too often we don't even notice how hard good people and good dogs are working.

Maybe I'm just pissed at Dan's daughters. Obviously I'm pissed, because I feel like using a lot of capital letters. OBVIOUSLY I'M PISSED.

Mom ran out of the house upset tonight, and I'm sure they're the reason. And—they could really mess this up, you know? They could. But, yeah, to answer your question, I *am* sure there are no airports on Bishop Rock! Ha. You should have seen them at dinner tonight, though. It was like middle school, when Gina Halverson and Whitney Fricks decided not to like me. Whispering behind their hands.

Most of the time you have mostly good people mostly doing their best, so how about a little generosity, huh? How about it?

And, yeah, your e-mail. Okay. Maybe it got me a bit worked up too. You know how I hate to fight with you. I don't want to fight. But, God. *That* was hard to read. If it's not what you want to do, "not at all," then why are you pressing me to decide? I've forced you to that position, I know. You're right. You need a commitment. It's unfair. Especially after what happened. But—it's all just a lot right now. Trying to figure out about school, moving, graduating . . . Please, I'll hurry. I don't want to lose you.

Please . . . wait.

Our story. You say it's painful *and* good to hear?
That probably says something twisted about your
psychology, and mine, too, since we've always
been just the same. But, stories . . . Remember
Anne Shields, English teacher extraordinaire?
When I worked for her after school over those
two years, she'd say the same thing Mom did
about them. I wonder if she ever finished that
book she was writing. Stories help you understand
your life, she'd say. Stories can heal. And I think
she's right, because why do old guys back from the
war tell their experiences again and again? Why
did people of long ago make up elaborate tales of
mythical beings? Why do people sit in a room and
reveal the pieces of their life to doctors trained to
listen, and why are they cured by doing that? Why
libraries? Come on, all those stories, pieces of life
told again and again. We *need* them. Stories are
a ritual that put all the crazy shit about life into
a form that makes sense. We're *all* like the little
kids that need to be read the same story over and
over again.

Plus, I like our story. I love it, actually.

After that day on the church grass came the
thing with my dad . . . Wait. I just remembered

something from before all that. Way before. When we were still all riding our bikes around together and making those elaborate forts in our family room out of sheets, with different rooms to sleep in. This was just before Jon Jakes moved in, when Mom was taking care of those two neighbor kids, Bella and Harrison. Remember those little monsters? God. She needed the money, though. She hadn't sold *Monkey M. Monkey* yet. Bella and Harrison. Wonder how they are? I can't think of them being whatever age they must be now. That was awful, though. Mom had been friends with their mother before that, but afterward she treated Mom like the hired help, which I guess she was. The woman's name was Janet, right? Why can't I remember? Probably blocked it out. One time we went with Mom to drop off the monsters at Janet's work. Janet showed off Bella and Harrison to some coworker but totally ignored us. Mom just hung back and pretended to fix the strap of her purse, and it felt humiliating.

The little guy threw the worst tantrums and the little girl was kind of a priss, and we'd all have to shove into the Bermuda Honda with their car seats and bags and toys whenever we went anywhere. Mom took Ben and me to counseling after the

divorce, and they'd be sitting out there in the
waiting room hanging off Mom's lap, reading
our old Elmo books. Harrison would scream
every time the sun got in his eyes, and whenever
Mom would put on Bella's red shoes instead of
her pink ones or give her a cereal snack instead
of fish crackers, she'd use her Janet mother voice
on Mom. "It's okay to make a steak, Daisy,"
Bella would say, which should have been cute but
somehow showed how she'd treat every waiter or
salesperson for the rest of her life.

But we'd sometimes have fun with them. Okay,
rarely, but we did. We'd play store, invite them
into our rooms to pick through our old Happy
Meal toys and crap we didn't want anymore. We'd
let them bring the stuff home. Sometimes they'd
cuddle up to us when we played them our old
favorite video, *The Land Before Time* (otherwise
known as the Screaming Dinosaur Movie), and it
was actually kind of nice.

That day, we were out back with them while
Mom was making grilled cheese. They had our
old kitchen toys with the dishes and the plastic
food spread out all over the lawn. I let Bella use
the child-size apron Gram had made me, and

Harrison was wearing Ben's cowboy vest from
our former dress-up box, and you and Ben were
the restaurant customers. You guys were maybe
thirteen, and you wouldn't have been there except
you were waiting for Mom to feed you. You two
were always together then, cracking each other up
over something stupid. I remember you bent in
half a lot, laughing. Holding your stomach.

You were sitting at our old kiddie picnic table.
You looked hilarious stuffed into it, your knees up
high. Bella made me pour the "coffee" from the
toy coffeepot, and Harrison was fixing you
up a plate of rubber bacon and pizza. The
monsters sat down next to you with their plastic
plates and plastic glasses that looked like fancy
goblets, and you asked for more coffee, please.
Ben thought that was hilarious, and Bella and
Harrison also lifted their goblets in the air for me
to fill.

"Dank you," Harrison said, and I suddenly looked
at his golden head and smiled. I kissed the top of
it, and it was warm from the sun and it smelled
like fruit shampoo. Mom called us in for lunch,
and Harrison untangled himself from the bench
and took my hand. It felt like a sweet hand.

You looked over at me. Do you even remember this? You said, "I'd take that good of care of you."

It surprised me. Probably surprised you. Definitely surprised Ben, who said something like, "You can't take care of a fucking *fish*." He never said "fucking." Doesn't even say it now.

We went inside and had lunch; everyday life piled on top of the words, burying them. But maybe they were like those sunflower seeds we planted with the monsters—forgotten in their Dixie cups on the windowsill and then overwatered, but still there underground. And then, finally, a real plant pushing through.

I think it's cool your Mom's getting a new horse. Did she name him yet? I can see how you're going crazy there, though, after being away at school. You came back to see me, and I'm not even there, and I can see why you'd feel you should have stayed where your friends were. Your dad's getting on your nerves, but he's only worried because of his own past, right? Think of the stories he tells! Sex, drugs, and rock 'n' roll! Grateful Dead Daddy. He's a good guy, your father. He probably just doesn't want *you* doing drugs, sex, and rock 'n' roll. Oh,

God, wait. *I* don't want you doing those things
either. Please don't do those things. Except maybe
the rock 'n' roll.

Love always,

Cricket

P.S. I'm sorry if I sounded mad earlier.

chapter
eleven

Early the next morning I awoke to Rebecca shouting. "Guests!" she called upstairs, to whoever might hear.

I put the pillow over my head. I didn't know who we were expecting that day, except the cake guy. I stayed there in my bed-womb and wished I could hide out for the next seventy-five years or so. That bed felt so good. A safe mini cave, a secret lair. Too bad everyone knew where I was.

Wait. Definitely *not* the cake guy. I could now hear a ton of commotion and a kid screaming. *No wanna! No wanna!*

"Someone find Dan!" Mom shouted down our hall. "I think his sister's here."

I tucked myself farther down into the covers. I shut my eyes and saw Ash's face and strong arms, and so I opened them again. God, those stupid raccoons kept me up all night again.

You could hear them tumbling around, thumping and—right, okay—humping, making some weird raccoon mating sounds. Two nights of no sleep, and I was exhausted. The fog was morning-heavy out the windows, but you could tell it was the kind that would clear away, leaving things blue and sunny. I wouldn't have minded fog all day. Fog was a good weather match with my mood. Why do they call it "feeling blue" when it is actually more like feeling gray?

I didn't want to see what the new day would reveal next. I didn't feel up for it. I glared at my laptop, which sat on the desk by the window. Its big mouth was shut closed, and I was afraid of what it might say when it opened again. Janssen was running out of patience. I needed to get my act together, quick. I had no idea how to do this. My act did not feel like it was getting together—it felt like it was coming more and more apart. Anxiety was shaking me like a dog with a knotted sock.

"Hey, Woof. Hey, Jupiter," I said.

She scrolled her eyes my direction, not moving her head from where it was, chin tucked into paws.

"Are you a regular dog or a superdog today, hmm, girl? You tired? Maybe you just want a rest from all this too."

She sighed through her nose. Her little warm, breathing self there—I didn't feel lonely.

"I sure like you," I said.

My phone rang just out of reach on the floor, and I grabbed for it. I thought, *Janssen, Janssen, Janssen.* Then I thought, *No, no. No Janssen.* Either way, I worried for nothing. It was Gavin.

"Aren't you supposed to be working?" I said. I ducked back down into the covers.

"Hello, sunshine," Gavin said. "I'm just calling to tell you that Oscar and me are driving up as soon as he gets here. We told Bob there was a death in Oscar's family and that I was going to the funeral too, for emotional support. Oscar's De Niro, man. Real tears. We heard from Natalie there were chicks there."

"Not your type," I said.

"Do I have a type?"

"You have a not-type."

"Hey, I'm open to anyone."

"I think that's what I mean. She's got a jock boyfriend."

"Oh," Gavin said. He thought a minute. A great idea apparently occurred to him. "Hey! She doesn't know I'm a geek! We graduated. I could be anyone."

I didn't want him to get his hopes up. "Yesterday, on the beach . . . she said something about the nerds who like *Star Wars.*"

"Cricket," he reprimanded.

"Oh, right. I'm sorry. I forgot."

"*Don't* forget."

I kept my mouth shut. Oscar and Gavin were two of my best friends. I loved them. They were kind and goofy and smart. But they had this strong, heartfelt belief that nerds and geeks were two different things. I could never quite follow the logic—something about how a nerd could just be a nerd, but a geek could fix your computer (ha—my words). Honestly? If you watched them do Wii dance aerobics or play War Worlds for three days straight, their argument was meaningless.

"I thought you guys had to work because of some big sale."

"Home Electronics, there's always a sale. Like mattresses."

"Well, great. Come on, then. Your brother let you borrow his tent?" Gavin's brother, Derek—asshole. *Not* a good guy. Actually, he was an athlete-asshole, which was worse than the regular kind. His gold sports trophies filled the shelves of Gavin's parents' dining room hutch. He was always putting Gavin down, in some verbal equivalent of "accidentally" stepping on the back of his shoe. One day in the future when Gavin got a job at Microsoft and made a jillion dollars and Derek was still working at Shuck's Auto Supply, Gavin could stand up to Derek with every ounce of his thin, muscle-free body and say, *Kiss my Boolean, Derek.*

"Nah. I bought a two-man at REI with that gift card my dad got me."

"Great," I said. Gavin's father gave him one of those cards every year. I guess he hoped Gavin might go in that store full of sporting gear and come out a jock.

"Do you know they got a big rock in there? In the actual building."

"I know. But you didn't have to buy a tent. You could stay in a room here. This place is big enough."

"Nah. You guys do your family bonding. I told you, Oscar and me are *camping.* I got some of that freeze-dried food astronauts eat. We'll come in and use the shower. Wait. Oscar's on the other line. Gotta go. He's probably here. Tell the chicks we played tight end."

"Your end is nothing but squish, idiot, from too many hours playing Lord of the Sword," I said, but he'd already hung up.

I called Ben next door from my phone so I didn't have to get out of bed. I asked him to pleasepleaseplease take Jupiter out so I didn't accidentally bump into Ash looking like I was looking. Actually, I didn't tell him that last part. He came over a minute later and got her. He's such a great brother, even though he's an idiot.

I lay there awhile until I came to the conclusion that what I wanted to hide from was still in bed with me. My mind could do the work of unraveling without my body moving an inch. It was time to leave the comfort of my sweet, isolated, feather-down cell.

The shower washed away some of my bad mood. This lasted until I went downstairs. In the dining room there was a pregnant woman with long dark hair, and a tall man with one of those beards guys wear to compensate for their bald heads. They both were looking down with gaga eyes at a little boy with a head of blond curls, who wore a bathing suit and no shirt and who was now putting a striped kitchen towel over Cruiser's head. Cruiser just sat there. He didn't seem to know what was expected of him. I felt bad for him. The boy yanked the towel and shouted *Boo!* and Cruiser flinched, startled. The kid put the towel back on Cruiser for another round, and

Cruiser spun his head to get it off. He caught it in his teeth, causing the bald man to snap *Hey now!* at him.

"Bad dog!" the man said, grabbing the towel back. But Cruiser was revved up now. He set his front paws on the ground, butt up in the air. He thought it was time to play. If Jupiter had stolen that towel, they'd have never gotten it back without a fight. She had the jaws of death, and you had to lift up her back end to get her mouth to open.

"Cruiser, come here, boy!" Mom lunged but missed, and Cruiser took off on a few racetrack-dog spins around the dining room table. I wished Jupiter were there. If she walked in, it'd be just like when our elementary school principal, Mrs. Benson, would suddenly show up in a class that had a sub.

"Cricket!" my mother said when she noticed me. She looked frazzled already, and the day hadn't even started. Cruiser was under the table now, wild-eyed and panting. "Jane, John—this is my daughter. Cricket, this is Charles."

"Can you say 'Hi,' Baby Boo?" Jane said.

"No wanna." The little guy even folded his arms. Wonder who did that at home.

I tried my talking-to-little-kids voice. "Are you going swimming?"

Which was obviously the wrong thing to say. John, the kid's father, suddenly thrust out a hand, stop-sign-fashion, at me, and the mother let out a little cry of alarm.

"Wanna go swimmy," Baby Boo whined. "Wanna go swimmy!"

Jane opened her mouth. "We promised—"

"WANNA GO SWIMMY!"

Mom flinched at the scream. So did I. It sounded like an electric saw hitting metal.

"I'm sorry if we're *bothering* people," Jane said.

"No, not at *all*," Mom said.

"Look, Baby Boo, lookey," John said. "Look at the pretty." He held up a crystal salt shaker from the table and shoved it into the kid's face, jiggling it back and forth.

Mom's smile was stuck. Her voice was singsongy. She sounded like Teacher Karen from my old Little Miracles Preschool when she said to me, "Dan's doing a hike today. To some cabin, where the original settlers of the island came from? Supposedly there are ghosts there. Gram and Aunt Bailey are bringing their cameras. Ben and the girls are going . . ."

I heard it for what it was—a plea.

"Oh, cool," I said. I hoped my tone said what I felt. She'd owe me big for this.

"Bus is leaving soon. I think Ben's waiting already in the foyer. After you grab breakfast. Look! Croissants!" She stuck a couple of them into a napkin and shoved them at me. She headed over to the big silver tank of a coffeepot in the corner of the dining room that Rebecca and Ted always kept filled for guests. She pressed the lever for the thin stream of liquid. Her hands were shaking. Too much coffee herself, or another bad sign piling up against the other bad signs. She popped the lid onto the cup, or tried to.

"Gimme that," I said. She was never good with things that required manual dexterity—lids on cups, keys in keyholes, driving, generally.

"I owe you," she whispered.

"WANNA HOLD PRETTY!" Baby Boo shrieked.

The smell of pot snaked through the dining room.

Ben stood with his arms folded, looking out the windows beside the front door.

"Dreaming of escape?" I said.

He turned. "She suckered you, too?"

"She owes us," I said.

"I already spent breakfast hearing how Hailey and Amy's mother makes elaborate gingerbread houses every Christmas, worthy of magazines. Castles. Victorian mansions. You can make icing bags out of Ziplocs, did you know? She's immensely talented."

"Hey, I hope you told them how Mom actually got the new vacuum cleaner bag in the vacuum that time without your help."

"Come on. She could make the Bodsky house out of mashed potatoes."

The Bodsky house was a piece of shit. I laughed. "Gavin and Oscar are coming today sometime."

"Thank you, God. I hope they're bringing their Xbox."

George came down the stairs, in another crisp outfit of khaki shorts and a polo shirt. I wonder how many of those he had. He looked tired, though. "Coffee to go?" he said, looking at my cup. "We are off to practice. To hit a few buckets of balls." I hooked my thumb toward the dining room.

"Bad night's sleep?" I said. I knew how he felt.

"Fucking raccoons," he said.

He might have meant this literally.

"On the roof," George said to Ben, who looked confused. Ben could sleep through anything. "Right above us."

"You might want to move fast," I warned him. "Screaming kid." He hung a left. I felt bad for him, getting stuck with us. Our family dysfunction was at least *ours*. Sure, I had a love-hate relationship with it, but I'd inherited it, same as, say, some ugly but meaningful vase. It had meaning to you, even if it scared the crap out of everyone else.

"Did you hear that?" Ben whispered.

"Yeah, I hear it right now," I said. Dan's angry, muffled voice somewhere above us, Amy's voice complaining back at him, a high-pitched rising whine and then silence, same as someone trying to start a chain saw. Wait. Two thoughts about saws in as many minutes. Bad sign.

"Not that."

"I saw Mom last night. She was pissed about something. Upset."

"Not *that*. You're not listening. Anyway, she can take care of herself—"

"You're kidding, right?"

"Cricket, don't be an ass. You know, you miss what's right in front of you. *George*. Right above *us*? What's up with that, huh? *Us*?"

"Oh, give it up," I said. "You bored or something? Please. Us, meaning our *rooms*? What are you trying to do? You sound like Gram."

"I know what I saw."

"Okay, right. Uh-huh." I started to laugh. "If what you're implying is *true*? If something like *that* happens? I swear, I'll go *with* Mom when she flees to some airport."

"Not without me, you won't. Anyway, no airports here." He sounded kind of sorry.

There was the sound of foot thumps on stairs. It was Dan, clapping his hands heartily. Dan was not the hand clapping type either, but he was doing it a lot lately. It made him look like a PE teacher. "Okay, guys. Change of plan. The girls are staying here. I'll be driving you guys to the haunted settler's house—"

"Dan?" Ben said. Dan stopped on the stairs. Ben contorted his face into a grimace. Dan took this in, and they had some kind of guy conversation that didn't require words.

"Absolutely. Go," Dan said. It was kind of beautiful, actually, the brief, knowing exchange. If it had been Mom and me, we might have talked for twenty minutes about what we needed and how we felt about it. Someone might have cried. There might have been hugging involved. I didn't necessarily work the way these guys did, but I could see the benefits.

Ben snagged his car keys from his pocket, dangled them at me like we were prisoners about to break. I felt a surge of glee. "Let's spring Jupiter, too," I said. "Who knows what that kid'll do to her."

"Good thinking," Ben said.

Gram came down the stairs next. "Ghosts! I'm so excited. Oooh-eeeh!" She lifted her arms above her head in a spooky fashion.

"Get a move on, Casper," Aunt Bailey said behind her.

Mom has always been insistent and sentimental about Ben and me staying connected "later." Whenever she discussed it, you heard the shadowy backdrop behind that word, the *Someday when I'm dead* that hovered there. It was more important to keep your ties with your sibling than nearly anyone else in your family, she would say, grasping our hands so we knew she meant it. She called her own sister once a week, and Aunt Hannah would be the person who stood up for her at this wedding, as she had also done at the wedding to our father. *Your sibling is your only witness to the train wreck of your childhood,* she'd say. *And that is valuable beyond what you can imagine right now.*

Train wreck—it sounded so cynical, a far cry from tender growing-up images of cookies and milk, birthday parties and paste eating. But from what I could tell, every childhood *was* a train wreck, or at least some sort of collision, small or large, every one. Natalie's mother takes medicine for depression, and Oscar thinks his father drinks too much, and Gavin's dad expects him to be someone he'll never be. Our father had an "anger problem," and our mother left men at airports. But how can it *not* be so? We get only imperfect people for parents, and then we get a dose of life thrown in—their bad marriage, a lost job, plain old sadness. Flawed Human Parents + Shit Life Throws At You = Childhood That "Builds Character."

I guess Mom was right about Ben. My brother was the only one who had our same parents and our same great-grandma, and those exact houses and that town and those particular school lunches. Only the two of us in Bluff House had our last name, McNeal. Dad's name. And I could feel all of that shared stuff as we got into Ben's truck and rolled the windows down and got the hell out of there. He was my witness, all right. Those were his frightened eyes next to me when we saw our father strike our mother in the kitchen once. Those were his joy-filled eyes too, beside mine when Mom and him and me snuck down to Marcy Lake and sat on the dock at midnight that one New Year's when we were kids. Yeah—sparkling cider in Styrofoam cups, fireworks exploding on the lawns around the water, his and Mom's faces glowing orange and red and gold.

So, my witness and my rival and my partner in crime. Also, my friend.

"Maybe Gram's gay too," I said to him. "I saw her and Rebecca hugging out on the deck."

"Shut up, moron," he said. But he didn't really seem to care. He popped in a CD of a band we both liked, and we shouted over it. It was the thrill of a narrow miss, a snow day, a test put off until the next week. Jupiter sat between us, her nose up in the wind, ears flapping. I swear she was smiling.

"We could drive home. Hang out for the day and drive back," I said. "Oh, wait. We don't have a home."

"We could drive south to Mexico," he said. "Eat burritos until our colons explode." See? Giddy.

"I saw some place that rented boats in town. You could take us sailing."

"Awesome," he said.

"Jupiter?"

She looked over at me at the sound of her name. She waited to see what was required of her. "We can put her below so she's safe," Ben suggested.

We parked in town and walked to the waterfront. As I said, Jupiter had never been very good on her leash (actually she was terrible on her leash), and she was yanking and pulling us forward, cruising around in a zigzag, sniffing and stopping to pee everywhere. We found the shack that rented the boats, and Ben paid, even though I offered to help. The guy handed us three life jackets: our two, and a yellow dog one. With it wrapped tight around her, she looked like a bright yellow pig in a blanket. We told her how pretty she was, and she wore it around proudly. She liked compliments as much as anyone.

Ben was one of those natural athletes—got it from our dad,

obviously, because Mom could walk into a tree on the street while trying to find her phone in her purse. (This happened once.) Any sport he tried, you'd think he'd done it a hundred times already. But Ben lacked the asshole quality that often came with putting balls into various nets, holes, and goalposts. He was just easy with himself, and the boat glided out and picked up the wind, and he seemed to remember the lessons he took once, even though that was several summers ago.

We didn't have to put Jupiter below after all, because there was a nice, deep, indented portion of the boat where we could ride. She wasn't so sure about the whole idea at first, and refused to sit on the smooth bench. She didn't like the feel of certain things under her butt (the seat of Mom's car, for one), and instead chose to balance precariously with her back end in the air if the surface wasn't right. I understood. I felt the same way about padded toilet seats and certain public bathrooms. I set her down on my lap and rubbed the tips of her ears and whispered that she was a brave sailing girl. She was a fat package in that life jacket.

"Guess who I talked to last night?" Ben said. He held the rudder in one hand, and the rope to the mainsail in the other.

"Oh, this is a challenging one. Go ahead. Tell me how much she misses you. She's cried every minute since you've been gone. No, wait. You are a god to her, I know. A sex god. Her life will never be the same now that you are in it."

"Janssen, idiot."

How many times in my life had I heard that name or

spoken that name or thought that name? Hundreds of thousands. Millions, even. More than my own name, I'm sure. So why did the sound of it send my stomach falling? A hurtling body off the tallest building?

"Go ahead. Tell me how much he misses me. He's cried every minute since I've been gone."

"He didn't even mention you." I had thought the hurtling body had reached the ground, but it hadn't yet. There, now it did. He didn't even mention me? "He was wondering if he could borrow some of my hiking gear. Is he going up to Rainier?"

"I don't *know*," I said. How could I not know? Jesus, I had needed a little time to think, that was all. That didn't mean a person completely went ahead and lived their life without you, did it? Okay, maybe it did, but at least they shouldn't live a life they didn't even *tell* you about.

"Hey. Don't get pissed at *me*."

"I'm not pissed!"

It was quiet for a moment. Maybe I was something worse than pissed. Maybe I was scared.

Ben put the sail down, and we bobbed around out there, and we poured some water from the water bottles into the plastic margarine container we always brought for Jupiter. She took a good, long wobbly drink and then got her courage up and walked around the deep, safe inset part of the boat. We tilted our heads back into the sun and sat there with the water sloshing against the sides. I made myself feel better with a nasty, selfish thought. It was all my doing with Janssen, so there. *My* decision. And I could un-decide if I wanted. Just like that, I could un-decide, and Janssen would be here in our next boat ride out and there'd be no hikes to Rainier that I didn't know about and no more uncertain futures.

Ben took his shirt off and jumped in. I got a little worried about that. I had a vision: him drifting off, me floating out to sea, unable to reach him and lost forever. But he stayed by the boat and climbed back in neatly. He shook his head like a dog after a bath.

"I'm getting sunburned," I said.

"I'm *hungry*. Let's head back."

Ben lifted the sail again. Jupiter, confident now, stood near the front with her nose up, like the mermaids on the bows of ships. Noble. Her eyes squinted at the wind, and her black fur shined. She looked very beautiful right then.

It was a fast trip in. The harbor was busy with whale watching tours and fishing boats; a huge sailboat arrived, and the passengers disembarked. Ben bumped us to the dock and tied us down, and he lifted out Jupiter. Her toenails clicked happily along the dock as we walked back. We headed for the nearest burger place, a shack at one end of the marina, The Cove, with outdoor tables set around that overlooked the sound. We ordered food, including double fries, and then headed toward the tables near the back of the place.

Wait—I knew that long hair, and those particular

shoulders. I knew that hair so well, I had grabbed it with my tiny fists before I could speak. (We had a picture of this, among others, on the living room wall.) Our mother was sitting by herself, eating fries of her own and drinking a Coke, contemplating the wide, wide ocean, and probably the distance from here to the next airport, by the look of it.

"Hey," I called. "You related to us?"

She turned, surprised. "What are you guys doing here? I thought you were hiking out to whatever that place was. Hi, Jupiter! Hi, girl! Where've you been?" She trailed her fingers down, and Jupiter wagged, happy to see her. Jupiter gave her salty-fries hand a lick.

"Dan set us free," I said.

"Went sailing," Ben said.

"Damn, I wish I knew," she said.

"What are you doing out here?" I asked. "Aren't you supposed to be cake-ing or something today?"

"Cake guy is later this afternoon. Had to get out of there for a while. This is great, though. You guys can give me a ride back."

"You *walked*?" I said.

"It's not that far," Mom said. She gave Jupiter a dog treat from her jacket pocket, where she always kept some. Jupiter crunched away down there. "I just needed to get a little air."

"Yeah, get away from all those people," Ben said. I shot him a look. Kicked his foot. What was he thinking? I remembered Mom, Ben, me, and Jupiter getting into the Bermuda

Honda and going on drives to get away from Jon Jakes and Olivia and Scotty. We'd go get Slurpees in the next town and then take the long way back on winding farm roads. We'd pile into the car to get candy bars at the Country Store down the road, and end up at the park at the Cedar River Watershed. We'd sit at the edge of the river with our shoes off for as long as possible, as Jupiter watched the treetops for squirrel action. Those were not the things you did when you wanted to be somewhere and with someone—you didn't try to escape. You didn't drive on every back road so it would take as long as possible to return. And, probably, you didn't walk miles down a beach without any thought to how you were getting back.

"Is Olivia giving you problems?" Ben said. He was digging into the bag to get his fries. He didn't even realize what he'd just said, but Mom did. It looked like someone had just struck her—her cheeks got red and she looked shocked.

"Ben, shit," I said. *"Olivia?"*

"Did I say Olivia? *Hailey.* Or the other one. Amy."

"They're not as bad as Olivia. No way," I said. "They're just *shy*. We're pretty overwhelming."

"Hard to get along with, yeah. I'd stay away from us too." Ben bit into his burger. "Grandpa is especially evil." I could read his damn mind, because he'd forgotten about Grandpa until he said his name. A grin started creeping up the corner of his mouth and he met my eyes, and I narrowed mine with warning.

"Adjustments," Mom squeaked.

"Dan's a great guy," I said.

"Great guy," Ben said. "Hey, as long as their mother doesn't show up at the wedding, you're fine." He was laughing, and not about Dan's ex, I knew. He was still thinking about Grandpa and George, and he was chuckling, the kind of chuckling that could turn into all-out hysteria. I knew what *that* looked like well enough, from a particularly serious moment during Great-Grandma's funeral, and from every time Mom got mad at him. I was going to kill him the second we were alone.

"I know he's a great guy," Mom said.

With Vic Dennis she started keeping her car keys in the pocket of her jeans toward the end. You saw the bulge of them there. I caught them having an argument once, and saw her gripping those keys in her hand. There'd been a lot of staring off into the distance then too, and she would run her finger across her mouth in thought, as she was doing now.

I stared off along with her. Maybe that's where a person found answers—out there. "Hey, wait," I said.

"What?" Ben said.

"I'll be right back."

It was him, I was sure—down by that fishing boat. Wearing those rubber overalls fishing guys wear. Walking up the dock, talking on a phone. Shutting the phone now. I jogged over. Looking back, it seems overeager. I didn't have much practice in those things. If it had been Janssen, I would have jogged right over without a second thought. I didn't know how to play games.

"Ash!" I actually called out, which was probably another thing not to do. Ordinarily, too, I would have joked about the rubber pants. Janssen and I always made fun of each other. "Is that you?"

"Cricket," he said. "Hey! Wait, don't come near me. I stink." We stood together on the dock. I felt a little dizzy. Either the dock was moving or the water and sloshing boats only made it seem like it was.

"You fishing?"

"Yeah. I work down here. Make some money this summer, you know? Good money, but I got to get up at four a.m."

"Ouch," I said.

"Got that right." He grinned. He had a zillion-watt grin. Warmth crept up my body, landed somewhere at its center. "But now I go home and sleep."

"Sleep is good." Oh, idiot. Nice one. It sounded like I was one of those lame people who thought sleep was an actual hobby. *I like to watch football and sleep.* I like to blink and breathe, too.

"Glad I saw you, though. I was thinking—we're having a bonfire down here tonight. Some people from school. Friends. Party, kind of. If you wanna come? Bring whoever. Mostly you."

"Okay, sure," I said. All right. I wasn't usually the party type. I didn't really like parties. Talking to drunk people—it wasn't my idea of a good time. But who knew? A bonfire, Ash, some beach town where no one knew me . . .

"Great. *Great.* Hey, I gotta get these rubber pants off." He snapped the suspenders like an old man.

"Or else get a rubber shirt to go with," I said.

He laughed. "You've got a beautiful smile, you know that?"

"*You* do," I said.

"See you tonight? Just come down here, over there—" He pointed. "After dark. You'll see where we are. Come and find me. Anyone else over at the house can come too."

"There's a toddler you'd love."

"Oh no . . ."

"I'm thinking up other uses for Cruiser's kennel."

"Got the picture," he said. "Hey, wait. Cell number?" He handed me his phone, and I typed it in. "All right. Later, Beautiful Smile."

I waved. Hurried back to my fries, which were getting cold.

"Who was that?" Mom said. She sloshed the ice in her cup in circles. She fed Jupiter the last bit of bun from her burger. "Is that Ted's son?"

"What are you doing, Cricket? Jesus, you should have seen yourself," Ben said.

"Can't I have a conversation with someone? Yes, Ted's son. No big deal, people. I'm not having his babies."

"Payback for Rainier? You trying to make things worse?" Ben said.

I stuck my tongue out at the back of his head.

"What happened at Rainier?" Mom said.

"He's wrong for you." This was not said in some big, overly-protective-brother way. Ben wasn't like that. He was stating a fact. The same way he'd say, *You got something on your shirt*, or, *It's getting late.*

"Did you decide to break up with Janssen all the way?" Mom said. "You guys don't tell me anything."

"I was just being *friendly*," I said. "He's wrong for me because he's not Janssen?"

"He's wrong for you because he's wrong for you," Ben said. He crumpled up the foil from his burger. "I think I want another one of those."

Mom reached for her wallet. "Here. I owe you guys."

I didn't know who or how I'd be without these people right here. If I went away to school, my own self might be left behind. My *home*, for sure. I knew them, and they knew me, same as a roof knows a house. We were connected like that, and they were my shelter, too. Could you be too known, though? What if, like Gavin said, you could be anyone now that you graduated? You could sit inside the warm, familiar room of someone's idea of you. Or you could step out the front door and see if they'd been right, or wrong, all along.

chapter
twelve

"I think that's Gavin's car," I said. I couldn't quite see over the dog.

"I don't have my contacts in," Mom said.

Ben hit the gas and swerved around the car in front of us.

"Shit, Ben!" I could see us making the papers. All of us dead in one swoop, and right before a wedding. The worst kind of horrible news story that stops you in your tracks for one second before you head into the kitchen to get yourself a bowl of ice cream. Close-up of the grieving groom, the dress spread out on the bed, the now-tragic yearbook pictures. So, chocolate mint or vanilla caramel? It makes me nervous, the way the biggest things and the smallest live together day in and day out.

The windows of the Kia rolled down, and arms popped out

on both sides, waving madly. That pasty white flesh could only belong to two people.

Ben *honk, honk, honked!* the horn. Mom rolled down her window and waved.

"They're camping on the beach," I said.

"Oh no," Mom said. "Is that safe? Have they ever slept outside before?"

"I don't think so," I said.

"They know there are no electrical outlets in nature, right?" Ben said.

"It's their big postgraduation adventure. Geeks Meet the Great Outdoors. Someone should make a movie."

"Reminds me of that time we slept in the tent in the front yard to watch the meteor shower," Mom said. "Remember that? They'll probably come running into the house in the middle of the night too."

"Freezing their butts off," Ben said.

Now that we were all back at Bluff House and my eyeballs had stopped spinning from Ben's driving, I could see that Gavin's car was jammed full of stuff. That back window was dangerously blocked, in my opinion. Gavin popped out of the car. He was wearing one of his usual T-shirts, the one with the wizard on it, but I was surprised to see him wearing a pair of shorts. I don't think I'd ever seen his legs before. Oscar got out too, and slapped Ben on the back, and Ben slapped him on the back while Gavin leaned into the car, shoving everything around in some sort of hunt. Finally his head emerged, his big bush of dark hair its usual mess. He was holding a box wrapped in birthday paper. He handed it to Mom.

"From both of us," Gavin said. "Happy wedding." For some reason Oscar wore a knit cap over his own longish blond hair. Probably to protect against the elements. He was trying to grow a beard or something, since I saw him last. There was an alfalfa sproutlike fluff on his chin.

"Oh, you guys," Mom said. "You didn't have to do that." She put her arm around Oscar's thin shoulders.

"It's a router," Oscar said.

"You fool! Don't tell!" Gavin said.

"That is so great!" Mom said. "How thoughtful. Dan is just going to love it." She had no idea what a router was.

"It's got WAP2," Gavin said.

"You're kidding!" Mom said. "Wow. I love it! *Thank* you."

"What's that on your belt loop?" Ben asked.

Gavin lifted up the dangling bit of flat plastic. "Cool shit, eh? Compass. They had 'em there right by the REI counter."

"Thank God. Now you dweebs won't get lost on the beach directly in front of the house," I said.

Gavin patted his new hiking shorts, struck a pose. "New me. Whattya think? Not bad for a guy voted most likely to have moobs, eh?"

Mom looked my way for an explanation. "Man boobs," I said.

"You've still got time, dude," Oscar said. He was obviously

trying on a new persona too. I'd never heard him say "dude" in my life.

Mom smiled, looked at her wrist where a watch would be, if she wore one. "I've gotta get going," Mom said. "Cake guy is coming. Thank you so much again for the gift. Hope you guys will have dinner with us later?"

"We're covered," Oscar said. "Beef stroganoff. Freeze dried, baby. Ice cream, too. Just add water."

"Want to come in and see the house?"

"Nah." Gavin brushed his hands on his shorts, like he'd already been getting down and dirty in the outdoors. He had some new look of manly determination, in spite of that same old fright-wig of black hair I'd known since the seventh grade. "We gotta set up here."

"So little time, so much to eat," Oscar said. I hadn't seen him this excited since War Worlds Six came out; his hands had been shaking so hard then, he could barely tear the cellophane from the box. "Later, y'all."

"I wonder how much stuff they bought," Ben said as we walked to the house together. "I saw an REI shopping bag filled to the top with foil packages."

"Look at them," I said. "Like us when we got our Aladdin tent for Christmas that year. Look how excited they are. I don't feel good about this."

"Good things don't always lead to bad ones, Crick."

"He just unloaded a camp stove! Oh no. I had high school chemistry with those two."

"Are they the ones that—"

"Yeah. And I don't know if that sub's hair ever grew back."

My mother had her own ideas about religion. A personal patchwork quilt of all the best stuff, the love, the watching over, everything comforting, minus the hell and damnation. Whenever we did a painful good deed, she'd say, *Well, at least you got some heaven points.* Her God was understanding enough to know that some situations required extra incentive to be good.

So I got heaven points for asking Hailey and Amy to come to Ash's party with me that night. I asked Ben, too, but he was going with Dan and Ted into town to watch an old James Bond film at the Bishop Grand (not so grand) Theater. Ben never met a gadget he didn't like.

I was glad he wasn't coming, actually. The night was wide open and smelled great, and I tried on three things before deciding what to wear. When you try on lots of outfits, you're probably going somewhere you don't want your brother to be. Your sibling is your witness and your rival and your friend, yeah, but also a spy. Even if they're not a spy, even if they're cool or don't even notice what you're doing, you're sure they notice what you're doing. Ben has never been my moral guardian, but I'm still pretty sure he's got some recording device embedded under his skin, like those tags dogs have in case they get lost.

I knocked on Hailey and Amy's door. "Ready?"

I gasped. Okay, that was a lot of flesh all of a sudden.

Not that I was a prude or anything; my school never sent anyone home for dress-code violations, so you see it all. Usually you don't go out with it all, though. Natalie and Kelly, even Shauna—my girlfriends stayed mostly dressed. But now Hailey wore a white skirt the size of a coffee filter, and a little crocheted doily for a top. We used to make Valentine cards out of those. Her stomach was bare. She was suddenly a good four inches taller, and, oh yeah, that was why. Those shoes. The kind Mom and I made fun of at Ross. Two stories high, gold glitter. Her perfume slammed into me, took me to the ground in some sudden champion wrestling move.

I hated judgmental bitchiness, but I was feeling it crawling all over me, like sand fleas. I did a mental slap-slap of myself. Sometimes you gotta keep you in line.

"Amy's not coming," she said. I could see Amy on the bed, head on her arms.

"She okay?"

"Not feeling well. Dad'll take care of her."

So much for James Bond. Who knew illness could get you such parental one-on-one? Slap again. "Okay. We've got to stop by and get a couple people before we go," I said. "Two of my friends are here, camping on the beach."

"Boys?" she said. The word was a joy-filled balloon, lifting up. I worried about those shoes in the sand. Could she get stuck out there as the tide came in?

"Yeah. They played tight end."

"Oh, I love football!"

We inched our way down the boardwalk. I pictured the twist of an ankle, me lunging to catch a body, no safe place to grab, yikes, the two of us sliding to the bottom in a broken heap. I could have run down there and back by the time we got to the ground, but we finally made it. Gavin's tent was a huge glowing ball out there on the beach. You could fit eight people in there. Yellow-orange lights flickered inside the globe. It looked as if a space vehicle had landed on our Earth.

"Gavin, Oscar!"

"What's that sound?" Hailey said.

Good question. A loud, vibrating thrum. Some kind of . . . shooting? The zing and zap of electronic *lasers*?

I flung back the tent flap. "What are you guys do—Holy crap!"

Gavin and Oscar sat crossed-legged on sleeping bags, which were laid out on cushy mattress-thick foam. Between them were two silver foil packages, sliced down the middle and spilling some brownish noodle-like substance. Piles of pillows made a cozy headboard. At the far end of the tent was a large flat screen TV, surrounded by speakers. A heater leaned against one nylon wall, shooting out waves of warmth, and a small lamp sat in the corner. It looked just like Gavin's room at home. All that was missing was the retro *Charlie's Angels* poster and the blanket with the digital-style lettering, reading, NO I DON'T KNOW WHAT'S WRONG WITH YOUR COMPUTER. Wait, actually, there it was, sticking out from his sleeping bag. I recognized that shade of orange.

"Cool," Hailey said. "Can you get cable?"

They both turned their heads at the same time, Gavin's big bushy-haired one and Oscar's with that stupid hat, and both their mouths gaped open at the sight of her. Their controllers went, well, *stiff*, thumbs frozen midair. Oscar's car crashed into a wall and exploded, and Gavin's ran off the road, smashing head-on into a video mountain.

"Why did I think camping meant flashlights and s'mores?" I said.

"Oscar's dad had a generator," Gavin said. "Hey," he said to Hailey. "I'm Gavin, and you're amazing."

Great. Just terrific.

"Oscar. Oscar Maya." Oscar held his hand out now. He was a genius and his parents were both geniuses, and sometimes geniuses could miss the obvious. Or else those folks had a fondness for hot dogs. Who knew? His name was a cruel parental misstep, I thought, given the crap he always got. But Hailey didn't notice either.

"This is my kind of camping," she said.

"Six-man tent," Gavin said.

"Plenty of room," Oscar said. He really needed to shave that stuff off his chin.

Hailey stared toward the TV. "I haven't seen my shows in two days."

"We got shows. Gavin doesn't have the satellite hooked up yet, but it just takes a sec."

Somebody had better step in there, quick, and I guessed

that somebody was me. Those two were in way over their heads. Someone was going to get hurt. "We're heading out. A bonfire down the beach," I said. "Party. You guys want to come?"

"Party?" Oscar said to me. "You?"

"What?" I was getting more irritated by the second.

"You never go to parties. You hate parties," Oscar said.

"You hate *parties*?" Hailey said.

"I don't hate parties," I said. "I just don't usually—"

"'Standing around talking to drunk people—,'" Gavin said.

"'Isn't my idea of a good time,'" Oscar finished.

The truth was, it was one of the reasons we all got along so well. Gavin and Oscar didn't like that stuff either. They cared about their brain cells.

"Come on, where is this party?" Hailey said. She took a pinch of Gavin's sleeve. "Let's go."

Was she *flirting*? With *Gavin*? In the years that I'd known him, I'd only seen that happen once. Holly Kenelly, and she didn't shave her legs. I think she went to an all-women's college to study feminist literature. I seem to remember reading that in the graduation program.

"I'll save our scores," Oscar said. He bustled around the tent, shutting things off. He didn't seem bothered by Hailey's attention to Gavin. He was used to it, probably. Gavin always got to the next level before he did.

The tent went momentarily dark, and then a large disc of light blinded me. I flung my arm to my eyes in protection.

"Sorry," Oscar said. "Emergency flashlight. It has a radio, too, and a siren with a bottle opener."

I sat in the back of Gavin's car with Oscar. He'd pulled off his hat, and now his hair stood up with wavy undersea tentacles of static. Hailey was playing with Gavin's radio dial. She fingered the tassel from Gavin's graduation mortarboard that hung from his rearview mirror. "I looove tassels," she said.

I was seriously racking up the heaven points now.

The walk from the car to the beach and then down to the bonfire was a long, slow trip because of Hailey's shoes. She kept sinking in the sand and giggling, and Gavin would take her outstretched hands and pull her out.

"You could take them off," Oscar suggested. He looked toward the bonfire's orange glow in the distance and to the crowd gathered there with an odd mix of eagerness and worry. We'd felt this same feeling, together, every time we'd stepped onto the bus for a middle-school field trip or into a gym for PE. Oscar was my partner whenever I needed one. He gave me a Christmas present every year, usually a girl gift—perfume, scarf, earrings—which he wrapped with tight, tight corners and a string of ribbon. He was a good friend.

"I can*not*," Hailey said. "I love these shoes. Aren't these sexy?" she said to Gavin, and stretched one long leg for him to admire. She sounded tipsy, but we hadn't even had anything to drink yet, obviously a flirtation tactic that had never occurred to me. I'd have thought Gavin would be having a coronary at the sight of those legs, but after the camping, wow, he was a new man.

"Sexy as hell," he said, and then he picked her up and threw her over one shoulder, and she shrieked and he ran. (Okay, this was awkward—an effortful lurching that made me worry he'd pulled some kind of groin muscle.) The bonfire was the finish line.

"Touchdown!" Hailey yelled, and Gavin swung her down.

"He's clutching his pelvis," Oscar said.

"I've never seen him lift anything heavier than a desktop computer," I said.

"Well, we sell a lot of those at Tech Time," Oscar said. "The fifty-six-inch big screens are pretty heavy too."

Hailey was waving her arms, down by the crowd. She was looking pretty chipper now, after all her earlier misery about her father and my mother falling in love and finding happiness together. She seemed to have forgotten about that. She already held a red cup in the air.

"Who are these people again?" Oscar said.

"I only know Ash. His parents own Bluff House."

Oscar looked at me, raised his eyebrows. "Did you and Janssen break up all the way? You never told me."

"No!" I said. I was entirely too known by *all* the people in my life.

"Cricket, are you okay?" he said. "You don't seem okay."

"I'm fine."

"You seem really off."

"I said I'm fine. Come on."

There were a lot of Valentine doily tops and short skirts and those squarish white manicured fingernails that always secretly gave me the creeps. Somewhere in the back of my mind I always worried I'd find one in my food. In my sundress and with my plain hands, I was practically the Amish wife in the crowd. I searched around for Ash amid the snapping fire and clinking glass bottles and people laughing. I felt out of place, like those times you went to watch a football game at a different school. It was the bleachers they knew, and their band, and you didn't even understand how the parking lot worked, and everyone kept looking your way with those little quick, appraising glances. Usually I had Janssen with me, though. I'd hold his arm. We'd sit together.

Oscar and I hung back. I tried not to feel awkward, although my covered chest and general party anxiety as well as my pale, shrinking companion with his uncertain chin fluff were making me feel infused with a sudden surge of geek. I felt dipped in geek, both inside and outside. It was the feeling of not belonging, and longing for your familiar couch and your familiar TV with all those comforting TV people who couldn't see you.

I felt a pair of hands on my waist.

"Hey," Ash said, and I was so glad to see him. He wore his jeans and a white T-shirt, and he smelled good, even in the smoky night air. Some kind of cologne. Something musky.

"Ash," I said. "This is my friend Oscar."

"Hey," Oscar said.

"You guys want a beer?"

"What else do you have?" I asked. "We're not big drinkers."

"Cool," Ash said. We edged our way through the crowd. The heat of the bonfire was intense. Maybe doilies weren't such a bad idea. The sea looked dark out there, though the waves coming in were frothy and white in the moonlight. A couple of coolers were set up against the sand bank. Oscar plucked a can of Mountain Dew from the slushy ice, and I poured some Diet Coke into a cup. "Really glad you could come. Let me introduce you to a few people."

Hailey and Gavin had disappeared into the crowd somewhere. I thought I heard her laughing. Oscar was standing so close to me, we could've won the three-legged race. We inched our way toward a couple with their arms around each other. It was Ash's good friend Alex and his girlfriend, yes, Alex, and we talked with them for a while. The male Alex was one of those big guys who are so instantly friendly that you like him right off, and his girlfriend was lively and interested in where we'd come from and why.

"These guys have been together forever," Ash said. "Look at them," he teased.

"If you had kids—," Oscar said.

"We'd name them Alex," Girl Alex said.

"You heard it before?" I said. I was starting to feel a little more comfortable.

"All the time," she said.

162

"Maybe that's just what we'll do," Boy Alex said, and pulled her hips toward his.

Well, of course I flashed on Janssen. How could I not. I felt so sad, and the shame of how hurtful I'd been shoved me hard once more. Another guy joined us. He had longish blond hair, and was holding a bottle of Southern Comfort. He shot some into my cup. "Fill her up!" he said merrily. "Big Alex, Big Ash!"

"This is Matt," Ash said.

"School's out for summa!" he sang. "My dudes, my buddies. My bosom pals. Boob pals." He cracked up. "You're gonna miss me when I'm gone."

"Not likely," Girl Alex said. She rolled her eyes at me.

Ash leaned over. His breath was warm in my ear. It made me shiver. "Wanna go for a walk? I can't stand that asshole."

He tugged my sleeve toward the beach. I looked over at Oscar. "It's fine," he said.

Guilt filled me, like in those movies where someone's trapped in a room and water starts coming in. I could feel it rising and rising, but I went anyway. I left Oscar back there.

"You don't have to drink that shit," Ash said.

I shrugged. I took a sip. Maybe I had some stupid idea that it would erase the guilt I felt about Oscar, about Janssen, about how badly I wanted to be alone on that beach with Ash. I was eighteen, and I wanted to walk by the shore under the moon with that attractive guy, just *walk*, for God's sake, and I wanted to feel large and brave enough to not care what that might mean. And so I tipped my head and swallowed that stuff like I was someone I wasn't. The drink didn't taste all that great, but it was pleasantly warm. Sweet-warm, like that whiskey drink Grandpa Shine made for me once when I had a bad cold. Lemon, honey, and water, but warm, and I slept so well. Now, it made my knees buzz in a soft, pleasant way.

"He's the worst," Ash said. "We've got some great people here. Great guys. And a few assholes."

"Like anywhere," I said.

The bonfire was getting smaller and smaller behind us. We walked near the shore, and I took my shoes off. The houses along the beach were all different, decks and no decks, small and shingled, huge and modern. In the windows where lights glowed, you could see the people inside, like they were onstage in a play.

Everything felt a little unreal.

Oscar was disappearing back there too, and I sipped from my cup and Ash walked close by me, and we talked, and then we were just quiet, listening to the *chsh . . . cshshh . . .* of the waves going in and out. You could walk and not realize just how far you'd gone.

Ash took my elbow, stopped us.

"It's beautiful out here," I said.

"It is," he said. "Your eyes are so bright in this moon."

I just looked at him, and we stood so close. His chest was there in front of me, a good place for the flat palm of my hand. I could really smell that musk now.

"Miss Cricket, I would really like to kiss you," he said. I felt so warm. So, so warm, and my whole body was buzzing now. "But I'm an old-fashioned guy. I like to wait."

He leaned in. I felt only his cheek against mine, and it was crazy, crazy how much I wanted him. Just that—*want*. I wanted that really good-looking guy and a meaningless, great kiss. He hugged me and pulled away. For one moment his cheek, my cheek, this unknown beach, I felt it. Free. Free from all the ways things could go wrong, and released from faithfulness and constancy and the ties that held me to everyone—Janssen, yes, but my family, too. Ties that felt like ropes sometimes, anchored to the ground on one end, to a hot-air balloon on the other, that hot-air balloon we saw that time, Janssen and I. Someplace inside of me felt that I needed to cut those ropes in order to rise up and see the countryside. That same place inside also knew how dangerous it would be to be so, so high.

"Maybe we should go back," I said.

I was afraid he'd take my hand. I tucked them into my pockets. My hands were mine, but they were also Janssen's. He'd held my hand after I'd gotten my wisdom teeth taken out, and at the movies, and when we'd lie quietly together. He held both of them that time, after my father scared us all so bad. Janssen held my hand under the table at that awkward Thanksgiving too, the one with my father and grandparents and aunts and uncles. He had to eat with his left hand, so he could keep hold of it.

We walked. Ash gave me a playful shove, and I shoved him back, and he hugged me again, and I felt that heat, that great heat, and then we were back. My cup was empty. I didn't know how long we'd been gone.

Oscar was sitting on a piece of driftwood by the coolers, holding his Mountain Dew. He lifted his hand in a little wave when he saw me. My insides felt like they were swirling a little.

"We'll probably be heading out," I said.

"Well, it was great. I'm so glad you came. I'll see you back at the house?"

"Back at the house," I said.

I headed toward Oscar. "There you are," he said. He stood. "Cricket? Are you all right?"

"Let's go back," I said.

"Did you drink that stuff?" he asked. "What did you do that for? What's happening to you? Okay, wait. Let me go get Gavin. Just sit here."

I sat. On the way down my head shimmered in a disturbing fashion. My butt almost missed the log. The wood scraped the back of my leg. There were some strange walls going in and out and up and down inside my head.

We all got back to the car. In the backseat Oscar kept peering at me. His little beard fluff looked very concerned. As the streetlights passed, his face shone with light and then went dark, light, dark. Hailey and Gavin were laughing and talking in the front. She was patting the top of his poofy hair. Did she actually *like* it? Everything was all loud and swarmy, like a carnival inside my own head—their voices were bright and wavy, and when the car turned into the driveway, it felt like we kept turning and turning.

Gavin and Hailey were saying good-bye. Some faraway piece of me was thankful there would only be two men in the six-man tent that night. Some far faraway piece knew how anything but that would hurt Dan and my mother. The idea of hurting people—it was so far away and small, I almost couldn't hear it. I felt a little wild and reckless, like I wanted to do something big. Huge. I could take Gavin's keys and drive back home and knock on Janssen's door and wake him up. I could say the words that would undo how I'd hurt him. We could stay together forever, and we could have babies that we could name Alex. I would never have to be afraid of assholes ever again. I wouldn't have to worry where home was—I would always be home.

"Cricket?" Oscar was breathing beside me. I could hear it, really loud. I could almost see wavy breaths. Were we holding hands? "Maybe I should help you in."

"I can go in," I said. "I'm going to bed."

"I want to tell you," he said. "Now that you and Janssen . . . I've always cared—"

His bangs were falling into his eyes. I brushed them off his forehead. There. He could see better now. The better to stare at me, which he was doing. "My inside walls are going in and out," I said.

Oscar put his arm around me, and I put my arm around his waist. Old Oscar. Good old Oscar. Great guy. I lay my head on his shoulder because my head was very heavy. Oscar's hand was on my arm, and then it wasn't, so finally I could leave. It released me, like ropes of a balloon being cut, and I drifted up and went inside and drifted up more, up the stairs, and the real walls were going in and out.

I went to the bathroom. I think I pretty much brushed my teeth, or something close. I was coming out and heading to my room, when I crashed into Ben.

"Cricket?" he said.

"Well, hello," I said.

He sniffed. "Cricket, for Christ's sake, are you *drunk?*"

"No!" I said. I'd never been drunk in my life.

He looked at me, stunned. Even then I could see the disappointment in his face. That disappointment—it cut through all the spinning and swarming, shot like a jet to the place that was me way down in there.

"Jesus, Cricket. What next? You're losing it," he said. "*Losing* it."

I went to my room. Jupiter was there on her pillow. She lifted her head and watched me. I imagined, or didn't imagine, worried eyes. Those white crescent rings under the milk chocolate as she looked up.

"I'm fine," I told her. "Go back to sleep."

I got into bed. The room was spinning in circles. I wasn't sure where I was, or, really, who. This is what happened too, when you cut the ropes. See? Here was proof. The balloon could get away from you. You could hurt and disappoint people. Home, it could drift far away. It would get tiny, and disappear. You could get lost.

It was worse when I shut my eyes. My stomach felt sick. It was swimming, and inside was a toxic mix of confusion and dread, and a very bad amusement park ride was happening in my head. The black lid of my laptop stayed closed on my desk. It kept its big mouth shut. *You*, I said to it in my whirling mind. *So there.*

chapter thirteen

Dear Janssen—

All right. My turn.

The Ways Dogs Show Their Utter Devotion:

1. They stay close, even if that means they
   sometimes get stepped on.
2. They watch you, always. They keep their
   eye on you, waiting for a change in your
   weather. When you are upset, they look
   worried. They sit right next to you then.

3. They try their very best. They will run too far; they will sit and stay and wait forever, all because you asked.

4. They are happy to see you again. If you're gone for five minutes, if you're gone for days. Every single time, thrilled.

5. They guard you against anything bad. Even though they are small, so much smaller than what might harm you, they are there, ready to protect you.

Jupiter is watching me now. It's morning, and she's lying on that stinky pillow with her blankie and Rabbit. Her little black self, with her white spot on her back. The sun is coming through the window exactly where she is, so she didn't even have to move to get there. It's one of those times I love her so much, I can hardly stand it.

I just realized something. She doesn't do that wild burst of insane running around anymore like she used to. You know, when it's like the devil bit them in the ass? Out of nowhere, she'd race like a possessed demon, sprinting mad circles around the living room, shooting up on the couch and flying across, then back down for another and another crazed loop. But when was the last time she did that? When was her last good lightning-fast run?

Wait a sec.

Okay, I'm back. I just tried to clap my hands and get her going, but, nothing. I said, *Come on! Let's play, kid! Let's go!* But she just looked at me, like, *Cricket, please. I'm tired, here.*

Why do they do that, do you think? Why do they suddenly let go of their usual, respectable selves? Do you think they just need to be wild, and suddenly there's no holding it back? They want to go, full speed. They want to *let* go. Feel. Feel the muscles in their legs and the wind on their back and their young, untamed selves leaping on some couch back of joy, *flying.*

Do you think we feel that too? Maybe when the music is on in the car and it's a great day and you want to push down the accelerator just to do life at full speed . . . You can feel so hungry for life sometimes; you want it all, all at once, now. You want to drink it up, every last drop. I do, sometimes. But then, shit. What would that mean? How would that change things? You could get hurt, running along up high on the furniture like that.

You should see her now, Janssen. She's still lying there, but her nose is in the air, sniff, sniff, sniffing, her little nostrils going in and out. I love that. I guess sometimes a dog needs to run like crazy, and sometimes a dog needs to stay still and try to understand what is blowing her way.

I noticed that you didn't answer any of my pleadings from my last letter. And I hate to plead. You know that. What's happening over there? What's going on, Janssen?

You know what's going on here? Me, remembering the Janssen and Cricket story, that's what. When we last left off . . . The church lawn. I was about fourteen, and you were about sixteen, and there was something happening between us. We both knew it that day, right? But I was your best friend's little sister, and I was *young* (your words). So you decided to forget about me (even if you never forget about me). You dated that girl! I hated that. I hated her. I didn't know her, but still. I'm sure she was a fine person. Aside from that annoying laugh. But then, well, we know what happened.

My father.

And that's when something huge shifted between us. It was right around when mom sold *Monkey M. Monkey* and then after that, *Monkey M. Monkey Has an Adventure.* She wanted to take us on a trip to New York, remember? Where she would meet her editor, and we would meet that tall chick holding a torch in the harbor. My mother gave notice to our father as required by the dreaded Parenting Plan (God, I hate those words), and then she bought the plane tickets. Ben promised you a snow globe with the Empire State Building in it, if I have that right. Maybe something else. But when it sunk in that we were actually going on a cool trip to celebrate my mother's success, my father went nuts. He refused to let us go. He said it was illegal to take us on a plane without his permission. He actually said that. So, yeah, it got a little crazy.

They had some heated conversations. (You always accuse me of understatement when it comes to my dad.) Mom was crying and calling her attorney.

Jupiter hovered nervously. Crying made her worry.
Ben and I were ready to run away. We went to
Dad's for our usual weekend, and he was sullen.
Pissed. He had some new girlfriend over for dinner
(can't remember her name), but it was awkward
because he was preoccupied. He wasn't always
that way, Janssen. We had a fun time over there
too, you know that. Camping, skiing, the kinds of
things Mom would never do.

But that trip. See, when he first left home? He
yelled this thing to Mom, right in front of us,
out in the driveway, where I'm sure even Mrs.
Washelli heard. A terrible thing. That she would
never be able to make it without him. She'd end
up in a tent in his backyard, he said. I don't think I
ever told you this, because it was an awful thing for
him to say. It was scary, too. I was embarrassed—
the mail lady was right there. But I also remember
thinking—could that be true? Is that what was
going to happen to us?

It wasn't working out that way, though, and I
think that's what made him furious. He hated that
her life was changing for the better. Ben had just
turned seventeen like you, but he didn't have his
truck yet. So that day Dad had to drive us home.

I think it's funny, you know. How we've never talked about this really. Ever. But anyway, he drove in through the electric gate, which Mom had left open for us. The stupid Mighty Mule. He drove up our long gravel driveway and parked by the house. He pulled the parking brake, and then he just sat there. Didn't get out, didn't move. We didn't know what to do. Ben opened his door, so I did too and we got our stuff out of the backseat. We said good-bye, but still he just sat there. We went inside. His car was still out there. Jon Jakes was living with us then—he was right upstairs! But there was no way *he* was going to get involved, after what our father did to him that time. There was some discussion about what might happen, who they should call or not call. Jupiter had been left out on the long front porch, and she was trotting back and forth, barking and barking, until Ben made her come in. There was that uneasy fear building. You didn't know this part. The who-knows-what-might-happen again. It was . . . creepy. My mother didn't want to call the police, she never did. Maybe she should have, but I was glad she didn't.

She went outside to talk to him. It was stupid. Maybe dangerous. We heard raised voices. Then

they stopped. All at once they stopped. Ben and
I peeked out the upstairs window to see what was
going on. We didn't understand the sudden silence.
We were scared, because, well, there could have
been a lot of reasons for that. But . . . not the one
we expected.

It was you.

Oh, my God, you were walking up the drive, all
casual. You said later that you were just coming to
see if Ben wanted to shoot some hoops. You said
that nothing special happened to make you come
down that day. But I still wonder. Because that
day, and every day after, you were always there if I
needed you. Always.

Dad was standing outside of his car with his
hands on his hips. He was parked on the
cement parking pad up by the house. Mom was
several steps away from him. I can see it now.
You walked up. You had a basketball tucked
under one arm. There were casual greetings. My
father, of course, had met you over the years.
You'd been to his house for that birthday party
he gave Ben. That cool party, where he had the
Reptile Man.

When Ben saw you from the window of the
house, he took off down the stairs, and out the
front door. I think he wanted to go to your house,
to get out of there. I followed, but I stayed on the
porch as Ben went over to greet you. I listened.
Dad still had that tight face, but he got his swingy
BS attitude, where he was playing with you but
was jabbing at the same time. Being good old
dad, but cruel. Like the one time he saw Grandpa
Shine after their divorce, at one of Ben's baseball
games, and he shook his hand and slapped him
on the back too hard, friendly-like, but then said,
"You're sure looking old." Joke, joke, as the skin is
poked with the tip of a knife.

My father was in a tracksuit, I remember. He
always thought he was a great jock, but great jocks
don't need to hurt their teammates on purpose in
order to win. God, don't ever tell him I said that.
Forget I even thought that.

I stood there on that porch watching you, and I
swear something changed right there. I hadn't
noticed it before, but I did then. You'd gotten
broad-shouldered. You were right across from my
father, and I saw that you'd gotten taller than he
was. I could see it—you were bigger.

I knew Dad was still pissed. That was obvious.
Mom was backing up farther and farther, heading
into the house. You and Ben were standing there
with him. And then it happened.

My father said, "What's this, little man?" and he
snatched that basketball out of your hand. He
bounced it. I can hear it now—*bank, bank, bank.*
So casual, so slow, but then you turned. You set
your back against him in a block, and you snatched
the ball back. You tucked it under your arm again.
And then you did the thing that still gives me this
feeling of thrill and fear when I think about it,
even now.

You looked him in the eye. "Don't fuck with me,"
you said.

I know I sucked in my breath and held it, and
I'm sure my mother did the same, and Ben, too.
I shut my eyes in a protective flinch. But when I
opened them again, my father had not done any
of the things I had imagined—grabbed your shirt,
hit you, pushed you down. No, he just stood there
looking back at you, appraising, I guess. And he
did nothing. Nothing. He got back into the car,
and he drove out of there. Slowly at first. Those

potholes, you had to drive slow. But when he was out of sight, at the place where our dirt road met the paved one, we could hear wheels spinning out, tires spitting rocks.

I felt sick with guilt, and I felt dread, and I felt like cheering. But even more than that, I felt like getting inside your arms and staying there. And something close to that happened. You and Ben walked toward the house, and so did my mother, silent and shocked. You saw me, saw my face, and you put your arm around me. I turned my face toward your chest. I won't forget, ever, the feel of your T-shirt against my face.

"Come on," you said.

We all went in. And we didn't talk about it. Not then, or even after that, probably because it sat too close to this fire, a house on fire, burning loyalty and love and fear and anger. Flames licking up, destroying the pictures and the walls and the furniture that hid the shame—shame because you loved, shame because you didn't love, shame and guilt about wanting him to pay and wanting him to be forgiven.

Instead, Mom made cookie dough, and we sat
around and ate it off of spoons. I don't think she
ever did make the cookies, did she? Jon Jakes was
still upstairs, playing on his computer; after Dad
drove off, he'd probably gone back to writing
chatty letters to his children or reading Mom's
e-mail, which I caught him doing once.

And, of course, my father dropped his argument
about us going on that trip. Here's the confusing
part. I felt guilty that she had "won." It meant
that we had won too. It made him seem small.
He could be so cruel and you could hate him,
but then he'd seem small and you'd feel sorry
for him.

The guilt gave way to excitement then, though.
The night before we left, Mom and Ben and
I played New York songs and slid across the
wood floor in our socks, arms out like Broadway
dancers. We spent my fifteenth birthday on the
airplane, and Mom snuck a cake in her carry-on
bag and surprised me with a party. A little
flame made out of paper for the candle. They
announced it on the intercom. Birthday on aisle
six, and there was a smattering of applause, and
we shared cake with the passengers around us.

Later you got your snow globe. I bought you a small Statue of Liberty. There seemed to be some metaphor in that.

And when we came back? Everything was different between you and me, wasn't it? Katie what's her name was gone.

We sat on that bench out by the library. I was waiting, and then it happened. You leaned in and kissed me. Your mouth—that was the mouth for me. Somewhere in those years I had kissed Josh Gardens after a homecoming dance, but I'd hated it. Have you ever accidentally put your slippers on the wrong feet? Your feet know in a second without looking that there's been a mistake. But then you switch them around and everything is the way it should be. There's that fit, a feeling of rightness.

"There," you said.

There.

Love always,

Cricket

chapter
fourteen

Everyone had let me sleep, I guess, because the next morning I saw that Jupiter had been quietly let out of my room. Rabbit had been ditched a few feet away from her bed. He looked like I felt.

I saw something else on the floor. A small bit of paper folded in half. Shoved under the door, probably. I tried to reach it without getting out of bed, but that became one of those moments you're glad no one sees. I got up (harder than it sounds) to look. It was a torn-off corner of a piece of notebook paper. It had only one word on it.

Tonight?

It was unsigned, but I knew it must be from Ash. I groaned. I wasn't sure what the hell I was doing. *Why* I was doing. God, I was complicating things. I knew I was making a mess. It was like that time Janssen and I had one of our few big fights. I can't even remember what it was about now. But I'd been so upset. I was stomping around, pacing. I'd gone into the garage and found a can of paint, and decided I needed a change. I started in on my room, and after one wall, I was tired of painting and the job seemed enormous and my mother was going to be shocked and the rug had been dripped on. But I had no choice; I had to finish what I'd started.

But wait. Another bit of paper? A wrapper, for some kind of nature-trail-hiking-bar thing called Aspen. *Energy for the Outdoors.* Also by the door. It was folded in half too, creased deliberately. I opened it. There was writing on the back.

I hope you're feeling better, it said. *Last night meant a lot to me.*

I felt a sick hit of confusion. *What?* Totally different handwriting. Ash's—even in that one word note, I could see that he had the kind of cursive that developed somewhere in the second grade and stayed that way. I should know—mine was just like it. Rushed, because recess was waiting. But the second note—I knew those careful squared-off letters that looked like they'd been written on graph paper. I'd always given Oscar a bad time about it. Old ladies took less time with their needlepoint.

Nothing monumental had happened with either of them the night before, right? RIGHT? Oh no. This is what they said would happen if you drank. It always went this way in the movies, too. Some stupid girl doing things she regretted and didn't even remember.

There were three people in the dining room when I got down there. Three *beings*. Cruiser and Jupiter and Amy. Jupiter was eating Cruiser's breakfast out of his bowl as he sat there, crying and whining like a big baby. Amy was on the phone.

"Gotta go. Talk to you later," she whispered when she saw me in the doorway. She shut the phone, set it on the table next to her. She stole glances at it like it might sneak off without her.

"Jupiter, what are you doing?" I said. "Now, this is just taking advantage."

Jupiter finished crunching. The bowl was empty. I picked her up, found Cruiser's bag of food on top of a nearby cabinet, and gave him another scoop.

"Hey," I said to Amy.

"You look awful," she said.

"Thanks," I said. "I appreciate that. Where is everyone?"

"My baby cousin ran away."

"Baby Boo?"

"I only have one baby cousin."

Oh, you could want to say things you'd regret. It would feel *so good*. But the timing was bad—my head hurt. I wouldn't even get the complete satisfaction I craved. It was true—if you drank, you did feel like shit in the morning. My head really did ache like you hear and my stomach *was* still queasy and my brain felt like it was a slab of that laundry lint you're supposed to take out of the dryer vent before it becomes that slab of laundry lint in the dryer vent. In our house Ben was the

185

only one who ever remembered to clean it out. We could have crocheted afghans out of the stuff.

Cruiser was done eating, and I set Jupiter on the floor, petted her with my foot as I tried to decide whether to have one of those muffins or not. They looked deliciously homemade, and there was a big bowl of fruit too. My body didn't know what it wanted, after that hit of venom.

But it knew what it didn't want. That smell. Lurking out of the kitchen, sneaking off. It made my stomach flip sickly.

"Smell that?" I said to Amy. "She's at it *again*."

"What?" Amy said.

"Pot? You don't smell that?"

"I thought it was incense," Amy said.

"That's not incense."

"Drugs?" Her eyes were wide. Horrified.

"Illegal drugs, right there in the kitchen. Not ten feet from you," I said. I may not have known my own mind, but maybe Jupiter did. She sat up straight next to my chair now, as if I were about to eat. She gazed at me with focused intent. Even her little white spot on her back looked serious. I guess I *was* hungry. I reached for a muffin. Dropped her a bit of it. She and Ben had the same appetite.

I heard the front door open and then close. Ted Rose walked in, carrying grocery bags in each arm.

"Morning, ladies," he said.

"Need a hand with those?" I said.

"Got it covered," he said, "but thanks." He headed for the

kitchen, then hesitated. He stopped and sniffed the air, same as Jupiter would. A shadow passed over his face, a speeding cloud, there and then gone again.

There were voices and footsteps and the loud lift of conversation and laughter now in the living room. Mom popped her head in the doorway.

"Found him."

"He ran off?" I asked.

Mom poured herself a cup of coffee. "Hailey must have gotten up really early this morning. She saw Charles crashing his trucks down here and decided to bring him out to Gavin and Oscar's tent. Did you know they have video games set up in there?"

"Baby Boo is allowed to play video games?" Amy said. She sounded envious.

"I don't think so. But he was having a great time. His frog even beat Gavin's monkey in Road Racers. Hailey felt bad. She didn't think Jane and John would be imagining him lost on the beach somewhere, or in the sea."

"*Hailey* was playing?" Amy asked. "Hailey's never played video games."

Mom sat down, sighed. "That explains why her teddy bear was in last place," she said.

"Mom doesn't think those things are good for you. Hailey's never done this *before*," Amy said. Before now. Before we entered the picture. Next Hailey would be shooting up heroin in seedy motels, thanks to us.

Mom ignored her. "They're going into town to see if they can find a place to buy more controllers. Ben wants in. We were hoping for at least one day of a family activity." She took a muffin out of the basket, laid it on a napkin and broke it in half.

"Tomorrow, maybe," I said.

"Since Saturday's the rehearsal, and Sunday's the wedding, that's probably our only chance. Is there something you might be interested in doing while you're here? Something we all could do?" Mom asked Amy.

"No," she said. She sat up straight in her chair. Put her hand on her phone as if we might suddenly grab her and take her hostage.

"Your dad says you like shopping."

Now, *that* would be fun. I'm sure Ben would love it. It reminded me of the time we all had to go to the cheerleading movie because that's the only one Jon Jakes's daughter, Olivia, would go to. Riveting pom-pom drama, the longest ninety minutes of my life.

"I don't need anything," she said.

"We'll keep thinking." Mom twisted her bracelet around and around her wrist.

"How'd it go with the cake guy yesterday?" I asked. After all, we were supposed to be having a wedding. Weddings were supposed to be *fun.*

"Oh!" Mom said. "It was great. *Unusual.* Friend of Rebecca's. Johnny B's bakery. Well, his bakery's out of his house. Big guy, Guns N' Roses T-shirt." She chuckled. "Drives a motorcycle. Can't quite picture how he's going to get the cake here, but okay. Maybe he straps it on the back. But . . . It'll be beautiful. White chocolate curls all over. I wanted to eat the *picture* of it."

Amy made a little *hmphh*, the verbal version of an eye roll.

I tried to keep my mouth shut, I did. "You disapprove of *cake*?" I said.

Mom shot me a look. Fine. All right. So my hand got a little shaky on the hostility volume control. But I guess Hailey and Amy's mother would never enjoy a picture of cake or any food, for that matter, not even those glossy images of heaping Christmas cookies in the holiday magazines. Not even those catalogs with cheese balls and towers of nuts and chocolate truffles that spell out "Happy Holidays." I loved those.

"I don't disapprove of *cake*," she said.

We all sat in the kind of silence that feels like you're wearing it—a wool coat, the heaviest, scratchiest, most unbearable coat. Mom stared down at her muffin for blueberry answers. "I love your earrings, Amy," she said.

"Oh!" Amy smiled. "I got these for my birthday last year. Ballet slippers. And they're dotted with my birthstone. Pink tourmaline. It's supposed to be lucky."

"They look great on you," Mom said. Ha. So she knew the trick too.

"My friend Kaylie gave them to me. I gave her the amethyst ones for her birthday. Purple. I don't think she's going to stay with ballet, though. She wants to quit now that I did. My mom said I need to at least do piano if I'm not doing dance."

"I saw a video of your recital. You're really good," Mom said.

Somewhere in the middle of Amy's story about the popular girls in her science class, I heard raised, scattershot voices in the kitchen. Ted, talking to Rebecca. Only a few phrases—or at least a few relevant ones. *High. Quit. At least not at nine a.m.*

Mom met my eyes. "They've got a little roach issue."

Amy squealed. She lifted her feet off the floor. "Eyuw, are you kidding? Gross!"

At the foot of the stairs, Jupiter stared up at me. *A long way up,* she seemed to say.

"Okay," I said. "You're lucky I love you." I carried her up, set her down at the top. She trotted down the hall. Her little backside looked so cheery. She stopped at the right door and waited. She looked at me with her melted chocolate eyes. "Very true," I said. "I'm lucky you love me, too."

It was a drizzly morning. I was glad. A tucked-in day sounded great, with everyone doing their own thing. I filled Jupiter's water bowl, and she headed to it. Man, she'd been going through the water lately. She was a noisy drinker. Now she had water droplets on her beard. I tossed old Rabbit over to her, and she scratched at her blanket and bed to make a snug nest. She turned circles and settled in.

"That's such a great idea," I said to her. "Just get in there and get cozy."

My phone rang. Natalie. I didn't even feel like talking but answered anyway. Every time I ignored a call, I had the disturbing feeling that the person somehow knew I was looking at their name and making a choice. I hated to hurt people. My conscience never took a day off. "I haven't talked to you in a million years," I said.

"I know it," she said. "I'm coming down Sunday morning, okay? But I thought I was driving with Oscar. He's not answering his phone."

"They decided to get here early. They're camping on the beach. You should see their place—"

"He's *there*? That asshole!"

"Wait," I said. "What happened?" We'd all been friends for years, and I'd never heard her talk that way and mean it. Except for maybe that one time when both Gavin and Oscar refused to go to Homecoming with her. They'd planned to sleep overnight in the Video Universe parking lot for the release of War Worlds Four, and nothing would change their minds.

"I just thought . . . Oscar and I . . . Whatever. Just, whatever. I'll be there on Sunday morning."

There was a soft tap on my door. Mom probably. "Hey, can I call you back?"

"Fine."

Great. Now Natalie was pissed. And I still felt awful. My

head wasn't throbbing exactly. More like my brain had grown too large for its container. "Come in," I said.

Jupiter stood when she saw him. She trotted over and sniffed his pant legs. She put her front paws on his knees.

"Down, girl," I said. "Hey, I thought you'd be at work."

What felt most dangerous is that he was beginning to look familiar to me. His eyes, those shoulders. They were thick and sloped, where Janssen's were strong and straight across. I had to think hard to remember how Janssen's voice sounded, because it was Ash's voice I'd been hearing.

A person could leave you so quickly. So much history and time and memories, but they snuck away from you, and other things took their place. How could you hold on? Wait. A bigger question. The biggest. How could you hold on *and* let go?

"I got down there, and Greg, my boss? He called last night and left a message, but I didn't even check. He was giving this guy I work with some extra hours. So, day off, but I got up early anyway."

"Too bad."

"You work?" He sat down on the bed next to me. "Bed" had a ridiculous amount of meaning for a piece of furniture. It was a flat surface to sit on, that's all, I told myself. But I knew that a bed usually had more stories than any other piece of furniture.

"One disastrous summer at this café, Carreras. I'm not meant to be a waitress. And then I worked for a few years for my English teacher, doing research. Spent most of the time in the library."

"Bummer," Ash said. See? Janssen loved the library. I did too. We'd go and sit in the squishy chairs by the magazines and read. He liked those legal thrillers. He wouldn't hear anything you said when he got to the exciting parts.

"Not working now, though. All this moving, and maybe going away to school."

"LA—sun, sand, surf, baby."

"I'm not really a sun person. I actually *like* the rain. No one likes the rain, I know. Don't even say it. But I love it. Rain, clouds . . ."

"Windshield wipers going . . ."

I laughed.

"I love that," he said. "It's so peaceful."

It surprised me. I don't know. Those big shoulders, the dark eyes—I wouldn't have guessed he was the kind of person to notice windshield wipers.

"So, you don't want to go there? USC?"

It came out before I could stop it. "Not *go there*. But *leave here*." I waited for him to laugh or narrow his eyes in a way that indicated he thought I was crazy. "Stupid, I know."

"Why stupid?"

"It's embarrassing. 'Don't want to leave home.' Sounds like I'm a baby."

"No it doesn't. Not at all." He looked at me. His eyes— they weren't just intense, I noticed. They were kind. He shook his head. "You know what happened to me? You spend the last years of high school dying to get away, right? But somewhere in there it hits you. It gets real."

"I know," I said.

"The, what, pieces of you that you're leaving."

I stared at him. That was it exactly. *Exactly*. No one had put it that simply before. That *rightly*. I nodded.

"Don't tell anyone I said that," Ash said.

"Don't tell anyone *I* said that," I said.

"For some reason no one says these things. You're not supposed to talk about that part. Why is that? It's wrong to love your family? The place you live? It's your *home*. It's all who you *are*."

"I don't know why, but you're right. You're not supposed to say those things out loud."

"I should punch something now so you know how tough I am."

I laughed. "No."

"I'm not the punching kind anyway. Hey, you okay?"

"I think it's this headache. Last night . . . I don't drink usually."

But it wasn't the headache. It was something much worse. Much, much worse. I had made Ash into some simple, hot guy in my mind. An idea I played with, more than an actual person. I had made him into a *type*. A nice, safe type. Now, though, as he sat in front of me, I saw that he was more than big, sexy shoulders and dark, intense eyes. He was warm. He was thoughtful.

Oh, God, I was in trouble now.

"Alcohol—that shit is bad for you," he said. "I don't know. I've never been much of a party person. All that standing around and talking to drunk people. Hey, I gotta do an errand for Rebecca. You guys are having some barbecue tonight, right? She needs some stuff."

"We are? Okay. But I thought your dad just got back from the store."

"This happens every time she sends him. She wants a head of lettuce, he brings back a cabbage. He figures, round green ball . . . She's pissed, he's pissed. A chill in the air."

"No *F-I-T-I-N-G*," I said.

"He hates all the . . ." He put an imaginary joint to his mouth and sucked in. He shrugged. "You want to come?"

"I think I just want to hang out here," I said. My head, it was throbbing. God, no. I could like Ash. Really like. As a real, live whole person.

"Cool," he said. "I hope I'll see you tonight."

He grinned, headed out. Images whipped past. Ropes and balloons and my family and Janssen and the little bit of life I'd lived yet and all the life that was still waiting.

I fished a book out of my bag and fell into the deep, safe hiding place of *story*. It was a book about a voyage, involving magic and good and evil. Good guys and assholes (with swords, on horses). Safety and danger, and keeping the bad away with shields and stone walls and brave soldiers. My mother always said that our own stories were where we made sense of things, but I think *all* stories have that power. You could put your confusion and upset and worries into whatever book you were reading. You could sort of *set them down* in there, and you could come out with your head on a little straighter. I don't know why stories worked that way, but they did. They're an actual *place* where confusing things order themselves.

So I felt a little better when I went downstairs again. Jupiter *plomp-plomped* down the stairs behind me, and I let her out to pee. I gave her a biscuit, which she crunched happily. I loved giving her treats.

Mom was sitting in her sweats and having tea in front of a beautiful fire in that living room fireplace. She was reading, too. She set down her book when she saw me. The fog outside hadn't cleared, and the huge windows in there were filled with gray-white waves and gray-white shores and gray-white seagulls flying in gray-white skies.

"Do you think Jupe is losing weight?" I asked.

"I wondered it too," Mom said.

"She's eating a lot. She stole Cruiser's food this morning. He was so upset. But, still. Maybe we should weigh her."

Mom set her book down. "She does look pretty trim."

Jupiter loved her food. Once, she got so chunky, we had to cut down on her snacks and keep a weight chart for her on the fridge. It didn't help all that much. Maybe we should have put up pictures of thin model dogs by her bowl for inspiration.

"I lifted her up the stairs earlier, and it wasn't too bad," I said.

"Of course, she hasn't been to Gram's in a while. That's where she gets to eat all the good stuff."

I sat down on the floor, my back to the couch. Jupiter sat right next to me, leaned against my side. I think she liked when we sat on the floor, when we joined her world. Of course, whenever I was on the floor doing sit-ups or something, she'd climb onto my stomach. "Hey, remember her first birthday?"

Mom laughed. "Favorite things: underwear."

We'd had a party, just Mom and me and Ben and Jupiter. We made homemade dog biscuits. Ate hot dogs. Drew a poster too, and hung it over her water bowl. The poster showed her favorite things, which were mostly the stuff she'd chewed up that year. Garden hoses, underwear, socks.

Mom scooted down off the couch. Now the three of us were on the floor, Jupiter between us. Mom scratched her black velvet head, rubbed the tips of Jupiter's ears the way she liked. Jupiter was smiling her dog smile. We were together, and she liked together.

"Where is everyone?" I asked.

"They could only find controllers at some outlet mall on the mainland. Gram and Aunt Bailey—you know they'd never miss an outlet mall. The place had a Golf Universe, so Grandpa and George went too. Dan took the girls to get them out of the house."

"You could have had your family day. We're the only ones not there."

"You know how I love to shop." She rolled her eyes. Yeah. School clothes shopping was a twice-a-year, get-it-done marathon. Ben and I would end up whining and pleading for a rest, clinging to the comfort of a dressing room chair. One Orange Julius break, and that was it.

"Probably if you went, Hailey and Amy wouldn't go anyway."

She sighed. "Don't take it personally, honey. It's hard. Complicated. Dan's in a bind. They're just . . ."

"Old enough to have a good attitude," I said. It seemed pretty simple to me. Dan deserved that. Mom, too. You did your best, at least until you had real reason not to.

"We stole the food out of their bowl, you know? Like the dogs. Same thing. It's hard," she said again.

"Hard?" I didn't like the sound of that. *How* hard? Cancel-the-wedding hard? "But if you love him—it's supposed to be enough, right? If you have that . . ."

She tilted her head, looked me in the eyes. "Are you asking for me, or for you? Love . . . I loved your *dad*."

I could forget that part, but it had to have been true.

She watched the fire. She spoke, finally. "There needs to be love, yeah. *And* all the right reasons for love."

The fire popped and crackled. I smelled something cinnamon-y coming from the kitchen. I tried to concentrate on that. Because I felt so tired all at once, and I hadn't been myself, and I missed Janssen and my own home. My heart felt like it was being squeezed.

"Cricket, are you okay? You seem definitely not okay." Mom took my hand. "There's a lot going on for you right now. For all of us. All of this *moving on*."

Shit. *Shit!* Suddenly I felt like I could cry. I swallowed hard. I didn't want to cry.

"Crick?"

"How do you know what to do? What do I *do*?"

"Oh, honey," she said. "You don't always know."

Damn, it was stupid, but I was crying, and stupid tears were rolling down my face, and I had to blow my nose, and my heart hurt so bad.

"You wait there, not knowing, until you do know," Mom said. "Eventually you do."

"Maybe not me," I whispered.

"Yes, you, sugar. Knowing takes its own time. I swear sometimes you've gotta get really, really uncomfortable before it shows up."

"The thing is," I said. I tried to say.

"Sweetie, what?"

"I want the past. I want the past *with* the future." I was a stupid, sniffing, crying mess. "I don't want it to go away. I don't want to lose what we had." We, all of us. All of it.

"Oh, honey." I heard her swallow hard too. Her own voice was unsteady. "I know. I do."

She hugged me. My whole chest ached. I didn't have words

for it, for everything that was happening. Had been happening, since Janssen and graduation and those moving boxes and that wedding dress in Mom's closet. But I felt it all. Loss-life-hurt-change, I felt all of it.

My mother's arms were around me, and I was getting her shirt all wet with my tears, and Jupiter was squashed between us. I could feel her breathing, her dog chest going up and down. It must have been hot in there, but she did what a good dog would. She stayed, still and patient.

chapter
fifteen

"Something fishy's going on here," Gram said too loudly, talking over the music. She had worked her way next to me on the big deck overlooking the beach, where we'd all gathered for the barbecue. The weather had cleared just before sunset, giving us a raspberry mango sky. An outdoor fireplace was blazing warmth into the salty sea air of night. Lit lanterns hung from wires overhead, and small white lights twinkled from the palm trees planted in enormous ceramic pots. Rebecca had turned on some reggae.

"That's just the salmon," I said. Ted stood in the corner manning a big gas barbecue. Smoke billowed. He wore an apron over his Hawaiian shirt and jeans. Rebecca had set up a long table against the house, and platters of food—salads and breads and rice dishes—were heaped along it. Ben and Oscar were already snitching stuff over there, before it was supposed to be time to eat. An entire bread roll disappeared into Ben's mouth. Jupiter was lying on Cruiser's bed, which had been dragged outside for the occasion. Her own bed sat next to his, empty, and he crouched on the floor nearby, watching her nervously. John and Jane both tried to coax spoonfuls of macaroni and cheese into Baby Boo's clenched mouth, as he sat in a plastic chair shaped like an airplane.

"I don't mean the *salmon*," Gram said. Her eyes narrowed. "I mean that George. And *Mr.* Shine." She flung her head sideways to indicate Grandpa and George, who stood innocently talking to Mom, dressed up now in a blowy blue batik skirt.

"It's all fine, Gram," I said. Oh no. Not her, too. Then again, she once thought her neighbor was the same man she'd seen on *48 Hours Mystery*, who'd chopped his wife up with a butcher knife.

"He gave him *money*," she said. "I saw Grandpa slip George cash when we went to Subway. Why would he do that, tell me. Maybe George is a con man." I looked over at George, who had his hands in his pockets shyly. "Do you know your grandfather couldn't say no to a salesman to save his life? Fuller brush men, religious fanatics, whoever came knocking on our door, he'd let him in. We had vacuums, Amway, encyclopedias. People don't even have encyclopedias anymore. I should have saved them. They'll be collector's items one day."

"Maybe George was short on cash, Gram. Maybe Grandpa borrows from George too."

"I tell you, there's something those two haven't told us. I've got a *feeling*."

Aunt Bailey danced on over to the sound of steel drums. "Buf-falo sol-dya," she sang. "Born in Amer-ica."

"You guys look great," I said. They both had new sweaters on. Gram's was blue, and Aunt Bailey's was green.

"Outlet mall, super deal," Aunt Bailey said. "I found mine first."

"We also got running shoes. Half off. I promise you, I'm going to find out what the situation is here," Grandma said.

"Are you still going on about that?" Aunt Bailey said. *She* once was sure a painting she'd bought at a flea market was the work of a Renaissance master. An overactive imagination was obviously one of our family traits.

Ben and Oscar joined us. Ben handed Gram a wine cooler, and she twisted off the top and took a sip.

"Maybe they're an *item*." Aunt Bailey wiggled her eyebrows, and Gram nearly spit spritzer through her nose. But Ben caught my eye. *See?* his expression said. *Forget it,* I said with mine.

"Fat chance of that," Gram said. "I know that man. He's got a sex drive—"

"HOW ABOUT SOME CHIPS AND SALSA!" I shouted.

"Salsa has only fifteen calories," Aunt Bailey said. "You can eat all you want of it in Weight Watchers."

"Over on that small table." I pointed.

Gram and Aunt Bailey headed off, and then, Jesus, Oscar put his hands on my waist, gave me a shake, and sort of pulled me to him. It was the same move he'd seen Ash do the night before. "One love," he sang to the music. "One heart. Let's get toge-ther and be-all-right."

"Okay, that was fun," I said. "Let's play 'keep your hands to yourself' now."

"Cricket." Oscar looked hurt.

I ignored him. That note under my door, the handsy move— I'd deal with it with a swift kick of denial. I looked around. Took roll call in my head. "Where's Hailey and Gavin?"

"Playing Road Racers in the tent," Ben said. He wiggled his eyebrows like Aunt Bailey.

"Oh, my God," I said. "Dan is going to love that." I looked over at Mom, who was smiling and happy in the glowy light of the lanterns. Obviously she didn't hear the disaster-movie music, telling her that the shark was now swimming right by the bikini-clad swimmer. This party was going downhill fast.

"It's cool. They're not—"

"Doing it," Oscar said.

"She just likes the new joystick," Ben said, and chuckled.

"You're awful," I said. "You're as bad as Gram." Gram was going at the salsa now, sliding closer to Grandpa and George, trying to listen in.

"No, I mean it," Ben said. "Do you know she's never played video games before? She can't get enough. Gavin's dream girl.

I guess she never was allowed to eat junk food either, and you should see what's happening to those M&M's."

"Ted!" Rebecca yelled. "I need you!"

Rebecca waved a broom over her head, up near the roof. I saw him then. A big ball of gray fur, his black bandit mask. Little evil hands, wearing black leather-ish gloves. Cruiser spotted him too. He began to run and pace along the deck, and Jupiter jumped up and joined him, two against one, barking and howling.

"That's him!" George said.

"If I had my shotgun, I'd shoot the bastard," Grandpa Shine said.

"What are you saying, Arthur? We were always members of the Sierra Club. Always," Gram said.

"Oh, my God!" Jane shrieked, and John flung himself in front of Baby Boo, who started to cry.

Mom and Ben and I were trying to hustle the dogs inside, and Ted was shouting at that raccoon and waving the broom, and then Dan hurried out, right before we shut the door. His hair was wet, just out of the shower, probably, and he was wearing a green polo shirt, not his style. The dogs paced back and forth in front of the windows, barking as if we were under imminent terrorist attack.

"It looks *very* handsome on you," Aunt Bailey said. She stood next to Dan in her own new sweater. Both of them were as green as a golf course lawn.

"Well, it was very kind of you to get it for me," Dan said.

Dan was a T-shirt and flannel kind of guy. He looked like he was about to play nine holes, or maybe head on over to the clubhouse for their Sunday buffet.

"I can't resist a bargain," said Aunt Bailey. "We should have gotten more colors."

Green Dan kissed Green Aunt Bailey's cheek. His shirt still had the fold lines on it. He approached me. "Do you know where Amy is?" I hooked my thumb toward the house. I could see Amy in there, sitting on the living room couch, holding her phone and texting. Dan exhaled in frustration. "Hailey?"

"She's out in the tent with Gavin. Playing video games," I said.

"That's all they're doing," Oscar said. "They're not making out or anything."

Dan smoothed his hair back with the palm of his hand. "All right, okay." His eyes were distracted. Ted put the broom down. The raccoon was gone. Baby Boo had calmed down now, and was eating a strawberry like a little angel. Mom came over, took Dan's hand. "Hi, sweetie," she said.

"Can you get Hailey?" Dan asked me. "It's almost time to eat, by the look of things."

"No problem," I said.

"Everything all right, honey?" Mom asked him.

"I'll be right back," I said.

"I'll come along," Oscar said.

"No, I'll be right back *alone*."

I got the hell out of there, headed down the boardwalk

toward the beach. I could hear Dan's urgent tones, and Mom's *Oh no. You're kidding* in a clearly pissed-off way. I heard Ben shout something that made people laugh, and the door opened again, and there was the scamper of dog toenails.

I touched down on the beach. I wondered if I could take the long way to Oscar and Gavin's tent. Like maybe via Southern California. The music up there, the lights and the laughter and voices—it all seemed twinkly and merry from down here. Inside of it there were too many stories. People's pasts and futures colliding.

I took a moment to breathe in the smell of the sea. Seaweed and murky green depths, coldness and salt. The waves rolled in over sand. *Chshsh . . . Cshshsh . . .* Maybe some things *were* forever. The ocean was. Tides in, tides out. A beach just *is* and always will be.

I heard laughter and screaming coming from that glowing tent globe. "Knock, knock," I said.

Not loud enough, I guess, because when I pulled back the tent flap, I caught Hailey in Gavin's lap, and at the sound of my voice, she jumped back and shrieked, twisted her shirt around the right way, grabbing at buttons. Gavin had sort of flung her off of him, and now looked more triumphant than embarrassed. I could see the television. A teddy bear sat in a car with its teddy bear arms raised over its head. The video words "YOU'RE THE WINNER!!!" danced happily around to cartoon circus music.

"Jesus, you guys!" I said. I covered my eyes. "This is neither the time nor the place." I sounded like somebody's mother. "Your father wants to see you."

"I didn't know what I was missing all these years!" Hailey said. Her cheeks were flushed. The boyfriend back home had obviously been forgotten in the thrill of the high score.

"Stick with me, baby," Gavin said.

"We're *eating*," I said. My voice had turned prim. My mouth felt pinched together in some church-lady way. "You both need to head up to the house, *now*."

"Okay, okay," Hailey said. She stood, pulled a handful of shorts from her butt crack.

"I'm not all that hungry after astronaut pot roast and mashed potatoes," Gavin said.

"I'm stuffed too. All those *chocolates*," Hailey said. She made the word sound sensual. The top button of her shorts was unbuttoned. Maybe Gavin had done it, or maybe she had, needing more room after all those M&M's and sour gummy worms and—wait, nacho cheese Doritos—partied in her stomach.

"Gavin, jeez," I said. "This place is a mess!"

"We're having fun. Isn't that the idea? What are you so pissed about?" Gavin said.

"The idea is . . ." I didn't know. Not this. Not the kind of disaster upon disaster that could lead to frantic cab rides to airports.

"Come on, Gavin," Hailey said. She was outside already.

Gavin was rushing me along. "She's never had chocolate, so she's a little—"

"I love technology!" Hailey shouted.

"Never?"

"Carob," Gavin said. He mimed sticking his finger down his throat in a gag. "She really pounded those M&M's."

"I've decided something!" Hailey said. Great. Terrific. "No more fucking *organic*. No more diets. *Die yet*, get it? They're trying to kill us."

We caught up to her. Maybe pro athletes should give up those pesky steroids, because by the look of it, M&M's could work magic. Hailey was cruising, fast. She could probably lift a car with one finger. She leaped over a large rock. "Hey, I like a real woman," Gavin said. "I don't do bones."

Well. Who knew he had preferences? Before that day the thing Gavin looked for most in a female was one that would say hi to him after he said hi.

"I *love* it!" she said, as sugar and fat and monosudiolgludo-somethings rose in her like a roller-coaster car up a rickety ramp.

I needed an aspirin. I left them at the party and headed upstairs to hunt through Mom's purse for the bottle. I went into their room, found her bag on the bed. I rustled around in there, trying to hurry.

But, wait. Wait just a second. What was this? A glossy pamphlet folded in half. I opened it. It was wrong to snoop, but what did that matter when you actually *found* something? I sat down on the edge of the bed. I held that thing in my hands.

There was a picture of a beach, a grass-roofed umbrella, a

shadowy bikini-clad woman taking a solitary walk. My eyes stopped on the words. *Enjoy the blessed isolation . . . Escape to sunny . . .* Escape.

I knew it.

Daughters and ex-wives and arguments—bad signs. They could press and press you to the breaking point. A person might want . . . options. But you could have an invitation sitting there at your fingertips and not take it, right? The beach and the thought of escape and tropical drinks, of peace, it could all sit there with its finger crooked, beckoning, and it didn't mean you'd follow. It didn't mean there was enough reason already. Maybe you just wanted to look at the picture. Maybe you just wanted to know you *could* leave.

I shoved the pamphlet back into my mother's purse and headed back downstairs, forgetting all about the aspirin. I hurried back down. Dan had wanted us all there for dinner, and it seemed crucial to cooperate as much as possible. Things needed to go *right*.

In the hall I ran smack into him. Ash. He was just out of the shower too, same as Dan. His hair was wet. He took my arms.

"Well," he said. "How's that for timing."

God, he smelled good.

"Coming to dinner?" I said. My voice was hoarse.

"Let's try that again, the whole crashing-into-me thing," he said.

"Later?" I said.

"Later," he said. "Soon, later."

Janssen, Janssen, Janssen, my heart said. But the voice sounded so far away.

"Now that we're all here," Dan said.

Dan's black hair was shiny in the light of the lanterns, as black and glossy as a rainy street at night. His eyes were black too. Deep black and sincere. His face was serious. Everyone was gathered around on the back deck overlooking the sea. Gram wasn't paying attention. She had her eyes locked on Grandpa and George. Hailey wasn't paying attention either. I saw her run her pinkie along Gavin's thigh. He started to cough; he pounded his chest with one fist.

"I just wanted to take a moment," Dan said. "We've all been here, but scattered different places. I can't wait until *everyone's* together—my parents, Daisy's sister . . . But now. Tonight. Great food, great music, family, friends . . . And my beautiful bride." He held his hand out to her, my mother. And she went to him. Pamphlet or no pamphlet, she took his fingertips and beamed.

He kissed her cheek. It was . . . It was so damn sweet, and I felt choked up. You could see how much he loved her, and there she was, my mother, and she'd been through so much shit, she and Ben and me, all of us, and now here we were, and the night was beautiful. I could see Ted take Rebecca's hand. Ash stood by the barbecue, smiling. Ben was next to me, with Jupiter tucked under one arm. She loved being up high, and

Ben was watching out for her, making sure she wasn't over-looked down there in the crowd, as she watched everything with her shiny eyes. And Jane swayed back and forth with Baby Boo on one hip, as John looked on, loving them both. I could hear Gram sniff. She was feeling it too—family and love and all the crazy stuff you go through together in a life. But the point was, you went through it together, and you all stood there as witnesses and allies, and you gave your love over. During the bad times, but in the moments that were this good, too.

"I just want to say . . ." Dan's voice cracked. "I am a blessed man."

Ben's eyes were wet.

"Jesus," Grandpa said. He sniffed, and wiped his eyes with a handkerchief.

My mother, our mother, set her head on Dan's shoulder. I felt my heart squeeze. Gold lantern lights danced in her hair. Love felt like magic.

And then it happened. The metallic, urgent song of a phone. It stopped. Started again. Amy fished into her pocket, turned her back, and plugged her other ear with one finger. "'Lo?"

She listened. Dan started to speak again, but Amy stopped him. She held the phone out to him. "It's for you," she said.

"No," Dan said.

"Dad! *Please* . . ."

His teeth were clenched. "I'll call back."

Amy spoke into her phone and shut it, but the moment was

broken. Ted shouted a hearty "Let's eat!" and slapped Ash's back, as my mother's face turned stormy.

"What now?" I said to Ben.

"Amy's all upset because people are *doing drugs all around her*," Ben said.

"What?" I said.

"Rebecca," he said. "I heard Mom and Dan talking. Amy smelled pot smoke, told her mother *everyone's doing drugs*."

"Oh, my God," I said.

"It's a great big drug orgy," Ben said.

"Where?" Hailey said. She and Gavin and Oscar appeared next to us.

"How 'bout just an orgy for two," Gavin said, and pinched Hailey's butt. He was really pissing me off.

"Then it wouldn't be an orgy, idiot," Oscar said. Oscar had always been a master at pointing out the obvious.

I watched Ash help his Dad with the salmon, moving it to big platters which they set on the table. They joked around together, enjoying each other's company. Gram and Aunt Bailey made a beeline for a dish of grilled vegetables. The music went back up again, but somehow Rebecca still heard the doorbell. She disappeared inside, skirts swaying, bracelets clinking, and came back out again.

"Look who's here!" she chimed.

A little old lady stood next to her. The ancient woman was barely five feet tall, as if the years had shrunk her. She wore purple "slacks" (wasn't that what old people called them?), and a purple flowered blouse. Her hair was a neat silver bubble. Rebecca held her elbow.

"Mom!" Dan said. He rushed over. He hugged her, but gently. It looked like she could fall over with rough handling. "Where's Dad? I thought you two were coming tomorrow."

"Your father," she said. Her voice was the sound of eggshells cracking.

"What?" Dan said. "Hey, Sis! Daisy! Come on over!" he called.

Oscar and Ben and Gavin and Hailey headed toward the food table, but I was still standing there, and so I heard everything.

"Son, I have some news," Mrs. Jax said.

chapter
sixteen

Dear Janssen—

Wait—another one for your list. "Dog eat dog."
You're right, though—the expressions are
mostly negative. Yeah, "She's a dog." I don't get
it. Here's Bella and Gracie and Buddy and
Lucy doing their own innocent thing, and we
slam them. What's "dog eat dog" all about
anyway? Dogs in a dog park are pretty reasonable
with each other, if you ask me. They play nice,
and when someone doesn't, they basically tell
them to knock it off, and all is well. Unlike us.

Think mall parking lots during the holidays, for one example.

And what about people who say "It's just a dog" when a pet dies? They would never say "It was just your friend." Or "It was just a member of your family." But *of course* a dog is your friend and family member. All pets are. You share things. Over the years, you love each other and get mad and laugh and take care of each other and have memories. There they are, in your Christmas pictures.

Maybe I do get it. It makes some people a little nervous to have so much in common with a creature that licks himself, you know? We need to feel superior, and fast. So we say, "Hey, they eat grass and throw it up. We don't!" We say, "How smart can they be? They only understand a few words!" Gotta be at the top of the food chain, fine. And, yeah, it's true. They can't seem to hear music or recognize themselves in a mirror, and they try to bury a bone in the floor, pushing against the carpet with their nose, when it's obvious that the bone is right there. But we *drink* too much and throw up! And how much of *their* language do *we* understand? *We* can't see ourselves very clearly, in a mirror or in general! We can't seem to hear *other people*! We pretend not to see things that are clear as day all the time!

You're not supposed to say that you can tell what an animal *feels* either. This really gets people going. He's not feeling love! He's just watching his food source! He's not afraid of that stranger, *you're* afraid of that stranger! Whatever. When you have a dog—well, you know what you experience. You do.

So:

A Few People Feelings Dogs Definitely Show, Like It or Not (And There Are Plenty More, Too)

1. Fear: Turn on a vacuum, right? Also, there was that time that Jupiter became very afraid of a large potted houseplant Mom got at Fred Meyer. She walked wide circles around it and eyed it suspiciously, and why wouldn't she? If you were that small and something that big appeared in the living room out of nowhere, you'd be nervous too. Fear comes along with a beating heart.

2. Hope: If the car door is open, even

for a minute, Jupiter hops up into the
passenger seat and waits. Hope is what
you've got when you can't drive yourself.

3. Anticipation: Deer, in our very own
   yard some nights. Oh, the thrill and
   anxiety. And the next morning? She'd
   barely have her eyes open before
   running over to the window where we
   saw them last. Christmas morning,
   dog version.

4. Love: A million examples, but how
   about one? A chin, resting on your leg.
   The eyes that say, *You're there, I'm here,
   and we're both better for it.*

5. Willfulness: A million examples, again.
   Jupiter, barging into the bathroom.
   Butting her nose against any door that
   shuts her out with a distinct I-have-a-
   right-to-be-here shove. Standing by
   the treat jar and barking. Standing by
   her bowl and barking. Standing by
   the door and barking. Barking her
   head off on purpose when I'm on the
   phone.

6. Possessiveness: My food. My bowl. My
   parking spot, my father, my boyfriend,
   my . . . You get the idea.

Jupiter also just showed shame after throwing up in my room. It wasn't her fault—everyone probably gave her food at the party, not knowing everyone else had too. If you could call what we just experienced a *party*. A party implies fun and laughter and good times. This was more one of those twelve-car pileups you see on the news whenever it snows. Everything's a big mess here, Janssen. I wish they'd get married now, quick, before anything else happens. I mean, *I'd* even be questioning things right now. I would. So Mom will definitely question.

Jon Jakes, Vic Dennis . . . But remember Garret Hanks? I almost forgot about him. Jupiter hated him. Used to growl at the guy. How clichéd of her. The dog-hates-boyfriend routine. He went to some sales conference in Phoenix, and Mom broke up with him in the long-term parking area of the airport after she'd dropped him off. She turned in there accidentally, trying to find the exit. You know how confusing that airport is. Garret Hanks probably hadn't even gotten through security yet when she called him. But remember why she broke it off? She had a bad feeling. He'd ordered for her in a restaurant. That was it. That was all. And what's been going on here is a lot more than salmon fettuccine when you wanted the steak.

I wish you were here with us now. You understand
all of this. You know us. It's all my stupid fault
that you're not here too. You don't have to keep
reminding me. Okay, that's unfair. You're not
reminding me at all. You've gone silent on the
matter. You've said what you need to, I guess. The
ball is in my court. I hate that expression. Anytime
I've tried to play tennis, I spend the whole time
running around and chasing the ball. It's never
actually in anyone's court.

Fear, willfulness, possessiveness. Uh-huh. Dogs
and humans, we're ALL a big mess of feelings. But
love, too, and don't forget it.

You're not here, and it's strange, period, because
after that time when you stood up to my father,
you were part of our family. Don't you think? That
summer, after you and my father faced off in the
driveway, all of us spent time together. Ben and
me gave Mom that rubber raft, the SS *Monarch*,
for her fortieth birthday, remember? She'd always
gone on about how she loved the one she and Aunt
Gaby had when they were in high school. How
they'd float around Lake Washington. How she
inflated it in Aunt Hannah's room and filled it
with their old stuffed animals on April Fools' Day.

So Ben and I bought that raft and filled it with
our stuffed animals, and it made her cry. The SS
Monarch—I'm only guessing why she named it
that, but butterflies are trapped first, before they
are free.

But we all took that raft to Marcy Lake. We tied
it to the top of the Bermuda Honda. We almost
lost it on the way over, when it lifted up like a
plane taking off. We had to ride the rest of the way
holding on to it out our windows. I think that's
why Ben can tie anything down to any car now
and it won't move an inch. Right? Not an inch.
Doesn't want a repeat of the SS *Monarch* trip down
to Marcy Lake.

Then, ha—there we were, all packed in that raft,
floating around and trying to eat a picnic lunch in
there, elbows knocking against elbows. Mom got
out to swim, and barely could get back over the
round hump of the boat's side. We had to grab her
thighs and heave, as she tried to scooch, scooch
in, wet skin over inflated rubber. You were *really*
part of our family after that little scene.

And we floated around the river too, down by that
park a few miles from home. We hiked. You came

with us when we tromped up to Moon Point, where
the paragliders take off. I thought we were going to
have to call an aid car for Mom, but she huffed and
complained and made it all the way up there. We
spread out on the grass and watched the colored
parachutes lift up into the wind. The treetops and
the valley spread out down below in a landscape
quilt. We took pictures of ourselves out there. Mom
hung them in our kitchen too, remember? They're
packed in a box somewhere now.

You were part of our family, but finally it was just
you and me too. After that day in our driveway
with my father, we would get into your car and
drive. Your dad's old hand-me-down Mercedes,
the most odd boy-car match ever. We'd go out
toward the mountains, head to the pass just outside
our town. We'd get lost. And we'd park there, in
lost. Away. Escape. I loved that. But a lost-away-
escape that was more safe than any found.

You seemed to know where you were going
when you were driving. Did you? *How* did you?
You drove so responsibly, too. You drove like a
businessman. You never rode people's butts or
swore. You were very calm. You'd offer Altoids
like a businessman too. You'd turn off onto some

road that looked like it went nowhere, but there'd
be a hidden park or something. In your car, things
would get a little out of control between us. I
wasn't anyone's little sister anymore. I was yours,
you were mine, and . . .

"We have everything we could want," you said.

"More," I said.

We had to work hard at finding places to be alone.
Yeah, there were times when we were all together
with my family, and times when it was you and me
and Ben like the old days, and times at your house,
and with your friends, and at your swim meets and
games. But . . .

"There are always too many people," you said.

"Way," I said.

So we'd get into the car, or go to Marcy Lake, or
drive down some horror-movie dark road, just so
that it could be me and you and no one else. We'd
roll down the windows and listen to crickets and
coyotes and smell the deep sweetness of darkness
and nighttime rain and ferns rolling up for sleep.

The breeze would rustle the leaves and evergreen boughs, and we'd sit there until you'd grab my knee suddenly to scare me, biting the back of my neck vampire-like, which probably meant the solitary road and the endless dark was giving you the creeps too. Not that you'd admit it. Growing up out there, growing up around horses and with your father—you could handle an ax and chop wood and discard the remains of a dead rabbit, so you "had cojones" (to use your dad's expression). You hated when the right song could make you cry. Don't worry. Our secret.

Of course my father hated you. He never said it, but when he found out you were my boyfriend (that word—it still gives me some stupid, shimmery thrill), he was pissed. He purposefully left you out of any invitations. That one Thanksgiving dinner, yeah. And he didn't even speak to you the whole time. You spent the holiday pretending not to notice. We fought that night. Too many things we wanted to say to other people so we said them to each other instead.

I hated it that he hated you. I wanted to sit down and explain you to him, and him to you. But I'll tell you something, Janssen. I loved it too. I loved that he hated you. You were a stone wall, a fort in high, unreachable trees, an island, my own island, that no boat could reach. I loved that.

You hated him right back. You did the part I couldn't.

And then the salmon hatchery, remember that? We walked around and watched silvery little fish fly in the air and attempt the impossible. The odds against making such a long trip, surviving . . .

"It's a long way from here to there," I said. You had lifted me up until I stood atop a bench, and I was bent down toward you, and your arms were around my knees.

"Here?" You rubbed my lips with your finger. "To here?" You kissed me. Janssen, you're an amazing kisser, you know that.

"No, those fish," I said. But I could hardly concentrate on them anymore.

"It doesn't matter if we're young. If you love someone, and it's right . . . We can make it the whole way, Crick."

"Well, I know I love you," I said.

"And I love you," you said, and lifted me back to the ground again.

It wasn't the first time we said it. No, that was in your yard, by the horses. We'd said it many times by then. But it felt more important than it had before. We'd decided something.

I didn't think I could feel any closer to you than I did right then, as some game warden in tan clothes walked around the hatchery and as some little kid broke free from his father's hand and ran forward to pound on the glass windows where you could see the fish swimming underwater.

I was sure I couldn't feel any closer, or more bound to you. But I could. I would. Soon after that. Oh, God, you know where this story is going.

I'm glad you had such a good time on your hike to Mt. Rainier. But who is Alyssa?

Love always,

Cricket

chapter
seventeen

"A divorce? How can my parents be getting a divorce?" Dan's golf-course green back was bent over as he sat on the couch, his head in his hands.

"I'm so sorry, honey," Mom said.

She had her hand clasped over her mouth. She met my eyes, shook her other hand in front of her, to indicate that I shouldn't say a word. She was struggling—I knew the look. It was the same one she'd gotten during Ben's orchestra concert when Jonathon Yamaguchi was playing his difficult violin solo in that silent auditorium, and then someone's mother in front of us farted. It was the same look she got when that vigorous college recruiter came from Tufts and asked the crowd to shake hands with our neighbor and give three reasons why Tufts was terrific. It was the same look she got, that I got, that Ben got, whenever we had to go to a wedding or a funeral. She'd be trying to find the page in the church hymn book until the song was practically over, with her shoulders shaking up and down, and with that look, that very one, on her face.

"Stop laughing, Daisy," Dan said.

"No, I mean it. I'm really sorry," she said. She looked down in her lap, but I could still see the corner of her mouth tipped up.

"They've grown apart? What does that mean?" Jane said. She was sitting on the other couch, rubbing the knuckles of her hand. Her face was pale, and her makeup cried off.

"They've been married for sixty-five years!" Dan said.

"Maybe they stayed together for the sake of the *grand*children," Mom sputtered. She could only hold back hilarity and suppressed one-liners so long. She was really cracking up now. She had to wipe her eyes with the back of her hand.

Dan whacked her with a pillow.

Amy leaned in the doorway. "It's hardly *funny*."

Going out, I mouthed to Mom, and gestured outside with my thumb. Mom had sobered up quick with the rebuke from the endlessly disapproving fifteen-year-old who was about to become her stepdaughter. It was a sobering thought, all right, or else the laughter was gone because she was considering the jail sentence for walloping the kid. *Someone* should. Was Dan just keeping his mouth shut in front of a large audience, or did he not even see the war-torn land developing between his daughters and my mother, the dead bodies of soldiers gathering, the burning trees? Maybe he had some fatherly garbage chute, where snotty comments efficiently disappeared, and where the bad smell was waved away into the high, hazy sky of forgotten. Here was a worry: Jon Jakes never noticed those comments either.

Outside, the lanterns were still lit, but the party had ended quickly after Dan's ancient mother arrived. Everyone ate fast and disappeared. Gram and Aunt Bailey were "tuckered out." Grandpa and George were going into town to see if the Possession Point Pub was open. Ben headed to the tent with Oscar, Gavin, and Hailey to play Circus Racers with the new controllers. Amy eventually went to her room. I'd gone up to mine, too, but after I shut my laptop, it felt too lonely up there. *Me, Jackson, Devon, and Alyssa hiked up Rainier . . .*

I headed down the boardwalk. The tent gang was probably having the most fun. Circus Racers, why not?

"Hey," Ash said.

I was surprised. I hadn't even seen him down there, sitting on his sweatshirt, his back against the high sand bank. I hadn't even heard the sound of those strings—the music had gone out to sea.

"Hey!" I said.

"I was wondering where you went."

"My family is crazy," I said.

"Every family is crazy. If it's not crazy, *that's* crazy."

"Did you see that little old lady?" I asked.

"Yeah. I heard. She's getting a divorce. Everyone's all upset. But look on the bright side. She's not *pregnant*."

I laughed. "It's probably the whole unresolved toothpaste-cap thing."

He started strumming. Some old Beatles song, I remembered. One of Mom's boyfriends had given her the greatest hits CD. "Life is very short, and there's no ti-i-i-i-ime for fussing and fighting . . ."

"You have a great voice," I said.

"I'm a hack," he said. "My Dad's the one with the voice."

"Really?" I couldn't imagine it, Ted singing.

"He plays, too. *Not* a hack. You ever think about the fact that someday metal bands are going to be thought of as old-people music? Led Zeppelin and Metallica? Our kids' grandparents will have listened to that shit. Come and sit by me. You're pretty far away, standing there."

I sat. "You're not a hack."

"I don't mind. I'm realistic. I've got no grand visions. Just makes me happy to do this." His fingers trilled on the strings. Ash stopped. He looked into my eyes. "What's this?" he said. He put his fingertip to the bridge of my nose. "What are you worrying about?"

I smiled. "No worries."

"Your face is screaming 'worried.' You one of those people who always think the plane's gonna crash?"

"How'd you know?"

"It's all right here." He pointed to my nose as if he were reading my future.

"It's stupid," I said. "This stupid wedding."

"You don't want them to get married?"

"No, I *do*."

"Well aren't they doing that in, like, two days?"

The pamphlet in my mother's purse leaped to mind. I pictured a solitary bikini-clad woman, taking a three-panel beach walk during a glossy-papered sunset. "I think so. I'm pretty sure. She just sometimes . . . She has this mental scale. Too much goes wrong, and the guy gets ditched."

"Better than making a mistake."

"I just worry that the ditching's become a habit. Like, she won't be able to stay with someone forever because she's afraid."

"She's afraid of forever?"

"After my Dad and everything . . . Long story. But maybe something gets *broken*."

"Oh," Ash said. We were silent. I could hear the sound of the Circus Racers music coming from the tent, and someone shouting a losing *Aww!* I watched the waves. Grandpa Shine once said that every fifth wave was the biggest one. The problem was, you never knew where to start counting.

"I don't know," I said. "I'm sure it'll be fine."

"People work around the broken parts, right? Like a bad knee or something? Sports injury? People make mistakes, they learn. Fuck, I've made a ton of 'em already and I've barely gotten started. *I* got broken parts."

"I know. I do too." I shoved my toes again and again into the sand until I'd made a pair of sand shoes to rest my feet in.

"And aren't you?" he asked.

"Aren't I what?"

"A little scared of the whole forever thing? Hell, *I'm* scared of it. I'll just say it."

He was right. The word even—it felt like those film shots of the universe, the deep darkness, the stars rushing past. "Yeah. Permanently permanent? Yikes," I said.

"Nah." Ash shook his head. "The scariest part of forever is that nothing *is*." Ash tilted his head back then and let out a long howl. "Ahhh-oooooo! Fuck, man. You gotta leave, be left, face facts, move on. . . . Can't escape loss no matter how careful or how smart you are, and, Cricket, my friend, that *sucks*." He picked up his guitar. Started strumming, all silly and possessed. "You gotta lose someone," he sang. "Baby you gotta lose someone, sometime . . ."

"Are you making this up as you go, or is that a real song?" I yelled over his loud, loud singing. If anyone had been sleeping nearby, they weren't anymore.

"Making this up," he sang. "Does it suck, suck, suck," he belted. He liked that word tonight. He shook his hair as part of the show.

"Badly," I said.

He put his guitar down. "It sucks badly, did you say?"

"Worse than bad," I said.

He grabbed me, and we rolled off the driftwood log, and I was laughing hard and he was tickling me, but I hate being tickled so I yelled "Stop, stop," until he did.

A man's booming voice came from an open window of the house next door. "Keep it down, Ash-hole!"

"Like it's the first time I ever heard *that*," he said to me. "Use your imagination," he called loudly toward that open window. "*Reach* for it!"

I started to giggle. "Oh, my God, he's going to hear you."

"That's just Randy, the ex-marine," Ash said. "See his helicopter? You can't take it personally. He yells at everyone. Probably that stress thing from Vietnam, whatever you call it. He still wears those big glasses from the 1970s. Steals our garbage cans."

We were flat on our backs. I felt happy. The moon above was nearly full, and it was big and craggy and improbable. How could it be that we sometimes didn't even notice it up there? When you thought about what it was, what was above and around *every day*, you wondered how we could ever forget.

"Moon, beee-you-tiful moon," Ash started singing again softly.

"Oh no," I said. "Not you again."

"But does it suck?" It was a tickling warning.

"Best song I ever heard," I said.

He scootched closer to me until our shoulders and arms and legs were touching. That's all. Just that. Laughter came from the tent then; a loud group groan. I had been beside Janssen like this so many times. So many times, he'd roll over on top of me, and then we'd disappear into that great physical oneness of mouths and mouths and hands and hands and skin and skin. Ash propped on his side, and stared down at me. I was getting used to his face, but also it could surprise me—this different face than the one I knew leaning over me like that. He looked different so close up. This was a real him, a whole person, with his own nose than looked different than the one I was used to.

He rested his forehead on my forehead. I sat up before it happened, before he kissed me. There were things that needed saying here. Because I liked him again, right then. Even more. I really liked him. And I needed to do something about it. It had to stop. But just then the tent flap opened a good distance away from us, and Gavin's voice bounced merrily down the beach.

"Where'd the music go, dude!"

I could see Gavin's smile from there, where his head had popped out from the tent. He was having the time of his life. Hailey's head appeared below his.

"Sing that one about fussing and fighting,'" she called. "It wasn't half bad."

"Losers!" I could hear Ben shout. "You are all pathetic losers! I challenge any of you! Mr. Elephant kicks sweet circus butt!"

"It's a global challenge," Gavin hooted.

"That means us, Cricket Girl," Ash said as he stood and held out his hand.

• • •

When I woke up the next morning after playing Circus Racers until two a.m., a dog was staring at me. Apparently Jupiter thought it was time for me to get up. She had her paws up on my bed and her nose was right in my face, and she was breathing on me.

"Hi, funny face," I said. "Are you the alarm clock?"

Her big black nose was right there, and it cracked me up. I smiled. The rest of my life took a minute to return. I remembered the beach. Ash. That fun night. My Janssen, somewhere far. A sick remembrance of a name. Alyssa.

"I hate her," I said to Jupiter. She looked very earnest with her face in mine. I stared at her and she stared at me, and we both understood how serious the situation was. She licked my face.

"Guck," I said. "Help, dog kiss."

Friday. The wedding was on Sunday. If there were no more shocking divorces and stepdaughter barbs and phone calls from ex-wives, if there were no sudden disasters of fate, maybe my mother could throw away the pamphlets promising escape and settle into life with her one, good guy. In two days.

Alyssa. I imagined my Janssen, lying on a beach with her somewhere, tickling her until she begged him to stop. I imagined him playing hysterical video games with her and our good friends. My throat was sore, I had laughed so hard. I got out of bed, looked for my phone. For a second I was sure. Decided. I was going to call him right then, ask him to come. I needed him. That was all. And I missed him. I missed that boy so much.

I sat up. Jupiter hopped down, found a paper towel I'd carried a sandwich on, and started to chew it up. I snatched it from her.

"You probably have rolls and rolls of paper towels in your stomach by now," I said.

I picked my phone up and held it for a long while. It was strange the way your body and mind could shove you around against your will when you were confused. All you could do was stumble forward and do what they forced you to do, like kidnappers, until the day came when the blindfold was off, and you could see, and your destiny was your own once again. I put the phone down. On second thought (or third, or fourth, or six hundredth, depending on how you counted) I put it into my pocket. It would be like having Janssen right there. A phone call away.

Downstairs my mother's hands were folded around her cup. She seemed pleased with herself, but it was the smug, irritated kind of pleased. This look? I'd seen this one a hundred times too. It was the one that said she was about to be proven right.

"Miniature golf?" Did I hear that right? "Are you kidding?"

"Not kidding. It was Grandpa Shine's idea."

"I think I need coffee," I said.

"Pour me another cup too," she said.

"What's the problem? Miniature golf is awesome," Ben said. He was eating breakfast and reading some boating magazine of Ted's and following our conversation. "The mini castle with the drawbridge . . ."

"*Everyone's* coming?" I asked.

"John and Jane are staying here with Baby Boo. And with these two." She lowered her voice, nodded her head toward the tiny Mrs. Jax, who sat at one end of the big dining room table, picking a croissant apart delicately, and the silent little Mr. Jax, who'd arrived that morning. He sat at the other end of the dining room table, bobbing a tea bag in his cup. "They can babysit the dogs."

"Cruiser will *kill* them," I whispered.

"Mrs. Jax loves animals," Mom whispered. "She told me about it this morning. I also heard all about her cousin Betty's Parkinson's."

"*Amy's* coming?" I asked.

"Supposedly." Ah. There was the reason for that look on her face.

"Miniature golf and a coupla hot dogs. You have an attitude problem after that, you got deeper issues," Ben said. He shoved a doughnut into his mouth.

I didn't say anything. Mom noticed my silence. I don't know what it said to her. Disapproval, I guess. Maybe I *did* wish she could do this better. With less mess. This—love.

"I'm doing the best I can here," Mom said.

The room was quiet except for the *shlick* of turning pages, the slurp of Mr. Jax with that tea. So quiet that Gram's sudden shout made me jump. "Fore!" she yelled from the doorway. She was wearing peach pastel capris, a peach shirt, and a sweater tied casually around her shoulders. She abruptly noticed the silence she walked into. "What?" she said.

"Jesus, Ma." Mom had her hand to her heart.

"Do I look like a cantaloupe?" she asked. "Too much orange?" She plucked a bit of her shirt.

"You look good," Mom said as she grabbed for napkins. Mr. Jax had startled at Gram's yell too, causing a tea tsunami to spill over onto the tablecloth.

"He's always been careless," Mrs. Jax said.

"What?" Mr. Jax shouted. He cupped his hand to his ear.

"Careless!" Mrs. Jax shouted back. You could imagine how loud the television was at their house.

"*I* could care less," Mr. Jax grumbled. "I'm the one."

Giant mess. Insert golf balls. My mother and Dan were out of their minds.

The splitting up into two cars became as complex and calculated as a world war, with Ben playing Switzerland and Dan playing the weary, distracted leader whose country is truly run by his cabinet. Hailey claimed the front seat next to him, Amy got in back, and so did Ben and Aunt Bailey, who was passing sticks of gum to everyone for a little breath freshening. The rest of us piled into Grandpa Shine's big squishy Lincoln, George up front, me and Mom and Gram in back. Then Mom had to run back into the house, because it was also a family trait that we could never leave without forgetting something.

Grandpa Shine almost collided with a delivery truck as he backed out onto the road. I imagined the scene. Broken bones, comas. No wedding.

"Where's your husband-to-be?" Gram asked Mom when we were finally underway. Our thighs were touching in that too-close way. I could smell Gram's coffee breath.

"Never mind," Mom said. "This is supposed to be fun." She looked out the window at Bluff House, as if she were saying good-bye to something.

"Well, you can't take it personally. No matter who he picked, they'd have had trouble. You could be the queen of England," Gram said.

"She's not Dan's type," Mom said.

"Still, you don't want the same problem you had with Jon Jakes."

The expression, about an elephant in the room? The great big obvious that no one speaks about? Gram not only talked about elephants, she'd go on to point out the destroyed furniture and the big piles of elephant shit. Maybe she didn't believe elephants should be in rooms.

"You want in on the golf betting pool?" Grandpa Shine said over his shoulder as he drove. "I usually don't have a handicap."

"I wouldn't go that far, mister," Gram said.

I could see Grandpa Shine grin in the rearview mirror. All these years, he'd always been patient with the verbal sparring. "George has never played miniature golf, eh, George?"

"Never," he said. "May I turn on a little music?" The back

of George's head was serious-looking with his neatly combed hair. It made me think of boys in elementary school on picture day.

"You can do what*ever* you want," Grandpa said. "My car is your car."

Gram elbowed me in the ribs. All right, it did seem a little strange. George rolled the dial past Grandpa's news radio station, settled on some pink pop candy music about La La Love. Gram did a little car dance beside me. "La la love," she sang.

"I love this song," George said. He rolled down his window a bit. Smelled the air, same as Jupiter. He had that same sweet look, come to think of it. "Is it too windy back there?" he asked.

"Nah, we're fine," Gram said. Even she had to be kind to George. He had a simplicity that felt like goodness. Gram's carefully sprayed hair was blowing off her face, though, giving her a dueling look of carefree recklessness and alarm.

"What is it about the beach," Mom said.

Out the window it stretched. In spite of all disasters small and large, there was that infinite curve of rock and sand meeting the edge of the sea. The sky was so big, bigger than it was at home, so much bigger than in the city. The haze had mostly cleared but was lingering lazily along rooftops. The smell of the sea pranced into the car from George's open window. That smell made you want to greet something, or someone, with open arms.

"It is a beautiful dream," George said. "It feels like you are looking at a side of God. Something permanent."

"Maybe that's it," Mom said.

Grandpa rolled his window down a bit too. Now Mom's hair was rebelling cheerfully. I noticed the very same chin on either side of me. Gram and Mom both had it. I knew I had it too, that chin, and so did Ben. Whatever I had felt or wanted from Mom back at the house slipped away. The insistent force of genetics and generations—there it was, right on our faces. We all tried so hard to be as strong as we could, didn't we? All of us, with our funny, vulnerable chins? When it came down to it, we were all trying to do the same impossible job of doing our best in a big world.

Grandpa Shine was grinning, and La La Love was all around now, and the point was—the point of the car ride, or of the beach itself, or of the whole nasty, glorious, uncertain, forever-not-foreverness of life—you could feel it. Love. You could keep feeling love no matter what. In spite of gnawing losses and the dark, gaping tunnel of change, love's dewy, golden, bittersweet self kept appearing, same as the sun coming up every single day. The unexpected rise in my chest I felt—*that* was sometimes reason enough right there to face all the questions, to go forward and turn the next page. And these funny, infuriating people . . . Their stupid goodwill and stumbling intentions were the ways love showed up.

This was what I couldn't bear to leave. This, this all. Right here.

"Ben was just telling us about the time you locked yourself in your parents' bedroom and your mom had to get the hammer to pry open the door," Dan said as they all piled out of the car.

"I was *two*," I said.

"He said it happened last week," Dan joked. He was slapping Ben on the back.

"No, last week she stuck that piece of—"

"Don't even say it," I said. "You're dead."

"She was a *kid*," Mom said. "And we didn't have to go to the emergency room or anything."

"A toy. My nose. Don't ask," I said to Dan.

Ben cracked up. "Loser."

"You ate a bathroom sponge shaped like a whale!" I shouted in the parking lot. It was mostly empty, save for a minivan and a big camper with a license plate that read CAPTAIN ED. We headed toward the merry archway with the words PEE WEE GOLF! curving overhead in rainbow letters. Nearby there was a waterfall spilling from a fake rock wall, and a huge fake elephant with his trunk curled in a frozen fake trumpet. When was the last time we'd done this? Maybe when we were kids, with Mom and Dad? I felt a silly thrill. The silly thrill some of us get at very large fake things and childish games. Amy and Hailey and Aunt Bailey were behind us. Aunt Bailey was trying to show them pictures of her cat, Missy, as she walked. I imagined the scene—a stray rock, a sprawling Aunt Bailey, broken hips, canceled weddings.

"He was always eating things," Mom told Dan.

"And you cut his hair that one time and made him cry."

"Don't remind me," Ben said.

"God, I still feel terrible about that. I'll never touch a pair of scissors again," Mom said. "Honey, I'm so *sorry*." She'd probably still be apologizing for that when she was ninety and Ben was sixty-five.

Dan grabbed her hand, pulled her next to him. "Come here, wife-to-be."

"I'm playing without a handicap," Grandpa said again. I was surprised he didn't bring his own clubs.

"I'm surprised you didn't bring your own clubs," Mom said.

George looked through the gate. "It is like a small wonderland," he announced.

We gathered in a group as Mom and Dan pulled out their wallets. Grandpa Shine pulled out his, too, and so did Gram, and Aunt Bailey, and there was a small fight over who wanted to pay, as there always was in my family. You just had to expect it. It was one of our group rituals, the way some families pray before meals.

"I don't want to wear the ugly shoes," Amy said.

"That's bowling," Hailey said. She was skipping, throwing her arms around her father's waist from behind. She, at least, was having a great time already. I had the thought, I did, so maybe it was my fault. I was the one who tempted fate, same as those people who wash their cars and cause it to rain.

Maybe everything will be fine.

• • •

There were score cards and short stubby pencils. Ben started getting competitive sometime after the pirate ship and the Brooklyn Bridge. It got worse as soon as we were at the giant frog, and it only pissed me off because I'd started getting competitive too.

"The frog's mouth is the *other* way," Ben said to me.

"Shut up. This isn't the PGA, you know," I said.

"Quit it, you guys," Mom said. "Move aside. My turn."

"Mom, you're the purple ball," Ben said.

"She hit my ball!" Grandpa Shine said. "Everybody see that? You can't just hit the one in front because you like it the best."

"It doesn't matter," George said. "Look, we are here in this tiny, beautiful place on a beautiful day." My mother beamed at him, and he beamed back with his deep, dark eyes. Sure, she was ahead now.

"Amy's turn," Dan said. "Here, honey. You just put your hands around . . . A little higher."

Amy's hair dropped down to cover her face. The ball hit the wall surrounding the flat green in front of the frog, jumped the side, and rolled under a baby stroller of the people in front of us. "I can't do it," she said.

Dan fetched the ball, set it up in front near Grandpa's. "Hey!" Grandpa said.

"My turn!" Hailey said. She gripped her club. She swung it high behind her, brought it forward, and whacked the hell out of the ball. It went soaring, landed with a crack on top of the

244

paddle boat a few holes over. "Let 'er rip!" she shouted. I stared at her hard, and then I saw it. Chocolate? Was that *chocolate* at the corners of her mouth?

"Billie Jean King versus Bobby Riggs," Gram said. She arranged and rearranged her feet on either side of the ball. She put her hand up like a visor to see where Grandpa's ball ended up.

"Who are they?" Amy said.

"Tennis players. A big man-versus-woman battle in the seventies," Mom said.

"Whatever," Amy said.

"Feminists do it with balls," Gram said, and knocked it straight into the frog's mouth. The frog closed his mechanical jaw, swallowed, and spit the ball to the other side.

"Ehaw!" Gram said.

"Beginner's luck," Grandpa said.

"Like hell," Gram said. "Why was it you never took me golfing? Probably because of the floozies." From where we stood, Gram's peach pants and peach shirt looked like her skin.

"Gram's outfit looks like her skin," I whispered to Ben.

"I know," he said. "Are you watching Grandpa watching George?"

"You're crazy," I said. "You're making stuff up in your head."

"You don't believe me."

I snickered.

"Keep your eye on the ball!" Grandpa shouted to Aunt Bailey.

"Don't listen to him! I'm the one in first place," Gram shouted too. I think she was flirting.

"If you people would be quiet, I'm trying to concentrate," Aunt Bailey said. She swung, but the ball sat where it was. Fifteen minutes later Aunt Bailey was still on the wrong side of the frog, which was the same thing that happened to her at every hole. She chased the ball around the green, tapping it and sending it sailing in a mad, forever circle. We waited. My phone rang. I checked. Oscar. Shit. Ever since that note, I was trying to avoid him. It rang again. Ben poked me on my arm.

"Who *is* it," he teased.

"Lover boy calling," Mom teased.

"It's Oscar," I said, and they both wiggled their eyebrows at each other.

"God, you guys," I said.

I was getting that feeling you have on a long car ride, where the wait starts to feel endless, and you start poking each other and teasing, and then the teasing becomes irritating because you want the hell out of that car. We sat down on a bench by the hole.

"Maybe we could order a pizza while we wait," Ben said.

"This is kind of how she parallel parks," Mom said.

"Can't we just move on?" Amy said.

"Just one more!" Aunt Bailey called to us. She tried again, but the ball rolled with slow taunting back to its starting position. "Oh, I give up."

"Let me help," Ben said. He picked up Aunt Bailey's orange

ball and gave a sidearm throw toward the frog, who opened his mouth and swallowed gratefully.

"Finally," Amy said. Mom tried to catch Dan's eye, but he was looking somewhere else. Mom's face cinched up tight. And this time I knew that look because it was my own, too. I felt annoyance circling around overhead, looking for a place to land.

Grandpa was already at the windmill, teeing up. He popped the ball neatly through the spinning blades, and then George did the same.

Hailey's ball sailed through the air. You felt it more than you saw it, the sudden whoosh of air flying past your cheek. It was a defense missile shot toward enemy territory; it soared high in the sky and then vanished. "It's a bird! It's a plane! It's . . . superball!"

"Hey, it was my turn," Ben said, but Hailey only shook her arms in victory over her head.

"Whoo hee!" she shouted.

"I'll have to find that," Dan said.

"Remember which ball is yours?" Ben said to Mom.

"Never mind, smarty-pants."

Ben and I hit, and then Mom went, tapping her ball neatly through the windmill blades. Amy did better this time, scooting the ball through on the second try, and Grandma's beginner's luck held, but then Aunt Bailey set her ball on the fake grass and placed her feet on either side of it.

Amy was next to me. She crossed her arms. She sighed

dramatically. Rolled her eyes. "Here we go," she said to me.

The thing was, I felt impatient too, I did—we still had a lot of holes to go before we got to the castle, the big Cinderella payoff, with the actual moat. At this rate we'd have to sleep here overnight, two nights, miss the wedding altogether, as Aunt Bailey tried over and over again to get the damn ball through the upcoming clown's mouth and past the log cabin and from one side of the lighthouse to the other. Sure, I was feeling a little tense anyway. I was ready for my hot dog. I was ready to get the whole "family" expedition over with so I could be alone, and so that "family" could lose the tense step inter-plays of quotation marks.

But as Amy stood there with her perfect teeth and her hair as glossy as cat fur, I could feel it inside, something bad build-ing and spilling over. I felt some inner hand pulling me back, urging me to stop and think. Aunt Bailey was one of my own, though. Her good parts and her irritations too, they were all mine, and they deserved my protection.

"Jeez, Amy," I said.

"What?"

"Honestly? You don't know?" I demonstrated. I sighed and rolled my eyes the way she sighed and rolled her eyes. I crossed my arms and turned my back. Oh, it felt good too.

Ben appeared at my side. "Crick? Just, come on." He held my elbow. We'd done this before. You learned how to get away from something like that together.

"What?" Amy said again.

"You," I said. I felt furious. Maybe I was feeling everyone's anger, channeling it like some psychic channels the voices of dead spirits. My face was red, I could feel it. I started to sweat. "Your *attitude*." I dripped venom into the word, and then I sunk the word into her, same as she'd been doing with every fake smile and huff through those semi-closed lips. It felt so, so good, which I suppose is the problem with anger. Everything comes falling deliciously down, every wall so carefully constructed, every bit of polite back-and-forth, brick and mortar, destroyed. You reach a certain point, and then . . . No more.

Amy's frosty, perfect exterior crumpled, and her eyes filled. "I can't believe this," she said. Amy stared at me. Her eyes burned with injustice and devastation. She flung down her golf club, and it clattered to the ground. She spun, took off running.

"Oh no," I said.

The glorious kick of anger started to slink off, looking for some rock of regret to hide under. I should have known it. I should have known that Amy would crumple like that. There were two kinds of bullies. The kind like my father, who would come back swinging if you crossed him. And the other kind. The ones who went weak after their own veiled antagonism was called out. The ones who could dish it out but couldn't take it. They got the best of both situations—they got to be strong and nasty, and then fragile enough so that whoever crossed them ended up the bad guy. Their tears always made it your fault, no matter who started what.

Dan ran up. "What happened?"

"She was being such a—" I said. He took off jogging after her. I saw his back pass the big whale and then the waterfall and the elephant at the entrance.

"God, just let her go," Ben said to Dan, who was long gone.

"Cricket," Mom said.

"She was making fun of Aunt Bailey," I said. We both looked over at Aunt Bailey, who was now attempting to roll the ball through the spinning windmill. Gram was urging her on. Aunt Bailey was chuckling happily, unharmed. Grandpa and George were teeing off at the clown mouth.

"*We* were making fun of Aunt Bailey," Mom said.

"Different," I said.

"Whoo hee!" Hailey said.

"Oh, my God," Mom said. She put her face into her hands. "Look."

We did. "I don't think you're supposed to be up there!" Ben called.

Hailey sat on top of the paddleboat, swinging her legs. "Look what I found!" she said. She held up one of her pink balls.

"I know Oscar and Gavin are good kids. They've always been good kids," Mom said. "But . . . is there any chance they were doing stuff out in that tent?"

I didn't catch her meaning at first. Stuff, yeah, they were doing *stuff*. But then I got it. "Drugs? Oh, come on. No way. You know them!"

"You're right. I'm sorry. Just . . . look at her!"

"They gave her their box of Snickers," Ben said.

"Chocolate?" Mom said.

"It was *a lot* of chocolate," Ben said. "She has no experience with the stuff."

"Okay." Mom breathed through her mouth like women are supposed to in childbirth. "Ben, can you get her?" she pleaded.

"Me?"

"Please."

"Can't you ask . . ." He looked around at her other options. "Fine." Ben strode to the paddleboat. "Hailey, you gotta come down."

"Too high," she said. Yeah, that was an understatement. She kicked her hanging feet back and forth, same as a toddler enjoying the swingy feel of legs.

"How'd you get up there in the first place?" he called.

"I put my foot in that porthole," she said.

"Jesus, then put your foot in the porthole to come down!"

She peered over the side. "Can't." Her phone rang in her pocket, some hip-hop song done in electronic jingles. "Wait a sec," she said. "Gotta get this." Ben looked around nervously for some sort of miniature golf police. Ben was a good guy, and good guys followed the rules for the most part. Okay, there was that time when he and Janssen made that rocket . . .

Hailey answered the phone. "'Lo?" she said. "Fine, Ma. Great. Having a wonderful time." She pointed at the phone, mouthed *My mother* to Ben. "I'm sitting on top of a boat. Uh-huh. . . . No, I haven't taken *drugs*. You know, Mother, you don't even let me breathe. And I'm sick of it. Finished. *Fini*," she said. She snapped her phone closed. "There. She is going to freak out. And I mean *freak*."

Ben was up the side of that paddleboat in some Spider-Man move. He grabbed Hailey, flung her over his shoulder. "I love fireman's carry!" she squealed.

Ben stepped over the walls of the paddleboat green. The people with the stroller were staring. Hailey's butt was pointed at us, the skin of her back showing from where her shirt was scrunched up. "Where do you want her?" Ben asked.

"I can see the ground from here!" she said.

"Just . . ." Mom shrugged helplessly. "I don't know. Here, I guess."

Ben set Hailey down on her feet. "Dizzy," she said. She wobbled.

"That woman is going to go nuts," Mom said. "Dan's phone is ringing this second, I'm sure of it."

"Stay put," Ben told Hailey.

"Guys!" Mom called to the rest of our group. "Everyone! How about some lunch!"

Gram and Aunt Bailey looked up. I could hear Aunt Bailey, even from there. "Damn. I was just getting the hang of this."

Hailey's golf ball missile had landed on Dan's windshield. It now sat cradled on the wiper, but the glass had shattered in a complicated web, still together but obviously ruined. He was standing with Amy, and she was wiping her eyes as he spoke intently to her, his arms folded. I felt embarrassed standing there, embarrassed for my own self and for the rest of our group, which hung back like the losers in high school, not knowing whether they should stick around or leave.

We group-walked over to the food stand in front of the building, and Mom took orders, and we all sat at the picnic tables on the grass. Everyone took out their wallets again, and then we unfolded our foil wrappers. Aunt Bailey and Gram chatted cheerily to George and Grandpa, but Mom was quiet. I felt shriveled with regret, like I had shattered that windshield myself. Ever since the spring of my senior year, I'd felt the gnawing, painful promise of endings. The thought of actually leaving—it held me in one place. But right then I would have been happy if some plane swooped down to scoop me up and take me away to a leafy campus where I knew no one. Not my family, not Janssen, not Ash, not anyone. Something had been whole—an idea, this idea that Dan and my mother had gotten something right this time, completely and wholly right, and what I had done was to speak and break the spell. It was a translucent bubble—beautiful, but it required care, cautious steps and gentle words, and now I'd been loud and harsh and it had popped.

"Crick, Jesus, don't feel so bad," Ben said. He had gone to squirt more ketchup on his hot dog. It had that pickle relish that you pump on too, which is just wrong, in my opinion. "What'd you even *say*?"

"Her attitude." I huffed and rolled my eyes so he could judge the replay.

"You nipped her in the butt," he said, and snickered. "Don't try sleeping on her bed, though."

"Oh, you're hilarious."

"Come on, big deal. You could have said a lot worse. Who didn't want to? You barely said anything. People can say something and it's not *huge*."

"Remember when we used to do something bad? Mom would say, 'Go to your room and think about it.'"

"Yeah, and then we'd come out two seconds later and say, 'I thought about it.' We'd see Mom trying not to smile, and then it was over. You don't need to be punished for this, Cricket."

I hated doing the wrong thing. My words had felt like roaring lions and raging forest fires and toppling buildings. But maybe he was right. Was it possible my words had just been words, not capable of permanent destruction? Mom threw her foil ball and empty cup into the metal trash can, which was set politely away from the tables. She came behind me, set her hands on my shoulders, and kissed the top of my head.

"I'm sorry," I said. But what I wanted to say, what felt urgent, was what I didn't say. *Please marry Dan anyway, even if the windshield is cracked.*

chapter
eighteen

Dan's windshield held together in spite of those spindly lines in the glass. We drove back to Bluff House. In Grandpa's car the drive was quiet, except for the soft radio and the occasional snap-pop of Gram's gum.

It was quiet inside the house too. I didn't know where everyone had gone, but John and Jane and Baby Boo had taken off somewhere, and the old people weren't around, and even Ted's truck was absent from the driveway. I found Jupiter lying on Cruiser's pillow downstairs in the living room. I didn't know where Cruiser was either, but Jupiter trotted over when she saw me, wagging. I clipped on her leash and took her out for a pee and then carried her up the stairs to my room. I closed the door behind us. I lay on my bed. Jupiter stretched her paws out in front of her, butt up, then butt down. She stared at me.

"Want up?" I said. That always felt like a treat for both of us. I patted the bed, and she hopped up.

"I don't know," I said to her. I held her in my lap. I could only see the back of her, her silky head and her ears and her long back with the white spot. I took off her collar for a minute. I would have liked to have had that thing off, if it were me. I scratched her neck. I kissed her head.

She shifted around. She got into a nice ball beside me, and set her chin on my leg. "I don't even want to open that fucking computer," I told her. "He's probably run off with Alyssa because I'm too stupid to make up my mind."

She kept her opinions to herself, which was especially smart under the circumstances. It was good to be by myself but not alone. She was good and respectful company. We stayed that way until my foot started to fall asleep. I shifted her, and she leaped off the bed, sniffed the clothes spilling from my bag. "Where's your jingle, huh?" I asked. It was funny when she walked around without her collar and her tags, her very own sound. She looked out the window for a while, which she loved to do. I stretched out on my bed, and then she came over, and I patted the spot beside me, and she jumped up again. I put her collar back on so she could go back to being herself. She sniffed around the pillows and licked some spot on my bedspread where I'd spilled some Diet Coke, and then she finally got settled. It took some doing, but she stretched out too, her chin on her paws, her deep brown eyes watching me.

"I wish you could talk," I said. I waited. Sometimes I forgot that I wouldn't get a response from her. She held my eyes. "Do you think I'm with Janssen for the wrong reasons? Or the right ones?" I asked. "I hate to even say that. Because I do love him." We kept on looking at each other. Maybe it was stupid, but I felt she heard me and understood me and was responding in the way she could.

"What do you think, huh, Woof?"

Of course she couldn't answer me. But her eyes said, *Everything is all right*. Her eyes kept on saying, *I am here for you*.

"Cricket!" Mom pounded on my door.

"What? God, what's the matter?"

I opened the door. My mother's eyes were frantic, and her purse was over one shoulder as if she was heading out, wearing only socks. "We've gotta . . . Cruiser knocked over Mr. Jax while we were gone. He's been lying out in the garden for who knows how long. We just found him! He's crying in pain. God. Do you know where Ben is? Dan doesn't want to drive his car around with that windshield. We need Ben's car to take him to the emergency room."

"He's probably out with the guys in the tent," I said. "I can run and get him."

"That's okay." Mom raced to the top of the stairs, yelled, "Dan? He's at the beach. In the tent!" I saw it all, as if it had already happened. Ben, not in the tent after all. Dan, pulling back the tent flap. Hailey with her blouse unbuttoned, sitting in Gavin's lap. "No wait!" I said. "No, no—"

I shoved past Mom. "Cricket?" she said.

I heard the back door close, and I knew Dan was already on the way down the boardwalk. By the time I got down the stairs, Ted was walking in the front door with another bag of groceries. It seemed like all he ever did was go to the grocery store, but there was no time to wonder about that. Ted. Car. "They need you," I said to him. "They need you to drive. Just a sec," I said.

Cruiser was pacing downstairs, whining and barking; we were anxious, so he was anxious. I raced to the back door. Dan was running down the boardwalk, heading toward the tent. I swear that tent off in the distance was vibrating. I could see its shiny fabric whipping a little in the sea breeze, and from whatever was happening inside.

"Dan!" I shouted. "Ted's here with his truck!"

Dan turned and waved at me, a rushed *not now* wave. He couldn't hear me. It was one of the tricks of the ocean. It could be beautiful and endless and full of hope, but it could also pull you under and steal your voice and drag it far away.

I tried to reach him, but he was too far ahead. He got to the tent just before I did, and he pulled that tent flap back all right, and it was oddly quiet in there. Ben *wasn't* there, and neither was Oscar, but Hailey was and so was Gavin. They looked like one big body in that sleeping bag, until Dan yelled something and Gavin's big bushy head popped up. Hailey appeared too, and her hair was all smushed up, and I didn't even know you could get a bra in that color.

"Hailey!" Dan cried. Hailey was eighteen and had had lots of boyfriends by the sound of it, and Dan wasn't exactly Jon Jakes, with his prim, obsessive eye on womanly virtue. Still, by the look on Dan's face, it never quite occurred to him that his little baby had grown up. Or else, seeing evidence of that right in front of him was more than anyone really wanted.

"I'm just changing!" Hailey said. Well, I guess this was true in more ways than one.

She held up her shirt as some sort of evidence and then struggled to put it back on. Dan covered his eyes. His other hand was on his chest. Oh, God. I imagined him keeling over, a heart attack. No wedding, Dan's blue face and lifeless body. But it was a heart attack of a different kind.

Dan turned and fled, and I followed, like the idiot sidekick in the cartoon, always a few paces back, waving her arms.

"Ted is here. A car," I said. And I watched Dan's back once more. Defeated again, and carrying too much, again. That poor, sad ponytail. You wondered how love could thrive in this kind of mess, or at all. Love was such a delicate thing, requiring tissue-paper touch and the safest place, yet there it was out in the real world, where it got battered by storms of ill will and bad circumstance and demons of your own or of other people. Love didn't stand a chance.

Dan and Mom and Ted came back hours later with Mr. Jax, who now had his left wrist bandaged in a white cast. Hailey and Amy were in their room, in self-imposed exile. I heard them arguing. Ben had gone into town with Oscar and Gavin, but I was too pissed at Gavin to go. I never took him for the kind of guy that liked girls who played dumb, first of all. But, worse, he should have known we didn't need any more complications right now. Maybe he should have just driven Mom right to the Sea-Tac Airport himself! Besides, if I went I'd probably end up in the backseat next to Oscar, with him grabbing my butt or something. Obviously high school had been some version of a safe, snug prison, with the inmates mostly in their cells, and now we'd been let out. Freedom had led to wildness and rioting, and if you asked me, some of us should be locked back up.

That night Rebecca made heaping piles of Japanese dishes as a surprise for George, and she set out bowls and platters for everyone to come by and dish up their plates when it suited them. I thought I'd probably be seeing Ash—I was looking *forward* to it—but for some reason he wasn't around. Fine. Good. No problem. Where *was* he?

Rebecca brought all the food back out when Mom and Dan came home, but no one except Ted was very hungry. Jane fussed around Mr. Jax, and Mrs. Jax fixed the collar of his shirt coolly. His chin was still dirty from his face-plant in the garden. Cruiser had been closed into the kitchen. I saw him in there, checking inside his food bowl to see if anything new had appeared. I caught Dan on his way upstairs.

"Hey, Dan? I'm sorry," I said.

We'd had a good relationship before. Before now, anyway. When he came over to our house, he'd cook dinner and

I'd help him. He taught Janssen how to replace the brakes in his car. He was easy to talk to. He told stories about how he changed his major three or four times in college before deciding, because he knew I didn't know what I wanted to study yet. He went out and mowed that great big lawn of Mom's, and I helped him bag the grass clippings.

I realized right then that an apology was a pretty shabby thing. The same word was used for both small crimes and big ones—you said you were sorry for bumping into another person, and for destroying their life. It seemed wrong. I was sorry for what I had said to Amy earlier, and sorry about Hailey, and sorry about Mr. Jax, and sorry mostly that things had gone so wrong. But an apology too—you think you're giving something, but you're not. You're really asking for something. You're asking for forgiveness, you're asking for the other injured person to make it okay for you. Apologies were harder work for the person getting one than the person giving one.

"It's all right," Dan said. "It's not your fault." But his voice was husky from fatigue. He rubbed under his eye with the tip of his finger, that place where the skin is so thin that emotions show through, rising up in dark rings of fatigue or despair. "Everything will be fine."

I heard them arguing through my wall. It was the first real argument that I'd ever heard, two days before their wedding.

I couldn't make out Dan's exact words, but my mother's were clear. My ears had been trained to her voice, probably, from a long time ago, when she used to sing Stevie Ray Vaughan's "Pride and Joy" to Ben and me, dancing with us. "Wheels on the Bus," sure, that too. All the songs from Raffi, and from Mr. Rogers. "Baby Beluga" and "You Are Special." I remember her singing Springsteen's "Pony Boy" to Ben, when he was seven and going through that cowboy phase.

She wants to go home? Mom's voice cut.

Then the low rumble of Dan's voice.

Did you tell her that going home isn't possible? That everything is not about her?

A slam. The walls shuddered. Slamming meant she was really mad. Mad enough to go public with her anger, mad enough to forget that other people might hear. Another slam, downstairs.

Jupiter got up from her bed, stretched out her back leg, oooh so far behind her, and then the other one. She sat beside my door and looked at me. Who says dogs can't talk.

"You need to go out?" I asked. *"Now?"*

She would sit this way by the back door at home, too. Sometimes near the jar where we kept her treats. She stared insistently. "Your timing sucks," I said.

I searched around for her leash, and found it under yesterday's clothes. My phone buzzed with a text message. I looked.

Oscar. We really need to talk. Where ARE you?

What had happened between us that night? Nothing, I was sure. I ignored it. Jupiter wagged. I clipped on her leash, and opened the door like a robber would. I looked both ways.

When there was a fight in the house, you were as careful and quiet as a thief trying not to trip the alarm.

At the top of the stairs, Jupiter sat willfully. "Oh, come on," I said. "Really?" She wouldn't budge. "Fine," I said. I picked her up. She seemed so much lighter than she had been. There'd been times in her life when carrying her around took some doing.

Her butt was sticking out under my arm, which made me think of Hailey that afternoon. And that made me think of Hailey and Gavin, and that bra color, and the fact that Gavin was one of my best friends. I saw the bubble of the tent, glowing in some otherworldly way. I felt guilty about it being there at all; it had gone from the greatest-fun sort of tent to a tent that made you feel like you were looking at a bed people had just gotten out of. Guilt wasn't exactly a logical thing. It was more like a virus, spreading wildly and looking for places to land. I wondered if love, mine or anyone else's, wasn't safe anywhere near me. I felt like bad luck.

I set Jupiter down on the grass. My phone buzzed again. I knew it was Oscar, and so I reached to shut that stupid phone off, but it wasn't Oscar after all. *Any chance we can talk? Something I want to tell you.* Ash.

Something *he* needed to tell *me*? I didn't know what to say right then, I really didn't, so I shoved my phone back into my pocket without answering. I saw my mother sitting on the beach not far from that tent. She had snagged one of Rebecca's beach towels that had been hanging over the deck railing, and she sat on it, her arms around her knees, her long hair down her back, and her white sundress glowing in the moonlight. Her chin was set down on her arms, and she was rocking slightly. She stopped and looked over her shoulder when she heard our steps on the boardwalk.

Jupiter saw her there and began to pull on the leash. "Okay, okay," I said. She made a quick stop to sniff and pee when we reached a clump of some apparently delicious-smelling beach grass, and then she pull, pull, pulled again toward Mom.

"Let her come," my mother said, so I let go of the leash, and Jupiter ran full speed toward her.

"Oh, look who's here," Mom said to her. "You little one. Funny girl." She scruffed Jupiter under her chin and around her soft ears.

"You must be freezing," I said. "Are you okay?"

"I'm too mad to be cold," she said. "You can leave her. I'll bring her back later."

I took this to mean that Mom wanted to be alone. So I left them there. I walked back toward the house, which suddenly looked huge, those glass windows an enormous display case for every feeling inside there. Above me I could hear a chair being dragged against the upper deck, the squeak of a body settling in. I smelled the grassy tang of burning pot.

I climbed the steps to my room. I did not turn on the lights. I stood at my own window, looking out. I could see Mom's figure down on the beach, with Jupiter sitting beside her. Mom had one arm around her, her fingers stroking Jupiter's head.

Jupiter had always been there for me. She'd sit patiently when I would cry. She would trot around when I was excited. She gave herself to your grief and to your joy. But I remembered too the times when we had gone for our weekends with my father. Ben and I would leave, and it would be the two of them at home, my mother and our dog. "What are we going to do this weekend, huh, girl?" Mom would ask her as we packed our bags. "Slumber party, you and me?" Other times I would hear Mom talking to Jupiter down in the kitchen. "Do you think that chicken's done, huh? What do you think? You like chicken." When we were at school, I knew that Jupiter would lie by my mother's feet while she worked. And when we had that earthquake, when I was watching the lights swing in Mr. Jacobi's earth science class, my mother said that she and Jupiter had huddled together in our doorway.

And Jupiter—she would go into Ben's room too, when he was doing homework. She'd go through his garbage can, sure, looking for candy bar wrappers or Kleenex, or she'd hunt around in his backpack for the remains of his lunch. But she'd also just lie quietly under his desk while he did his math. She would lick the salt from his sweaty baseball-playing legs. She would tease him by stealing something of his and taking off.

I watched her and my mother out there. And I realized what a big job our dog had, looking out for all of us.

I stared at the wedges of light on the ceiling. My mind was playing a slide show, and I couldn't seem to interrupt it to get up and get ready for bed. After a while my mother tapped at the door softly and brought Jupiter back. Jupiter's nose was cold from being outside. Her fur smelled like night. She had a long, slurpy drink of water and looked out the window for a while into the darkness, and then she sighed through her nose and went to her bed, turning three circles before settling into her croissant-shaped circle.

My phone buzzed again. Oscar. Damn it! This time I remembered to shut off the phone. There were murmurs on the other side of my wall, and then it was quiet. I heard a toilet flushing upstairs. I had not opened my laptop all day. So I did. And what I read made my stomach feel sick. I held my pillow on my bed and rocked.

The slide show kept playing. My mother's sharp words to Dan, my sharp words to Amy, an old man sprawled helpless in a garden, a windshield destroyed.

A mess.

A new house, an old one gone, maybe a plane lifting off, changing things forever.

Janssen.

It was too big, too much. But mess and chaos love mess and chaos. Mess always gathers more, like dust gathers dust, like friends gather friends for support when they want to do something bad.

So of course I let him in when he tapped on my door and said my name softly. Of course I let Ash in.

chapter
nineteen

Janssen—

Wow—your list was full of amazing dog feats, just
like you promised. I loved that one especially about
the people who watched as their car went into that
lake with their dog in it, how he managed to get
out and swim ashore. I was so happy he made it.
But Jupiter has her own astonishing talents, don't
forget. She can open Gram's refrigerator door. She
carries her red ball with the treats in it to the top of
the stairs and lets it drop, so that the biscuits break
up and fall out. And, of course, there's that thing
she used to do with her food. Picking out the reds

first and then the yellows and oranges and leaving behind the tans. I wonder what was in those tans.

All right. My turn.

What Us Humans Could Learn from Dogs:

1. How to notice the small things: The smallest speck of cracker. Some tiny piece of kibble that's rolled under the stove. They *see*.
2. How to keep it simple: A meal. A treat. A walk. A friend. No need for big TVs and fancy cars and expensive clothes. Grass itself is joy.
3. How to make the most of what you've got: If all you have is the hard floor, find the spot of sun.
4. How to be a good friend: Play together. Have patience. Forgive. Be there. Listen carefully.
5. How to be hopeful: Keep checking your food bowl, just in case. Sit and stare, but if that piece of cheese doesn't come your way, move on.
6. How to be loyal: Stay near, never forget, and fight for what's most important.

the story of us

I was thinking about this last night—how
Jupiter is faithful to all of us. She drives Mom
crazy sometimes, going everywhere she does.
Mom gets up, she gets up. Mom goes to the
kitchen, she goes to the kitchen. But she keeps
her eye on her. And when Ben leaves for college
too, Jupiter is always so thrilled to see him again,
weeks later. She waits. You have the feeling that
he could be gone for years, and Jupiter would
keep on waiting. She keeps track of me also,
of course. She watches, and she listens to me
carefully, even if occasionally she yawns while I
talk. (Yeah, don't even say what you're thinking.)
She tries to protect us all from coyotes and deer
and strangers and squirrels, even though she is
small and old.

Are we even capable of that kind of loyalty? Dogs
don't have their line in the sand, where they say,
"That's it." Enough. I'm out of here. When my
mother got back from Great-Grandma Georgette's
funeral in California, when she flew home and my
father went to pick her up at the airport and she
told him right there it was over—it had to happen.
Sure, he brought flowers to welcome her home, but
there were all those other times. We saw him raise
his hand to her. We heard her scream. If loyalty

was a pure, finite thing between people, she'd still be there. Does an abused dog ever run away? God, I hope so.

Still, Janssen, doesn't it seem a shame? That words like "love" and "loyalty" and "forever"— beautiful, perfect words—can't just stand apart, always beautiful and perfect, untouched? Isn't it a heartbreak that the most beautiful words are the most complicated? I wish and wish and wish that they could just *be*. We mess them up so bad.

It seems wrong that goodness can't be permanent. That love can't just be love and loyalty can't be loyalty and forever can't be forever, without it all getting so wrecked.

Humans. We love our messes, don't we? Gotta make a big old mess in order to learn how *not* to make a big old mess.

But dogs. This is the very heart of why we love them, isn't it? Their goodness is goodness, and their love is love, and their loyalty is loyalty, and nothing you do seems to change that.

the story of us

So. Our story.

We fell in love.

God, did we. We would meet up at lunchtime
at school, remember? We'd ditch the cafeteria
and those tables in prison rows and those prison
mashed potatoes in ice-cream scoop lumps with
that brown, criminal gravy. We'd stick our
backpacks into our lockers so we would be free of
their weight. You would lift me up onto your back,
or we'd clasp hands and run, escaping to your dad's
car, your car now, since he gave up and bought a
new one. We'd run outside into fall and orange
leaves and drippy trees and the fast *thwick, thwick,
thwick* of your wipers, or into winter, stepping
carefully in the icy parking lot, or into spring,
when the air smelled so good you wanted to roll in
it, same as Jupiter with just mown grass.

I was glad to get out of there. So glad. Every time
we pushed open those doors, I relaxed. You used to
tell me that. Maybe school was just not my natural
environment, like it seems to be for some people.
You got your Emma Brightleys and your Ashley
Hills, Brianna Campbells—they live in it, they

flow. Friends drip off their arms, and their laughter is the right balance of cutting and self-assured. They'd come back to school after a weekend, talking about some party at Ethan Rivera's house, and I'd never even know how this worked. How did you get invited to Ethan Rivera's house? What would a party at Ethan Rivera's house even look like? My big moments were the slumber parties at Kate Ship's, back in the sixth and seventh grade, but she stopped inviting me and I never even knew why.

I did go to parties with Meghan and the orchestra kids. I think Ethan Rivera would have laughed at those. You would have laughed at those. Mr. Popularity, everyone loved you. The way it's supposed to work is that the popular boyfriend suddenly makes the girl popular too, right? Isn't that how it goes in the movies? But that never really happened. I was friends with your friends, but reflected glory, forget it.

Anyway, I would go to Mr. Clymer's American History class, or worse, Mrs. Bryan's Algebra II, and I would watch that thin black second hand ticking away the time until lunch. (Ben actually *liked* Algebra II, which shows for the millionth time what a loser he is.) I would hold my breath in

Biology, with all those guys from the track team,
reeking of BO from their early-morning run. I
waited, is my point. To get out of there. You were
like a vacation spot I was about to go to after too
many hours in a job I hated.

But finally I was let out, and there you'd be. Your
hand would go into mine, and we were there in the
real world, even if that was only the McDonald's
drive-through. Even if it meant just watching you
eat fish filet sandwiches and talking with your
mouth stuffed about the way Jackson's girlfriend
was always such a drama queen, crying over some
fight she had with her friend or having "talks"
all the time with him about how he was looking
at other girls. Or we'd sit out on the grass on
the back lawn of the school, way out on that hill
where no one went. We'd take our shoes off, and
you'd tell me my toes looked like a row of old men
standing together. Old men, waiting at a bus stop.

And after school we'd go to your room and study.
Study, right? We didn't get much studying done.
I'd have to wait until I got home, away from you,
to do anything but pretend to look at words until
we both tossed our books onto the floor and rolled
into each other.

It got really hot between us for a while. Remember kissing until our lips were numb? Shoving, pressing, rubbing. God. That time we went to Marcy Lake and we were on the grass . . .

Supposedly it goes this way, right? The girl says "Wait, wait," and the boy either pressures her or is "understanding," a good guy, someone who tells her he'll hang around until she's "ready," as if sex was something she reluctantly hands over, a prize he's earned for his good behavior and patience. Not that you didn't have good behavior and patience. HOW long did we know each other? But it's like . . . A certain number of gold stars on the sticker calendar and he gets to go to the prize box, just like in Mrs. Mosher's kindergarten class. Was it just me? Am I the one girl who felt like I did? Because I wanted you. We would kiss, and kiss, and then I wanted you so bad. Not just my hands under your shirt or unzipping your jeans, but all of you.

When you're a girl, desire means you're a slut, but when you're a guy, it means you're normal. What's up with that? Don't say a word, I'm warning you. Still, you have to admit, it's a societal contraceptive device if there ever was one, and an effective one too, given that girls and guilt go together like boys and freedom, but, whatever.

We tried to be a responsible couple, didn't we? We *were* a responsible couple. We "talked" about it. Maybe *you* talked about it. Remember? We were in your car, driving to school. Ben was one of the sweaty guys running track early in the morning, and he wasn't with us.

"Cricket, lately," you said. I knew it was serious, because you always cleared your throat a certain way before you were going to say something important.

We were driving down Cummings Road, heading from home into town. We'd already passed the Country Store, and Johnson's Nursery, and the secret shortcut where Bob, Betty, and Louise walked. It was a dangerous road, fast, curvy, so you kept your eyes forward. As you drove, I was busy admiring your cheekbones and your caramel brown hair and your collarbone. That dip, the small crater at your throat. "You are gorgeous," I said.

You grinned. "Okay." You snuck a glance at me. "Terrific. But I need to talk to you, okay? Stop looking at me like that. Lately we're getting so close, you know. Physically."

"I've noticed," I said. The thought of it made me want you to pull over right then, drive that car off to some forested roadside like we'd done before. That damn parking brake.

"Do you think maybe we should turn it down a little? Wait, or something?"

"No," I said. "I don't want to wait."

You nodded. "Okay . . ."

"I want you to make love to me," I said. The words sounded silly. Stupid. Something a person would say in a pink-covered romance novel, or in a movie where a glamorous, heavy-breathing couple is standing dramatically on some terrace with city lights all around.

But you didn't seem to mind. You reached over the seat and took my hand and tangled our fingers together and squeezed hard.

"Us," I said. "Each other."

You brought our hands to your mouth and kissed.
"Oh, Cricket," you said.

Remember that pharmacy we went to? We even
went together. Who does that, J.? We might as
well have worn T-shirts printed with "VIRGINS"
and a big slash through the word. Of course we did
that old trick of buying other stuff too, to cover up
the obvious. I guess everyone does that. We waited
for the guy clerk to be available, because somehow
we were sure the forty-five-year-old woman would
judge us. Like she never did it herself. But the guy
would understand.

It was just after Thanksgiving, and there were
Christmas decorations up and those men ringing
the bells outside the stores that always made me
feel guilty when I walked past (see Girls and Guilt,
above). You bought a box of candy canes because
they were cheap, and a pair of those stretchy
mittens that look like they'd gotten shrunk in the
wash, which is pretty much how everything ended
up looking if you let my mother do the laundry.
What else? Those gingersnap cookies you like.
You and the spice stuff. You're the only one I know
who wants spice cake for his birthday. Anyway,
Christmas music was playing. I was so excited and

mortified. It was this huge step we were taking together. Crossing over to everything adult, which sounds corny. Teen big moment drama. But I really felt that way.

We got back into the car, and you gave me those mittens, which I still have. I pulled them on, streeeetched them on, and shook the bag around and wiggled my eyebrows, but you were serious. You made your face so still, and your eyes grave.

You said, "Cricket, this is a really big day." You held my hands. You looked into my eyes solemnly. "It's our first time buying candy canes together."

Ha. Oh, I do love you. Even if the terrible thing I did messed this up, that very fact stays true.

I know the guy in Rite Aid probably thought we got into the car and did it right then, but we didn't, did we? That's when we waited. We both had some idea of "the right time," even though we didn't talk about what "right" would look like. "Special," that's the other word. Maybe it's like any other big decision. Right is something you feel, not something you necessarily have words for.

It was a snow day. Like the first day we met you, all those years ago, that day you rode by on your mother's horse. So many years, you. But this day we were messing around outside, you, me, and Ben. Jupiter ran outside, and the snow was up to her knees, and then Mom brought her back in. You and Ben shoved snow down each other's backs and pushed each other to the ground, in that foreign language of guy affection. Your cheeks always get so red in the cold. Mine must have too, because you put your gloved hands to either side of my face, and that's when Ben said, "Hey, guys, I'm out of here." He loved us both, but Ben was never really into public displays of affection.

He went in. I ran in too, and changed out of my wet clothes. I yelled to Mom that we were taking a drive into town. We both knew that "right" had come, didn't we? The sky was that blue-blue that comes after it snows, and everything was sparkly, like God had taken huge handfuls of the tiniest daylight stars and threw them into the air. The roads had already gotten a little slushy. You ran up the gravel drive to your house and got the car, and when you drove back, I saw the blankets in the back, something big rolled up.

I knew where we were going too.

We found it accidentally one day, after we'd parked out there, just off Cummings Road where the trees closed off into a patch of forest. It was fall then, and we'd sat out there and kissed, and just as you started the car to head back, I noticed it. Far off, hidden by evergreens and blackberries and ferns— a tiny shingled house. Not a house, a shed. No, bigger than a shed, but not much.

"Look," I said.

"Let's go see," you said. That's how you are. You always want to get in there and investigate. If there's someplace you're not supposed to look in but can look in, you'll do it. Funny, because I always think of you as being so responsible, but you've got this other side too that will commit a minor crime in the name of curiosity.

Which you did then. We hiked over to the shack, blackberry stickers clinging to my pant legs, and we looked into the two small, dirty windows and found this wonderful, empty hiding place. There was a bench built into one wall but other than that the place was bare. It wasn't obvious who it

belonged to, or even why it existed at all—maybe
a storage room for one of the houses up the road.
Who knew? It looked like something you'd see
high up in the mountains, where hikers could rest
to get away from the cold, or where a forest ranger
could stop to take notes on whatever forest rangers
take notes on.

"Cool," you said, and then you messed with the
latch and shoved at the door.

"Janssen," I said. I looked around. Frogs were
bllleeep, bllleeeping, but that was about it. Maybe a
few crows were watching.

"Oh no! I hear a police car!" You grabbed my
arms in fake panic. "They're coming for you,
Crick. See that tree? It's got a spy cam, like in
the stores."

"You're hilarious," I said.

We went inside. It smelled like cedar planks. I
love that smell. We sat on the bench, our arms
touching. There was that great feeling, the feeling
I love, that you're hidden and safe, but that no one
knows where you are.

"Listen," you said.

I listened. It was hard to believe.

"A rooster?" I said. "Am I hearing a rooster?"

Yeah, there it was. A curdling cry. There were
all kinds of things out where we lived. Head over
the hill to Dad's house, and you had suburban
neighborhoods with those neighborhood parties
where the kids run around the yard and the adults
barbecue things and get drunk and hit on each
other's wives. But there, out past Cummings road
where we both lived, well, *you* know it. There were
more crazy animals than people. Bears, mountain
lions, those goats. Our own yard had a variety of
creatures we named: John Deer and Gauca-mole,
and Dan and Marilyn Quail, and the salmon in
the creek. There was that llama farm just before
town, the one we passed every day heading in to
school. They stood around blinking their long
eyelashes as we drove by. There was a roving
band of chickens, which we would see on various
stretches of the road on various days.

"Aren't they supposed to do that in the morning?"
I said.

"So, he's a fucked-up rooster," you said.

Anyway, that snowy day, that's where we were
going. It was white winter and glittery, and the
tree branches were drooping and heavy, and I
knew we were driving toward that cedar shack.

We didn't even speak. You held my mitten-hand
with your glove-hand. It took a while before the
car got warm. We hated the way your heater
smelled when it got going. Like someone cooking
corn dogs. I didn't care right then. Your car was
shit in the bad weather, and I could see us getting
stuck somewhere and having to call for help before
or after this big moment. But the car did fine, and
you pulled off the road and drove up the trail and
parked. Snow would slip off evergreen branches in
big slushy clumps, and the branches would snap
back up to their regular selves again.

"Kiss me," you said. I leaned over and did, and
then you hopped out of the car and got all the
stuff out. It was so quiet out there. Snow-quiet.
We hauled all of that warmness and softness
you brought up the hill. You planned that ahead,
didn't you? But I was glad because, God, it was
cold in there, when you shimmied open the door.

I could see my breath, and you got to work with all that camping gear you have. You laid out a thick foam pad, sleeping bags, blankets. You even brought juice boxes, those little square ones we had in elementary school with the plastic straws attached. Your mom probably bought those for your lunch ten years before and still had them in her cupboard.

"Oh, my God, it's freezing," I said.

"Get in," you said.

I took off my shoes, and got under all those layers of slippery nylon sleeping bags, and so did you, and when we finally got warm and when I remembered that it was just you, familiar you, I relaxed and we got undressed, and you were there naked next to me, and on me, and in me, and then you held me in your arms in that cedar shack and that stupid rooster crowed again, and I leaned in close to your ear and whispered. "That's one fucked-up rooster," I said, and you kissed my cheek with your cold, cold lips and told me you loved me, and there we were, on the other side.

You said I broke your heart after what I did. And I would take it back if I could. I'd be so much more careful with you. People always say, "You can't undo the past." It's one of those expressions you hear so often that the words lose meaning. But it's true. You can't undo the past, and the minutes tick by and even the things that deserve to stay, especially those, can't be held forever, even in hands more careful than mine. I feel it in my chest, deep and painful, this truth, a terrible truth—time goes forward and things are left behind. There's no way around it, Janssen, and my problem is that I stepped to the other side of adulthood and realized that fact. I turned my tassel to the other side of my cap, and there it was, this truth I never felt before. Loss is the price we pay for life.

How are we humans supposed to go around with that knowledge? And can I just say that, unfairly or not (okay, unfairly), you are making it worse? You don't admit that you're interested in Alyssa. Instead you answer my question about her with two lines. I've read them a hundred times. *Maybe we should see other people. You can't expect me to put my life on hold.*

Jesus, Janssen. Am I standing here at the fucking
Sea-Tac Airport?

Love always,

Cricket

chapter
twenty

"I can't keep my life on hold," I said.

"What?" Ash said.

"I can't. I can't either."

"Are you okay, Cricket?" Everyone was asking me that lately. I was asking me that. Ash's hands were shoved down into that sweatshirt I had worn. His head was tilted sideways in question. The room was still dark. I could see his face in the light from the moon. He sat down on the edge of my bed, shoved my pillow aside. It seemed intimate, touching my pillow. Like touching me, or my most private clothing. I was territorial about my pillow usually. It was one of my weird things. When Ben or Mom was in my room, I'd hate it when they'd fold my pillow in half and lie on it.

He took my hands. Jupiter was sniffing his pant legs. He

was pulling me toward him, but she was in the way, and he gave her a little push with the side of his foot.

"Hey," I said. "Don't." We all had to get Jupiter out of the way sometimes. But a foot seemed disrespectful.

"I'm sorry," he said, and he seemed to mean it. "Just, come over here."

I sat down next to him. I really liked how he smelled. You could believe in those things you read about, smell and attraction, some whatever-something we give off, a particular whatever-something that attracts you specifically. Maybe we had our own version of a dog's nose without even realizing it.

"You smell so good," I said.

"Thank you." It sounded formal. And he had his hands in his lap, folded like a schoolboy hoping to be noticed for his good behavior. And he didn't even realize how he looked— sweet, and it made me laugh. I forgot all my heart turbulence and just laughed. "What?" he asked. He was grinning, ready to get whatever joke I had to offer.

"You," I said.

"Oh, I'm funny, am I?" He held his arms up, werewolf, monster-movie arms, ready to tickle.

I set my mouth into a serious line. "Not funny," I said. "Not the least bit funny. Hey. You weren't at dinner tonight."

"I know. It's stupid. But I was thinking about how to tell you something. Did you get my message?"

"I did. I guess I was thinking about how to tell you something too."

"There's all this chemistry between us . . ."

"I know."

"I wanted to tell you . . . I'm not the kind of guy that does casual hookups. I don't want you to think that. I want you to know I don't just go doing this all the time." He leaned in close to me. I could feel his breath on my face. "Forget what I said about waiting to kiss you, okay? Because I can't think about anything else."

"Wai—" I said, but he shut me up. His mouth was on mine, and his lips were warm and he tasted like fading peppermint. He held my face in his hands, held it hard, and it wasn't something that Janssen did really, and his tongue was different, the kiss itself was, but it was good, and I felt myself folding into it, and it would have been so easy to relax and love this. It was dark, and darkness could make you feel like you were anyone. A different kiss—even as I was kissing I thought this, and I was shoved up then against a hard truth—there were a thousand different kisses out there to experience, different hands, different moments with different people. You could cut the strings to that hot-air balloon and could see and feel more than you would even guess from the ground.

I pulled away. "Wow," he said. His brown eyes were holding mine. "I was nervous. About kissing you. I wanted to tell you—I've only had one serious girlfriend. . . . Let's do that again."

I started to speak. The bad thing was, I almost called him Janssen. The name sat right there in my mouth. It almost slipped out. I stopped myself in time, but I had a crazy moment of hunting around in my head for his name. If not Janssen, who? Nothing was coming to me.

"Ash," I said. Thank God, there it was. "I want to. I do. I really like you. Really like. But—"

"Oh, I hate buts." He groaned and put his hands to his head in mock pain. "No . . . No buts."

"I'm in this strange place right now. *I've* only had one boyfriend. For years. And now we're . . . I don't know *what* we're . . ."

"Taking a break?" Ash said.

"Taking a break," I agreed. It was as good as anything.

"That's not a bad 'but'," he said. He looked crushed, though.

I had hurt Janssen that day. I had done a terrible thing. I'd never been disloyal, though. I'd never done what I just did. I could permanently damage us, and some great big hand, a huge Hand of the Future, slapped me hard.

"I need to get things sorted out before I'm with *any*-one. I'm so sorry. I don't go around doing this either. This, you—confusing."

Ash stood up. "I think I'm going to hope that you're a fast sorter outer." He smiled. I thought it was really brave of him to pull that smile off. He took a pinch of my shirt and pulled a little, playfully. "So. This is awkward."

"God, it is. I'm sorry."

"Okay." He opened my door.

"Okay."

He shut it behind him. My chest hurt. I felt awful. I had that feeling that sometimes sits oddly around you. *Where am I, and how did I get here?* Of course, I knew how I got there. I brought myself right to this place, to see what it would look like. The view always seems like it will be better at the edge.

In a book, in a movie or something, I would now have had some great moment of truth. A wrong kiss, which would send me back to Janssen. A right kiss, which would send me away. Or Ash would suddenly reveal himself to be a bad guy, making my path clear. The thing he did with his foot with Jupiter would have huge meaning. But it wasn't that simple. It's not how it happened in my own life.

In my own life two truths coexisted, and that seems to be how it goes. If I've learned one thing, it's that. There were a thousand kisses out there, but there was also the one that mattered. There was the one that mattered, and also the one that never had a chance.

It was the day before my mother's wedding, a day to believe in love. The clouds lazed around as if it were a Sunday morning and they were wearing cloud pajamas. Soon they would drift off with better things to do, you could tell. I felt two truths inside of me, but under that roof there were too many truths to count, and it seemed that Jupiter and Cruiser were the only ones that had worked out their relationship. Things were very clear between them. She was smaller, she was older, but she was still the boss, something they both understood without long talks and arguments and history. I bit your ass. We know where we stand. End of story.

"Let's go outside," I said to Jupiter. She tilted her head at the word. Wouldn't it be freeing to be able to ignore all the words that weren't important, like dogs did? Boring stories, painful ones, all those hurtful comments people flung your way—the rhythms and tones would wash over you like waves until you heard only what you needed to: *walk, treat, good girl*. You'd only have to listen for your own name, and the few things that mattered.

"Outside, then breakfast." She put her paws up on my knees. "You hate those stairs. I'll carry you. Don't even have to ask."

I tucked my phone into my jeans. Oscar had quit calling. I needed to go see those guys. They were my best friends, even if Oscar had turned into my stalker and Gavin had brought Hailey to the geek dark side of technology and junk food. Natalie was coming that day too. It would be good to have her here, to have all of us together again. I loved familiar.

I looked down at Rabbit, Jupiter's familiar, and decided to leave him there. "You're okay without him, right?" I asked. She licked the side of my face. "Oh, guck," I said. "You goof. Silly girl."

I could hear voices downstairs already. We'd all have a day to ourselves, but the rehearsal (if you could call it that) and the rehearsal dinner would be that night. My stomach fell at the thought, though I don't know what my problem was. It wasn't me getting married. Still, I had that lurch of nerves you get when the something big that had been off in the distance is now in front of you.

"Do you remember how you used to always bring us something when we came back home?" I asked Jupiter quietly. "You'd run and get your blankie or Rabbit or some chew toy, and you'd greet us with it, and drop it at our feet?" She was riding down the stairs, under my arm. "You were always enough by yourself, you know. We never needed anything else."

We almost bumped into George at the bottom of the stairs. He was rifling through the pockets of his jacket, which had been tossed over the banister. "Headache tablets," he said. His accent reminded me of the plucking of banjo strings.

"Oh no, again? What happened, George?"

"Fucking raccoons. They are a curse. I sleep, and then there they go. Arthur says ignore it. He says, *Go back to sleep.* How can you ignore it, I want to know. It is worse than cats fighting."

Well, of course I heard it. *Go back to sleep.* This could go two ways, right? An after-the-fact piece of advice, or a right-there-in-your-own-bed statement. God! Ben couldn't be *right*, could he? I mean, we never did get the whole story about George and Grandpa, how and *why* they were friends. No. No! I was born after Gram and Grandpa had divorced, but they'd been married for nearly thirty years. We'd known two girlfriends of his—the real estate agent with blond hair and manicured nails, who smelled faintly of cigarette smoke, and the thin, nervous golf pro. We met her once when they all went to my fifth-grade play. Gram had said, *Adult anorexic*, when they got into the car to go home. *She's an athlete, she's thin*, my mother said. She had practice keeping parents separate too.

When George went into the kitchen, I stuck my hand into his jacket pocket. I don't know why I did it. I was hoping to find some proof, maybe. But all I felt were several loose coins and the smooth, thin wood of a few golf tees. Even my hand felt guilty. My brother was an idiot.

My mother sat at the table, wearing her Chinese robe with the dragon on the back. Her hair was all flat, and her face looked blank without her makeup. Either she was getting really comfortable here, or she'd stopped caring. Rebecca sat across from her, and they both had their hands around their cups and were leaning forward in conversation.

"It's a damn shame, but 'safe' is just a sweet dream," Rebecca said.

"Nooooo." Mom groaned.

"Love, our shaky triumph over uncertainty." Rebecca sipped her coffee. "'Shaky', key word."

"I'm glad I'm not the only one," Mom said. "You sure we should do the ceremony outside, not in?"

"Absolutely." Rebecca nodded.

"Sorry to interrupt," I said. "Dog's gotta go out."

"Go right ahead," Rebecca said.

On my way out through the kitchen door, I saw a different spot of grass, ha, in an ashtray on the kitchen windowsill. I don't have any experience with the stuff, but I was somehow surprised by the ashtray. It looked 1950s formal. Less Age of Aquarius or the guys in the back parking lot at school, and more martinis and boofed-out hair.

And then, right there, looking at that crinkled stub, something hit me. That pathetic little joint spoke to me. I'd never respected the act of doing drugs. It felt like a cop-out. And I still didn't respect it, but all at once I *got* it. We used anything we could to protect ourselves against fear, against the ways life felt too big. We put God in front of terrifying things, and we knocked three times, and we took drugs and shopped too much and obsessed about food or success, so that the scary stuff would look farther away than it was. We worried, because maybe if we worried enough, it would act like a spell of safety. All those things, superstitions and addictions and anxiety, they were all about hiding from what scared the shit out of us.

And, say it, Cricket. Be honest: a relationship. A relationship could be a place to hide too.

I set Jupiter down, and she squatted on her narrow back legs. Her legs wobbled, I noticed.

"What's wrong, girl?" I asked, but she averted her eyes. She was quite private when peeing, and I usually tried not to look, out of respect. When she finished, she did her usual pride-restoring act, the vigorous back kick of dirt, but even that was done slowly.

We went back in. Jupiter gave Cruiser's empty bowl a lick. I gave her a few biscuits to tide her over, and she crunched away. "Aunt Hannah is coming today," my mother said. "My sis," she said to Rebecca. "God, I can't wait to see—"

She was interrupted by a pounding on the front door, and a deep voice, shouting, "Hurry, hurry, hurry."

"Yes, okay!" Rebecca hustled out. Her caftan caught on a chair and knocked it over. Mom stood quickly and righted it. I could see George out on the deck, watching the sea.

"Look what's here!" Rebecca said.

"This thing's a bitch. Watch out."

"Oh!" My mother gasped.

"Where do you want it? Yi, yi, yi, gotta set her down."

It was a man. In jeans and a sloppy T-shirt, a rough beard. He had a red bandana in his dark hair. Huge muscles. No wonder he could carry that thing himself. "Beautiful as the bride," he said. He had the rough voice of a smoker.

The cake. Mom's wedding cake. And as he set it down, slid it from his palms onto the table, I could barely hear their words anymore. He was talking to Mom and Rebecca and they were exchanging stuff, receipts, money, whatever, and then he left, the unlikely baker, and Rebecca was walking him back to the door and saying something to him. But I couldn't even make out their words—it all felt underwater.

Because there was this beautiful, huge white cake, three layers of roses and swirls and new life starting, and my heart was in my throat and tears gathered in my eyes before I could stop them.

"Honey?" my mother said.

"I—" The word barely escaped.

"Oh, sweetie." She came and put her arms around me. I started to cry. If I had to explain why even now I couldn't. It was all just too big.

"I'm sorry, it's stupid . . ."

"It's change," my mother said. She stroked my hair.

I sniffed into her shoulder. And then I pulled away and looked at her, and saw that she had tears in her eyes too. "I thought it was just me," I said.

"How, oh how could that be? You leaving, and—" She waved her hand all around. "This. So much happiness. So much left behind."

"The cake and everything . . ."

"It's beginning now," Mom said.

I nodded. I sniffed hard. I wiped my eyes, but the tears kept streaming. "I'm happy," I said. I didn't want her to get the wrong idea.

"I know. It's not that."

Well, of course my stupid brother had to walk in then. But he knew how to handle us. "Oh, great. A blubber party," he said. "What's the matter, guys? Did they get the cake color wrong?"

"Shut up, idiot," I cried.

"Come here, you," my mother said.

And he did. He reached his arms around us both, and we reached our arms around each other.

"I love you guys," Mom said.

"I love you too," I said.

Ben's voice was hard to hear, spoken into Mom's shoulder. "Love you too," he muttered. He wasn't much for mushy stuff.

I would miss this so much. These people. The eighteen years before now. My own bed, in my own room. Waking up every day knowing that I was *home*.

"Frosting roses," Mom said. We all looked at that cake. She took my hand and then Ben's. She held each up and gave our hands a kiss. "My babies," she said.

"I never knew you could get a bra in that color," Natalie said.

"I know. Right?"

"I'm stuffed," Natalie said. We headed out of Butch's Harbor Bar restaurant, leaving behind the smell of frying burgers and onions and the ghosts of cigarettes past. We pushed the door open into the sun. I was glad the girlfriend contingent had arrived. My Aunt Hannah had come that morning too. I saw her and Mom walking far off on the beach, both carrying their shoes and heading toward the lighthouse.

Sea air, ahh. "God, I love the way it smells here," I said. "I could live here for the smell."

Natalie grabbed the pooch of her tummy. "How am I going

to get my little friend into my dress tomorrow?"

"Love your belly," I said. "You're not going to become one of those girls that talks about food all the time, are you? We hate that. Being *good* or being *bad*?"

"Yeah. I'm going to the dark side. Lettuce leaves and ketchup on a spoon are definitely the way to moral superiority."

"If brownies are a sin, then, I'm sorry, I'm a sinner."

"I'm a sinna!" Natalie said up to the sky. "You better stay straight yourself. If I hear you use the words 'freshman fifteen,' I'm friend-divorcing you."

"I don't even know what that is," I confessed.

"Oh, my God. They were all talking about it on the campus tours. The fifteen pounds you're supposed to gain from dorm food the first year. If we count up all the hours we talk about food and think about food and put that same energy somewhere else . . ."

"Let's have a no no-fat movement."

Natalie stopped walking. She looked over at me, her face serious. "I've been doing a lot of thinking since graduation," Natalie said. There she was, Natalie, another loved person to miss. Natalie had this curly, curly brown hair that she hated but you wished you had. That hair alone was character. But she had relaxed smarts, too, and she was someone who always remembered what you said, who *listened*. She would bring you some great book because she was a book matchmaker, because she loved books the way other girls loved clothes. And when you were sick, she didn't even worry about catching whatever-it-was herself. She was one of those friends you knew you'd have forever. Or you *hoped* you would.

"Yeah. I know. All I've been *doing* is thinking," I said.

"If I don't do something about this now, it might be too late. Promise me you won't laugh."

"I promise," I said.

We were standing out there on the sidewalk, with the marina stretched out in front of us. I tried to spot Ash's fishing boat out there, but I couldn't tell which boat was which.

"I think I'm in love with Oscar," Natalie said.

A sound escaped my throat—an embarrassing bodily noise that fell somewhere between a gasp and a gulping swallow. Sometimes it was harder to keep your promise than others.

"Cricket, shit. You're laughing."

"No, I'm not," I said.

"Quit it."

"Look. I'm not laughing." I faced her, tried to look solemn. Wrong move. The corners of my mouth were creeping up like some sadistic marionette player was yanking my strings. See? Laughing inappropriately, family trait. Mom, Ben, and me—we all had it. Probably our kids and grandkids were all destined to bust up whenever someone's stomach growled in a quiet bookstore.

"I knew I shouldn't have told you."

Okay, that hurt. I'd always tried to be a good friend to her, as she'd been to me. It was hard too, because of Janssen. When you had a serious boyfriend, you were aware of how often your friends felt second. But Natalie put up with me and Janssen. She could handle it without getting her feelings hurt. I sobered up quick.

"Of course you should have told me," I said. We started walking again. Natalie looked pissed. She gave me a doubtful look.

"It makes sense," I said.

And when I thought about it, it did. All those times she'd gone to Tech Time to look at laptops . . . She looked at laptops *a lot*. But it was more than that—Oscar with his shy eyes under those bangs and that dweeby scarf he never took off all junior year, and his quick mind. He had a shyness that was sweet. Maybe even attractive. Not to me, but I could see it. If I squinted a little, ha. No, okay. I really *could* see it. Maybe what Gavin had said was true—after graduation you could be anyone. Or, rather, you could be *you*.

Natalie started talking fast. "It does make sense, Cricket. You know how hard it is to find a good guy. You look at their Facebook page, and their photo screams 'Asshole.' They pose with some stupid beer bottle, or with their shirt off. Or you go to Starbucks, and they order a white mocha decaf with one vanilla shot, extra foamy."

"High maintenance coffee drinker. Reject."

"Oscar's picture? It's just him, standing on a rock. He gets a regular Americano. No one has to bend over backward to kiss his butt."

"I know. And no insistence on sushi and foreign films."

"He's just himself."

"You're right. I think Oscar is a great guy."

It hit me then. That note. That confusing note. All those calls.

"What?" Natalie said. "What's that face about?"

"Nothing. Really, nothing. You and Oscar—"

I stopped, now. I grabbed Natalie's arm. "Oh, shit. Wait." I pulled her into a doorway, under an awning. Some taffy store. Ladies dressed in pink.

"You want to go in *here*?" Natalie said. "I'm trying to talk to you. I don't care about *taffy*."

"No, no. Just, up ahead. It's Dan. And his daughter. They're sitting on that bench right there!" Right on the street. Not four feet away.

"Is that the chocoholic?"

"The other one. The one I yelled at at the golf place."

"I wouldn't call that *yelling*."

"Shh."

We stood with our backs to the window of the taffy shop. Behind us some taffy machine was spinning slowly and pulling a gooey pink slab back and forth, a jaw-dropping spectacle any tourist would be riveted by.

"We could be here awhile," Natalie said.

"Shh!"

"She doesn't *seem* like she likes me," we heard Amy say.

"Who?" Natalie whispered. "You?"

I put my index finger to my lips. *Quiet!*

"Of course she does," Dan said. He was turning his watch in circles on his wrist. "That was the first thing she said. That you seemed like sweet girls."

Your Mom, Natalie mouthed.

"That was before she spent four days with them," I whispered.

"Shh," Natalie said. She craned her neck, listening.

"I just want to *go*. No one likes me here."

"Yeah, I wonder why," Natalie whispered.

"Shh," I said.

Dan looked up toward the sky. "Look, Amy. You've got to put forth some effort, here."

"I didn't ask for this," she said. "I don't even know these people."

Dan rubbed his forehead. He blew out his breath in a loud sigh. Finally he put his arm around Amy, and she leaned into him. "I'm sorry this is so hard for you. No one can take your place with me, right? You know that."

"I just want to go home, Daddy." Natalie elbowed me. Mouthed *Daddy* and rolled her eyes. I nodded my agreement. Natalie wasn't the daddy's-little-princess type, and neither was I.

"Amy, it's important to me that you're here," Dan said.

"It's important to me to go home."

Come on, Dan, I urged. *Come* on. I don't know what I wanted him to do. What *could* he do? Nothing, really. *Some*thing! Something more than *this*. I thought about that pamphlet, the tiki hut in sunset. Blessed isolation. For once maybe I could understand my mother's second thoughts. Maybe she had good reason.

"They're getting up!" Natalie whispered. "They're coming this way!"

"Oh, shit!"

The bell on the door tinkled merrily. The smell in there—like walking into an aggressive linebacker of sugar and butter.

"How can I help you ladies?" chimed the Mrs. Claus impersonator behind the counter.

"We'll have a pound of mixed," I said.

Ha. Wasn't *that* the truth.

I liked to imagine disaster, to see it coming. Ever since I was a kid, I was on the lookout for it. I remember riding in the backseat of the car at night on long car trips, with my parents in the front. My brother slept beside me, but I always stayed awake. I'd kick the back of my dad's seat, to make sure he wouldn't doze off. I guess I thought our safety was up to me. If I was vigilant, if I spotted disaster before it arrived, it would have to turn and flee. Disaster likes the element of surprise, right? So I saw car crashes and heart attacks, falls, and acts of God. But this time Mr. Disaster—the biggest asshole of all—snuck around every one of my careful moves. I didn't even see him coming.

chapter
twenty-one

"So, a quick run-through, everyone, and then the important part . . . Par-tee!" Rebecca said. She swiveled her wide hips a bit, and her skirts swirled. Ted whistled with two fingers, and everyone who had gathered in the darkening living room laughed. Rebecca had already lit the hanging lights over the deck, and a fire was going inside. Bunches of helium balloons were tied to the corners of the deck posts. Out on the beach Oscar and Gavin's tent glowed, and they had a small bonfire going. I hadn't seen them all day. After Natalie and I got back, Natalie took a walk on the beach, and I went to my room and wrote to Janssen. I hadn't seen Ash or anyone all day, either. Now we were all here except for those three—Oscar, Gavin, and Ash. John and Baby Boo were missing too. Cruiser was tucked safely away in his kennel up in the hall, and Jupiter was in my room with a super dog chew and Rabbit. The celebration was officially starting.

"The bride and groom—" Rebecca said.

"Yip! Yip! Yip!" Ben called, and everyone laughed again.

Rebecca gave it a second try. "The bride and groom, after much discussion, have decided to have the ceremony *outside* on the back lawn, at seven p.m. tomorrow evening, as scheduled."

"Oh, hell, let's just do it now!" Dan said. He lifted Mom up and spun her around. She wore her favorite long, layered orange dress she'd bought on our trip to New York all those years ago, and her cheeks were flushed with happiness. Dan looked happy right then, happier than he had in days. I scanned the room for Amy and Hailey, who stood with their Aunt Jane over by the French doors. I looked for Ash. I wanted to see him. I didn't want to see him.

"Is there a judge in the house?" Grandpa yelled. George grinned at him. Now that this wedding was almost here, everyone was in high spirits.

"I'm quick to judge," Gram said.

"I second that," Aunt Bailey said, and Gram socked her arm playfully. Gram was dressed up that night in a wild-patterned dress, and Aunt Bailey was looking fancy too. She wore a blue print skirt and heels, and her sapphire stud earrings.

"Good enough. Get the job done, Ma," Aunt Hannah said. She stood right next to Ben, and ruffled his hair like he was still seven, even though he was taller than she was now. We loved Aunt Hannah. She was Mom's older sister, so she was like a sensible spare mom to us. You ever needed advice, a ride, a person to interview for career day, you called Aunt Hannah.

"Witnesses!" Rebecca said. Aunt Hannah and Jane raised their hands like the A students they'd both probably been. "Make sure you have your driver's licenses—"

"So you can drive the bride the hell out of Dodge!" Ted yelled.

Not funny, I thought.

"That's not funny," Natalie whispered beside me. "You know your mom—"

"I know," I whispered back. "She prefers airplanes, though."

"She prefers airplanes!" Grandpa shouted. Everyone laughed. I watched Mom—it could have been hurtful. But my mother just shook her head and screwed up her face in an *I'm going to get you* look.

"Driver's licenses for the *judge,* all you smart-asses. We've got to make sure this is official."

"No loopholes, Daisy," Dan said. A look passed between them that I couldn't read. Dan leaned in and kissed her. Amy was staring intently at her ballet flats.

"We all clear? Then, let's turn on the music and *dance,*" Rebecca said.

Ted flung open the French doors, and we all moved like cattle out toward the deck. I could smell chicken barbecuing. I saw him. Ash, manning the barbecue. His lean waist, and those wide shoulders.

"I can't hear a thing," Mr. Jax said next to me as we pushed forward with the group. One of the arms of his sweater lay limply across his cast. "What'd she say?"

"We're all done," I said loudly to him. "We're going to have dinner now. Dance."

"Ants?" he asked.

Mrs. Jax was on his other side. She wore a lavender dress with a sparkly pin at the shoulder, and small, tidy heels. "William, really. Turn it up."

"It *is* up." He seemed to hear her just fine, but he could probably read her lips after sixty years of marriage.

"Give me that," she said. "You don't even know *how* to turn it up. Or where the gravy boat goes after all these years. Or how to make a pork chop."

"I make a fine pork chop. If you'd stop with your gabbing and interfering."

Things were getting a little heated. Dan was glancing over. Jane, too. They looked alarmed. Like they'd never seen their parents argue before. Ted carried out a huge platter of chicken and set it on one end of the table, next to the salads and breads Rebecca had brought out.

"Food, everyone!" Rebecca called.

"Am I going to have to take care of you for the rest of my life?" Mrs. Jax snapped. She reached toward his ear, popped free his hearing aid. "Look!" She held up the small, pink offending object. "The volume is set at low!"

"Give me that," he said. He tried to snatch it back, but she held it away. The music blasted on. It was some goofy eighties dance cha-cha. *Come on, everybody, let's do the conga . . .* Ash must have felt my eyes. He turned away from the barbecue and stared at me, and a rush of warm-energy-thrill toppled every sort of certainty I'd managed to build.

"I'm fixing it, you old fool," Mrs. Jax said.

"Who you calling a fool?" He heard *that* perfectly too, even with the music blaring now. He lunged for her arm again with his good left, and the hearing aid flew with a small pink mind of its own. It rose high and then lost the thrill of flight, descended and bounced on the edge of the table and rolled underneath.

"Now look what you've done," Mrs. Jax said, proving to me forevermore that it always, always took two people to screw things up.

Dan was now conga-ing Mom happily around the crowd, and Mrs. Jax's floral rear end was sticking out from underneath the drooping table cloth. Dan stopped Mom mid-dance, and they all started hunting around for the little hearing aid. With the situation under control, I moved away—Natalie was talking to my brother, and Ash stood alone, the kind of alone that was an invitation. And then I noticed that Hailey had her palms pressed against her eyes. Her shoulders were bent over. She was crying.

"Hailey?" I asked. "Are you okay?"

Amy stood beside her. She was still punishing me with silence and with twelve million miles of icy terrain.

"Gavin says he thinks we need to slow things down. The whole thing with my father freaked him out. . . ."

"Well, I can understand. . . ."

"He's probably just got someone else. Does he have someone else? Every girl he knows is probably after him," she cried.

I kept my mouth shut.

"*You* have someone else," Amy said. "What about Brad?"

She had a point. "Right," I said. I nodded to Amy. This second of agreement between us opened a possible door, a secret entrance to the icy land, and I opened my mouth to apologize to Amy, to make some outreach, but just as I did, her stupid phone rang again. She answered, plugged one ear, and turned her back to us so that she could hear over the pounding music.

"Do you want me to call Gavin?" I asked Hailey. "They were supposed to come to this thing tonight. He should be here soon. You guys could talk. . . ."

Amy turned back around. She handed her phone to her sister. "Mom," Amy said.

"For God's sake!" Hailey shrieked into the phone. Her tears were gone. She'd gone from a sad, drippy rainfall to a raging hurricane in less than a second. "I'm not taking your calls for a reason! We're away from you for five minutes, and you think we're in danger of completely fucking up our lives!"

Amy gasped.

"No," Hailey said. "I will not take Amy to the airport. I don't care if Amy wants to go home. *I* want to stay! No, I am not on some kind of drugs!" Hailey held the phone over her head. I could hear a voice way up there, a shrill, panicked Mom-God voice, a tiny but all-powerful phone trill coming out of that speaker. "Blah, blah, blah," Hailey said.

"Give me that," Amy said. She grabbed for it. *Here we go again,* I thought. It was bound to go flying just like that hearing aid, but I was wrong.

Hailey brought the phone back down to her ear. "I'm running off and getting married, Mother," she said. Then she flipped the phone closed and chuckled. "*That*'ll get her riled up."

"Oh, Hailey," I said. I was shaking my head, *No, no, no.* "I think you better call her back. You need to tell her—"

There was a crash then. A small yelp and a cry. Ted's butt had joined Mrs. Jax's under the table, and as he backed out, he lifted the table up ever so slightly with his weight, tipping it enough so that the chicken plate started to slide, caught by Grandpa, but not before a few pieces had dropped to the ground. The other dishes slid and banged and gathered together like a sudden food traffic jam.

"Ow, shit!" Ted rubbed his back, but he held the hearing aid up like a winning lottery ticket.

"Whew!" Rebecca said. "Near miss." She rubbed her temples. We were stressing the poor woman out.

"You!" Hailey said suddenly. I followed the direction of her finger. Gavin and Oscar had arrived. They had both dressed up too. They were wearing their button-up shirts and good jeans.

Oscar's blond hair was combed down and shiny. They were heading our way.

"You," Gavin said as they approached us. "Father or no father." He took Hailey in his arms and kissed her then, right there in front of everyone, and it was a bold move, but kind of revolting, too. I'd never seen Gavin kiss anyone before, and maybe it was like watching a relative making out. I averted my eyes, and they landed on Oscar, and before I could take in what was happening, he followed Gavin's lead as he had always followed Gavin's lead as long as I'd known them.

"You," he said to me, and suddenly his mouth was on mine, *Oscar's* mouth, a mouth I didn't want at all, and it was the same feeling you get when you are at some buffet and you eat some slightly unidentifiable food you think is one thing but is another. Mayonnaise, but it's horseradish. Potatoes that are actually parsnips. There's the shock, and then the urge to spit it out. It doesn't necessarily taste bad, but you hadn't expected it, and to your stunned mouth it's just *wrong*.

I shoved him away. His eyes were glazy and oddly triumphant, and then I was aware of someone pushing past us. Natalie. I was aware of Ash, too, who just shook his head as if I was someone he couldn't believe, as if I were *too much*, and he set down the barbecue fork.

"Cricket, I don't get you," he said softly as he went by me, went inside, and shut the door as the chicken kept smoking and the flames leaped.

And then I heard a scream. And then another. Coming

from somewhere near the table. George. And what was that? Something *on* him. Partly on him, and hanging from the tall potted palm near the table. Something large and gray. George was shrieking and screaming, and so were the ladies, and Grandpa had taken off his hat and was whacking whatever it was, and yelling. *Goddamn you!*

A raccoon. A raccoon had dropped from the roof and was reaching for a piece of the chicken that had dropped into the large pot of one of the palm trees. It had its little black leather-gloved claws on George's back, and George was hopping around with his hands covering his head, and Grandpa was whacking the shit out of them both.

The animal released itself from George, ran onto the roof and away, a rolling gallop, and then George had his shirt off and Grandpa was examining the scratches.

George was gesturing and breathing wildly, and that stupid conga song was still going, or another one just like it, and everyone had stopped, and their eyes were on George and Grandpa. Grandpa was examining George's back. But then he must have felt the sudden stillness in the room, and he turned around. I'm sure he could feel us all staring. He looked back at us all, caught. He held his hands out, a helpless gesture. It was so clear then. There was something between them, all right. Something important. The two of them shared a secret all right, and we all saw that, and they knew we did.

"Well, George and I—" Grandpa said.

"George and *you?*" Gram gasped.

My mother, suddenly beside me, might have been hyperventilating.

Two truths? Could I have been more wrong?

A hundred truths. A thousand. Truths—they can't even be counted.

chapter
twenty-two

Janssen—

Really? Did you make that up? Anywhere you
find humans in the world, you also find dogs?
Wow, those little guys get around. Okay. While
we're on the whole topic of shocking canine
truths . . .

Astonishing Dog-Human Communication Facts:

1. Scientists have discovered that we read our
    dogs' emotions and they read ours. (Ha, we
    knew that all along.) They've found that

dogs scan our faces for different feelings, and that *we* can identify different types of barks and what they mean. Researchers played tapes of barking, and people could tell what was actually happening when the bark was recorded. They knew the dog wanted a toy, for example, or was watching a stranger approach, or was trying to say that they hated your new girlfriend. Okay, I made that last one up.

2. In the wild, dogs only have one kind of bark—a warning bark. But domesticated dogs have developed many different kinds of barks, in order to better communicate with us.

3. Dogs may think more like us than even the chimpanzee. (This will be a relief if you watch chimpanzees for more than five minutes at a zoo. Kind of disgusting. Kind of like sitting in our school cafeteria.) Dogs are the only animals that understand a pointing gesture. We take it for granted that they understand our pointing. They even understand us "pointing" with our eyes. But apparently this is really unusual. No other animal knows what we mean when we do it. Dogs don't use pointing

with each other, only with us. It's like
they've learned a second language.

4. There is a dog in Germany that can
identify three hundred objects by name.
If you tell her to go get her rope, she will
bring back the rope. The bear, the ball, the
pig, etc. Three hundred. But even more
amazing? If you show her the picture of the
object, she'll go get it. Some days, I think
Ben isn't even that smart.

5. Dogs tilt their head to listen better for
the words they know. (Well, this is just
something I noticed.)

If you think I'm over here looking up stuff for
hours just in order to fascinate you, you're wrong. I
found that all in one article about a NOVA special
they had on dogs. So there. Five minutes, and that
was it. The rest of the time I've been spending not
keeping my life on hold, same as you.

It's interesting, though. Obviously dogs and
humans have some kind of evolutionary
determination to make something special work
between us. And isn't it great? We have this
mystical, outlandish success—two different species

doing what we can to communicate with each other. Jupiter always gets so excited too, when we get it right. Food? Pee? Outside? When we hit the magic word, she does a little dance of glee, like a winning game show contestant.

Of course, there were plenty of times we didn't get it right with Jupiter. Miscommunications. She'd bark and bark a warning, and we'd look outside and . . . nothing. We'd even try to tell her there was nothing! We doubted her. What are you barking at? There's nothing there! Quit it! But if we looked again more carefully, there it would be. Some raccoon. A rabbit. A stunned deer family in the dark, hooves pressing quietly on the lawn as they passed, but never quietly enough for Jupiter. She must have been frustrated with us, as we were with her. They probably sounded like an army troop passing through, or maybe just smelled like one. They were eating our blueberries and fallen apples! But we missed her message. We didn't see or understand.

It's both harder and easier without words.

And maybe it's another miracle that *human* communication works at *all*, ever. So many ways to misunderstand. All the wrong directions, the wrong roads of tone and gesture. Or, yeah, an ill-timed laugh.

Of course, you know where I'm going with this. Of course you do.

I'm sorry. So, so sorry.

We were in love, and then . . . Janssen, I keep telling you, it was an accident. But you call it one of those accidents that *reveal the real*. You love that phrase, "reveal the real." I still don't think (or want to think, that's what you'll say) that you're right. It was a miscommunication. I've said I'm sorry every way I know how. I didn't mean it, Janssen.

I felt even closer to you than ever, after that first time in the shed. I felt so, so close. You felt that too, right? We both did? We went back there a lot, in different seasons. It was like having our own little house. Our own *home*. Is that corny? I could feel us pretending it whenever we walked through that door. We'd set our things down, sigh. Home, dear. Some future of ours. Of course it wasn't just about sex after that—we were there for each other, with each other, always. You'd come by our house

before school for breakfast. I'd be over at your
house for dinner. I knew you so well—someone
could say something and I knew it'd piss you off
before you even showed it. I knew you had to have
your apples peeled because you hated the skin,
and I could look at a menu and guess what you'd
order. I knew how you'd get grumpy after swim
practice because you were hungry, and knew how
you could almost choke up with emotion when you
saw the Cascades on those days when they were so
craggy and snowy and unreal. You believed in God
when you saw those mountains. And you didn't
whenever you heard about some natural disaster.
Thousands of people being killed.

You knew me. You *know* me. I can't imagine life
without you, without someone who knows me that
well. You know I'm always cold, and you reach
for my hands to warm them whenever we've been
outside. You know I get anxious talking to my dad,
and know I get lost when driving and hate water
chestnuts and believe in God when the Cascades
are so craggy and snowy and unreal. And I don't
whenever I hear about a natural disaster.

I sat through those zombie movies you love, and
you brought me books from the used-book store.

We could sit on the couch all Saturday together.
(Especially during the period when I had that brief
fling with the Classic Movie Channel. You were
very patient.) But we also went on drives over the
mountains and went swimming at Marcy Lake.
We'd swing on the swings there, remember? My
hands would smell like metal from holding tight
to the chains. We'd go on fancy dates, not many
of those, but a few. Where we'd dress up and go
out to dinner. We valet-parked, even though we
weren't sure how to pay the guy and it ended up
being sort of embarrassing. *I* was embarrassed. You
were totally cool about it all.

You and Ben graduated. You moved into your
dorm. I was scared it would change things, and it
did for a while. I was sure you were going to meet
some college girl and leave me. I'd visit you and
go to your classes, and I felt like I was wearing a
sign that said "YOUNG" around my neck. When
Thomas was gone and we had your room all to
ourselves, though, it was magic. A bed, a room
of our own without the cold and discomfort of
our shed . . . I'd have to leave, and it was so *hard*.
Stupid curfew. My mother, always worrying about
me driving back from the city. Two years until
we would be free! No more rules, no more of my

mother waiting up at night, no more feeling like a kid—God, I couldn't wait. I COULDN'T WAIT! It couldn't come fast enough. It seemed forever until I'd graduate.

We had anniversaries. That's when we'd have our "fancy dates." Like a married couple. Okay, maybe I liked those more than you did. And, sometimes, let's be honest, we fought like a married couple too, didn't we? Having the same arguments over and over again. About me not asking for what I want, about you not listening sometimes. We'd have those days where we just got irritated with each other. You'd pick around in the popcorn bowl, or I'd refuse to cross the street until the walk sign came on. I'd confess that I hated that T-shirt of yours with the guitar on fire. You'd wonder why I always waited until the last minute to get working on something. My mother told me that maybe we needed to spend more time apart, and we both got mad about that. This was what happened after you'd been together with someone a long time. You loved that it was old and worn and comfy, but sometimes it was old and worn and comfy.

Still. No matter what, I could always, always count on you to be there. I loved you. Love you.

Change—sometimes it's some great big event, right? One major episode that means nothing will ever be the same. Birth, death, meeting you on your horse, a wedding, a hand striking, an announcement. But more often, I think, change is slow and quiet, it sneaks in like the seasons, where you don't even notice the shift until the trees are all orange or snow is falling, or it's so hot that you are desperate for a swim.

My senior year, though—I felt every shift of every season. How can I explain this to you? I noticed the first leaf that turned orange. I smelled snow in the air before it fell. I felt spring approaching under my skin, in my body somehow. I felt it all. You go, go, go, but sometimes you stop and it all catches up. You start thinking. You feel what it means to be alive and what it means for time to pass. That's what happened.

We got rid of the Bermuda Honda. My mother had bought her beloved Jeep long before that, but the old Bermuda Honda was kept around for Ben and me, until one day every piece of it broke down, as if it had cancer or something, an illness that crept around and ravaged it. The cancer had spread to the brakes, then the carburetor, and then to the back windows, which wouldn't roll down, and the tires were balding and there were those bangs and bashes along its body where people hadn't been careful with it.

That stupid car, that evil Bermuda Honda—it was still trying to get us, all the way until the end. It started emitting noxious fumes that probably would have killed us. The last ride was spent with the only working windows down, and it was probably a miracle that the car didn't have the last word somehow, veering off into some telephone pole, or blowing up with us in it.

We took the car to the wrecking yard, the car cemetery, my mother called it, all that over-and-done-with glory and all those stories, buried in unmarked heaps. Every one of those cars once had the thrilling new upholstery smell.

And then we had it put to sleep.

I feel choked up to see it go, my mother said.

I didn't say what I thought—being sad to see the Bermuda Honda go was like being sad when Jon Jakes and his nasty kids left, but she had been sad

then, too. You'd think saying good-bye to crappy
cars and bad relationships would be easy. Still, it's
a time in your life that you're leaving. And you
know what? Leaving that blue metal piece of shit
gave me a lump in my throat too. I'd learned to
drive in that car. That car played the starring role
in so many of our stories, even though we hated
the thing.

So, the Bermuda Honda was gone, and Jon
Jakes and all of them were long gone, and Ben
had moved out to go to college. One day Mom
decided to paint our bathroom. *I realized it was
still decorated for little kids,* she said. It was true. It
had been decked out for years with our framed
art: a crayon lizard Ben had drawn, clay masks I
had made. Various objects were hanging from the
ceiling—a papier-mâché globe I'd done in the
fourth grade, and a mobile Ben had done in the
sixth. Folded stars and origami dangled from
strings. *I realized you guys were grown up,* she said.

I guess I realized it too.

It hit me, filling out those college applications.
The year before, the idea of the future, of moving
out—it was hurry, hurry, hurry! Get here! You

had shown me how it was done. Ben, too. It was natural, easy, except for what you both left behind. I saw Mom staring out the window of Ben's room sometimes, and Mom and I would eat dinner standing at the counter every so often, like a couple of bachelors. Jupiter slept on Ben's bed. I couldn't just walk up the hill to see you whenever I wanted, but I could drive into the city and be in your dorm room within an hour, a private place, the two of us out in the world together.

You were a shield for me, even then. Even about change. I watched, and you made moving on look possible; it made me think it could be merely practical, a series of steps, forward motion that was only ever a welcome thing. You taught me that the inner shifts could be ignored. Or didn't matter. Or didn't exist. I didn't see your inner shifts. Did you even have them? Was this a guy thing or a you thing? Both you and Ben moved on to the next stage of life without a tear or a hesitation. That you showed, anyway.

I thought that's what would happen. I didn't expect the interior noise, the clanging and banging that looming change brought. Or my bravado just wasn't loud enough to cover it all up, like yours.

The college applications made it real, though. I filled them out, and it felt like I was going through the motions, faking this thing that was supposed to happen—going away to school, being a college student, moving out. Applying to out-of-state schools, places I didn't know. Cities where there were no coyotes crying out in the night or the Taco Time right there on the corner where I knew it was, or where there was no little kiddie bathroom that had just been painted but still had the tack marks in the ceiling where the globe and the stars had hung. Where there was no you, a car ride away. Where my mother wasn't in the kitchen, eating cookie dough from the bowl, talking to the dog so it wouldn't look like she was talking to herself. Where would *us* go, all of us, where would home be, if we all weren't here anymore?

The awareness slapped me, Janssen. I was faking it, but I knew it was real, too, a big huge real, sitting out there in a future that was tearing toward me, heels smoking from speed. Too-much-ness was hurtling my way, and the brave thrill of the year before seemed childish and naïve. I was putting stamps on envelopes and not wanting to put stamps on envelopes. I mailed those things with both a sick and excited feeling in my gut.

You . . . You had always made the future feel safe. As long as you were in it too, beside me, I could be okay. From first days of school, to awkward school dances, to scary, dark nights, to car trips when we were lost . . .

The future, this big step out of life as I knew it, the whole piece of childhood, I tried to keep it all at this shiny, golden distance. But the symbols of time passing were piling up. The last homecoming, the last holiday concert, the last, last, last. The bittersweet arrival of summer, the air smelling like warm cotton sheets. Prom, and there you were, looking so crazy handsome in your tux. We were there at home just before meeting Natalie and everyone. Mom was taking pictures and her voice was wobbly, like she might cry. I suddenly wanted to get rid of the dress and the hair and sit on the couch and watch movies.

These shoes are too high, I said.

Those shoes are perfect, you said. *You look like a princess.*

Beautiful, Mom said with her wobbly voice. *A grown woman.*

I can't walk, I said.

Look, you said. You held your arm out for me to take. *No problem.*

And of course Mom had met Dan by then, and she was so happy and so in love, and they started talking about moving, getting married. . . . She was in her own world. *Everything* felt like an ending. I wished we could fight more, Mom and me. Don't you think that would have helped? She was too happy to fight, and I was too scared. I want to say that everything was fading into the past, but it was actually fading into the future. I didn't know whether to hold on tight or to let go. There were too many opposites at once, scenery speeding past, flying past, as if I were in a high-speed train. The desire to go, the desire to stay. My old blankie, my birth control pills. I noticed that my father was going gray.

No one talked about this. Did anyone else feel this? Of course they must have, I realize now. Because that's what all the college drinking is about, right? The drinking and the eating disorders and the super-achievement or its opposite, the purposeful failure. It's all about the

panic of time passing, the strings of a balloon
being cut, the height.

But I didn't know that then. I could only feel
panic. What would happen to me at a distance?
Would my safety net, you, my family, even be my
safety net? Would I want a net at all?

And then came those acceptance letters. One here,
one away. A choice. The crazy indecision. And
then, that night. The night of graduation.

This is hard for me to write. But I need you to
understand.

Most of my class had loaded onto the buses for
the party, but I didn't want to go, as you know.
You know me and parties. We went out to
dinner instead, a big family dinner, with Gram
and Grandpa and Aunt Bailey, the whole gang,
and then they all got into their cars and said
good night, and you and I drove to Marcy Lake.
My cap and gown were still in the backseat of
your car. You brought a blanket, and we walked
out to the dock, the same dock my mother and
Ben and I sat on when midnight struck that one
New Year's Eve.

The night was warm. The stars were a billion brilliant speckles. The water smelled mossy and deep. Black, beautiful warm summer night. You spread out the blanket, and we sat. We looked out at the warm yellow lights of the houses all around the lake.

You kissed me. It was familiar, so familiar, but the big thing that just happened made it feel a little new. I felt the familiar stirring too. Want.

You did too. "Skinny-dip?" you said.

But I ruined the moment. Instead of being drawn further in to the summer night and the liquidy dark, my head was spinning with images of purple gowns and good-byes. Surprisingly meaningful ones, the sense of a bond to people I hadn't even felt that close to, honestly, in the four years of high school. My heart was still thrumming with the excitement and the energy of the night. All those families and photographs. My father standing there with roses. The sad-happy, the thrill and high, the good-bye to teachers I cared about, more now that they'd be gone, and those stupid, boring hallways and lockers, and that cafeteria that all at once felt permanently memorable and somehow important.

"I only wish I knew what I was going to do," I said.

"Cricket." You groaned. "Not now . . ." We'd been through this a million times.

"No one else is this stuck," I said.

"Lots of people are."

"Did you see that program? Every single person had a plan. Where they were going, what they were doing."

"Your name said 'USC' beside it. You looked decided too."

"I don't want to go to USC," I said. "I just don't want to. I don't want to do something stupid, though. Where will home be if I go there, Janssen, *where?*"

"Cricket!" you moaned. "Look!" You set your palms up toward that incredible sky. "Be here now."

You were right, of course. I'd built up all that angst like a wall between me and you and my family.

It was handy—a PROBLEM I could focus on so
I didn't have to feel all of these feelings. I knew
I should give it a rest, at least then, that night,
or else, even *those* last times together would pass
too fast. I stared into your eyes, those same eyes
I'd been looking into for years. I just wanted an
answer so bad.

You took a big breath. You stepped into my
question and need and you filled it.

"Cricket," you said. "You know, maybe we should
just get married."

I sucked in my breath—shocked. What I saw
was, you meant it. We'd joked and talked
aboutit countless times. Named our six kids,
pretended we were old people who'd been together
for years. But this time you *meant* it. You set it
out there on that dock, under those stars, as a
real possibility. An option. A choice we could
make.

And I panicked.

I thought, *Wait. Oh, shit. Is this some moment,
here?* Were you going to take out a ring from your

pocket? But that didn't happen. It was just you and me, talking about what could happen if we wanted it to.

And, here's where . . . I know I've apologized a million times. But have I really explained? Have you really heard?

I laughed.

I laughed and then the words jumped out: "No *way*," I said.

God. God, Janssen. Words. Words, and their power and their permanence.

I understood how bad it was right away. How cruel. Your eyes—they were hurt. So openly hurt. I'd never seen you look like that. You got up, strode off. I called out, "Wait!" I followed a moment later, after I stared out to the little houses with their golden lights and said *shit, shit, shit* out loud to all the night creatures who might be listening. All the crickets and owls who'd cringed when a thoughtless girl broke a wonderful guy's heart. I've said it to you a hundred times before, and I know all the things those two words were saying to you, but I was just surprised, Janssen. You'd set it out there like it was a possible, practical thing. But no one does that anymore, you know, gets married so young? That's where my reaction came from. No one talks like that, makes a decision like that at our age anymore. Grandma did it, but we don't. We don't, because forever is hard enough without it beginning now.

I'm so sorry I hurt you like that. Janssen. I am.

When I got to the car, you were already sitting inside silently. You drove me home silently, dropped me off silently. We didn't know there could be all this silent, dangerous territory of *unspoken* between us, did we? We didn't know that words could do that kind of damage.

Humans, with our comments thrown like spears, or even just our fumbling, offhand talk, our careless laughter—maybe we should have been the ones sentenced to wordless communications and tail wags. We should have been the ones.

You said in your letter that you loved me as much as ever. That you missed me so much it hurt. That

I wasn't at the Sea-Tac Airport, and neither were you, yet.

Yet.

That dog, the one who understands three hundred words—I think even he can hear the one that matters most.

Love always,

Cricket

chapter twenty-three

"Oscar! My God. What did you do that for?" I yelled.

"You didn't . . . *want* that?" Oscar's face went from triumphant to confused. He stuck his hands into his pockets, rattled around some loose change like we were two strangers having an awkward moment in an elevator.

Grandpa and George were hurrying inside; Rebecca was rushing around, using words like "tetanus shot" and "antiseptic." "George and I . . . We have something to tell you. I'll explain later!" Grandpa said over his shoulder.

The doors shut behind them. "Are you gay?" Gram shrieked toward Grandpa's disappearing back. Subtlety wasn't her strong suit. "All these years?"

"Mom!" my mother said. "Mom, stop that right now!" She was getting a little hysterical.

"Perhaps he's one of those bisexuals," I heard Mrs. Jax say somewhere behind me. "My friend Marguerite's boy was one. She told me when she was on those pain pills."

"I thought we had a *moment*," Oscar said. "That night of the party. You put your head on my shoulder. I thought you cared."

"Of course I care! I've always cared! You're one of my best friends." I was getting a little hysterical too.

Next to us Gavin and Hailey were going at it again. I flinched at the glimpse of dueling tongues doing a scene from *Robin Hood* with pink swords.

Oscar looked their way too. "I guess I was just hoping for . . . something *big*. Something to *change*."

"I'm not the one, Oscar. I'm not."

"Okay." He accepted this without drama. Jesus. I got the feeling he'd be more upset if he lost his wallet.

"But maybe Natalie is."

"Natalie?"

"She's cared about you *that* way for years."

"She has?" His eyes got wide. So wide, I might have just told him that Bill Gates himself wanted to be his personal pen pal. E-mail pal. Whatever. "I would've thought she was out of my league."

Oh, and I wouldn't have been? But there was no time for that. Hits to the self-esteem would have to wait. "So, something big, right? Bigger than you thought, even," I said. "But, God, now she thinks . . ."

"Hey, Crick, not to be rude, but I gotta—"

"Go. Go! For God's sake," I said.

He dashed inside. That stupid music was still playing, but Dan now sat in a deck chair, his head in his hands, and Aunt Hannah had her arms around Mom's shoulders, saying, *For all we know, George could be his long-lost son*, and Aunt Bailey was fanning herself with her hand. The wind was picking up out there—Rebecca's wind chimes started going wild, and the lanterns strung above began to swing. Ben came over to me, eating a chicken leg. How anyone could eat at a time like this was beyond me.

"I told you," he said.

"I've got to get out of here," I said.

I needed to find Ash. I needed to fix something I could fix. What he'd said—it was a misunderstanding with the clearest explanation. What he saw—well, Oscar was only the fourth boy to kiss me ever. If it even counted. Will Maxwell, sixth grade. Out by the 7-Eleven after that thrilling field trip to the Woodland Park Zoo, when our parent helpers were still inside, fitting caps onto spilling-over Slurpee cups. Josh Gardens, after a homecoming dance. Janssen, of course. And then Ash.

I went inside, tried to avoid seeing anyone. I headed straight for the stairs. I only wanted to talk to Ash. Right then every relationship in my life felt weighted with complexities and communications gone wrong. Stories were where meaning ended up, stories could heal, but stories too had different viewpoints. Layered motivations. Subplots you didn't know existed.

So of course I ran into Grandpa on the stairs. Maybe I didn't know him anymore, or maybe I never had.

"Cricket!" he said. "I think George will be okay. The scratches aren't deep. It's a miracle." It was Grandpa's voice coming out of Grandpa, but it was a man standing there. Not just a funny golfing caricature in a cowboy hat, but a man with a life led over the years. He had pouches under his eyes, and his gray hair was thin where that bold hat usually sat. His eyes were blue, like Mom's. Maybe I never even could have told you what color they were before. I probably never really looked at them. I could see his old pink skin in the open collar of his polo shirt. He'd been in the marines years ago. He'd been a young father, who held my mother in a baby blanket.

"I guess you're relieved." I didn't know what to say.

"Relieved, hell, yes. I could just see it. Him getting some disease. Tetanus, turning to sepsis, hospital, deathbed. Him kicking off . . . Goddamn. Maybe it was the wrong thing to do, but I got my whole future wrapped up in this thing."

I was listening, trying to listen. I felt so embarrassed. Grandpa and George, really? But something felt off. It wasn't exactly how you talked about a relationship. "This thing?" I said.

"With George. I'm afraid to even tell everyone. They'll think I'm an old fool. But we've got a secret. I guess everyone will know sometime or other. George and I—we're building a golf course."

"A golf course? A golf course!"

"I don't want to hear it. I know it's crazy. But George has got a lot of money in this, and I do too. We bought some property out in Carnation. We're looking for other investors. The family, they're all going to lose their minds when they hear it. They will. I know how risky it is. Me, this close to retiring! But hell, do you know something?"

"What?" I said.

"I hated the insurance business. Every damn day I hated it. But I was scared."

"You were? You were scared?" It didn't seem possible.

"On the ranch, growing up? We were poor. My father? Always poor. Making ends meet. Insurance business, see? I had this paycheck, and I wasn't going to give that up. I kept imagining me without a job, all of us on the street, no food, sick, who knew. Some disaster out there . . . But look at me, I'm old. If I don't take a risk now, when the hell am I going to? I've always dreamed of something like this."

A golf course. That stupid ass Ben was wrong all along. "That day, when you and George went golfing. You came back all . . ." I spun my hand around. "A mess."

"Don't ever get in a golf cart with that guy, I'm telling you. Crazy! We wanted to talk to a few people, see the grounds. But he can't steer worth shit. Talking, looking over his shoulder— Jesus, we had to bail at the sand trap on the ninth hole. Drop and roll—I thought he was going to get us killed."

"I'm glad you were all right."

"Believe me, I don't want anything to happen *now*. Have

some heart attack, whatever. I wake up every morning and feel *purpose*. I feel *meaning*. Well, Munchkin, I guess I better break the news and face the music. You know how this family is. Knowing them, they probably think George is my long-lost son or some damn thing."

I kept my mouth shut again. But inside I felt like singing. Grandpa Shine, he was cutting those balloon strings, and he was going to fly. I never even knew he had balloon strings of his own. I hugged him. I hugged him so hard. He was the same old Grandpa, the golf shirt under my hands, his cologne smell. The man with the big laugh who always gave the biggest toys under the tree. Who sang country music at the top of his lungs (painfully, too), who roped cattle when he was a kid—we saw him do it in those pictures. But he was new, too. Stories took twists and turns down fairy-tale paths or down very human everyday ones. You think you're at the end of the book, and it's only the end of a chapter.

I climbed the stairs. I needed to see Ash. On the third floor I saw Ash's closed door, but I had no idea if he was in there or not. I thought I was alone in that hall. The commotion downstairs sounded far away. The stillness up there made me step quietly, the way quiet asks for more quiet, the way you whisper sometimes in a forest. I crept down the hall, listening for guitar strings or rustling in Ash's room, but I heard nothing.

But I was wrong about being alone. All at once, and loudly *wrong*.

"What are you doing?"

Ted. Ted and Rebecca's bedroom door was open. He was shouting.

"Nothing." Rebecca.

"Are you *hiding*?"

"It's crazy down there. Please."

"You're *smoking* again."

"I'm sorry!"

"You think I won't know? Jesus! How much of that stuff do you have? Where'd you get all that? You stockpiling in case of a *war*?"

I was frozen there, in that hallway. I tried to move, but the floor creaked under my feet.

"Johnny B gave me some." The baker? "And Butch. Butch's giving it up. Everybody gives it to me when they quit."

"Goddamn it!" Something slammed down hard. *No F-I-T-I-N-G*, I thought. "You know, Rebecca? This isn't working. This just isn't. I'm in some fucking contest with that stuff. A triangle. A love triangle! And I'm done. You've got to choose, because I'm *done*."

He was coming. I heard his shoes on the wood floor. I ducked into the open bathroom door next to me, the second duck-hide-flee maneuver I'd done in one day. The taffy shop, this bathroom—I was a character in my own video game, those shooting ones that Gavin and Oscar sometimes played, where chicks in combat uniforms darted around ominous empty rooms.

Shit. He'd see me shut the door. I didn't want him to know I'd heard anything. Too embarrassing for both of us. I stepped into the tub, pulled the shower curtain across. I heard him storm past. But then the footsteps came back my way again. Another round with Rebecca, probably. An apology? A zinger that he couldn't pass up?

But, wait, no.

He *was* coming my way, directly my way. Oh, God, he was there in the bathroom, and he was shutting the door, and it was worse than a video game because it was real, and I was stupidly hiding in the bathtub trying not to breathe and trying to keep my feet still so my shoes wouldn't squeak against the porcelain. What were my options here? Come on! Speak up, stay quiet, do neither and be found out? Could he see my shadow from there? Stupid, stupid, stupid!

There was the loud sound of his peeing, a zip, a flush. The water running. *Please be done,* I begged him. *Pleasepleaseplease.* The water shut off. I was sure he would hear my heart beating, my breathing. He would *feel* my presence, he had to. But no. I heard a towel thrown softly to the tile and then a quiet sound.

"Ah," he said softly. It was the sound of defeat, but also a cry of awareness, when you realize your life might be changing, going a direction against your will.

There was some strange storm front blowing in. I heard the high whine of a whistling wind outside the bathroom window. And it was raining broken hearts.

Ted left the bathroom. I exhaled. Thank God. I would

wait there for a minute, until he was definitely gone. I'd wait, and then I'd get the hell out of—

What was THAT? A herd of pounding feet, rising voices. What now? Shit! I crouched. Someone was running down the hall. Footsteps going one way, and another pair . . . Were they? Were they turning right into the bathroom? The shower curtain was flung aside.

"Aaaaaaaahhh!" Dan Jax screamed.

"Aaaaaaaahhh!" I screamed.

We stopped screaming. Dan had his hand to his heart again, but so did I.

"Cricket, for God's sake, what are you doing?"

"What are *you* doing?" Sure, I was the one hiding in the bathtub, but who was the screaming, unreasonable one here?

"Looking for Baby Boo!"

"I was—What? Where is he?"

"We don't know! John was upstairs with him, and then John fell asleep. He woke when he heard all the noise with the raccoon, and he realized Baby Boo was gone."

"Oh, Jeez. I'll help look."

Okay, yes, it was another humiliating blow to my self-esteem, lifting my knees up high and stepping out of that tub, leaving a set of shoe prints behind, but there was no time for ego hits right then either.

"The tent," I said.

"You're right," Dan said.

"That's where he was before."

"Christ, the ocean . . ."

Mr. and Mrs. Jax stood at the deck railing looking over, and so did Gram and Aunt Bailey. Hailey and Gavin and Ben and my mother had already had the same thought I did, and now they were rushing toward the beach, calling Baby Boo's name. It was getting so, so windy out there. The waves were high, and water droplets were rising up and you could hear the clang of a flag on a flagpole, and the high pitch and whine of wind.

We were running down the boardwalk, me and Dan, Dan in front of me. Hailey and Gavin and Ben had already reached the tent, and we saw their backs disappear inside of it, and then they emerged. We were there now too.

"No," Ben said. "Nothing."

"I thought for sure," Hailey said.

The tent nylon was flapping in and out, *whick-whick, whick-whick*, flapping kind of crazily, it seemed. But I had no time to register that fact in the narrow, logical part of my taxed mind right then, because there was a shout and a cry from up above, at the house, and we saw Jane and John on the deck, and George, who was lifting little Baby Boo in the air in a Lion King moment. You could hear the joy up there. Jane was shouting something down to us, but I couldn't hear what she was saying.

"He wanted to see the Goddie?" Hailey said. Hailey lifted her shoulders, held her palms up to indicate to Jane that she didn't understand.

"The Goddie!" Jane's voice traveled down to us. She hooked her thumb toward the French doors, where Jupiter came trotting out. She stuck her head between the deck rails.

"Ah." Dan Jax sighed. "Ah."

"Thank Goddie." I laughed.

He laughed too. He crooked his arm around my neck and around Hailey's in relief. "I know. I thought . . . what next?"

Which is a stupid thing to say. You never want to say that, ever, unless you want to tempt the cruel and black-humored Goddies up above, the ones wishing to liven up the dull human poker games by upping the stakes.

"Whaaa!" Gavin shrieked. He saw it first, went grabbing for the nylon that lifted up as easy as a kite on a breezy day. A large, domed kite, an alien vehicle returning home by rising up into the dark sky. Gavin's hands—they grasped only at air, and so did Ben's, they were reaching up into black nothing, because the tent lifted up, up, up and out toward the sea, out for a wild outdoorsy tent ocean adventure, back out to wherever home was. It lifted high, and you could hear the collective gasp of our group even through the whistling wind. The tent rose and then slowly set itself down upon the waves, the window flap waving a mad good-bye as it drifted farther and farther out.

The contents of the tent sat exposed on the nylon floor. A vulnerable TV, and electric cords, a red cooler, sleeping bags and blankets. An M&M's bag lifted in the wind too, and went running, end over end, down the beach. It all looked for a moment like the news footage after a tornado, missing roofs and the embarrassments of ordinary living exposed.

"How the hell did that happen?" Gavin said.

"I'm so sorry," Hailey said. "Back when I was mad? I undid the snaps. Those ones there." She pointed to the now gaping halves of metal, which had once connected the secured tent floor to its dome. "I'm sorry, Gavey."

"Hailey!" Dan Jax said.

Ben made a choking sound, a gasp. He was doubled over. He was laughing. He held one hand up in some sort of apology as he cracked up. "Shit." He laughed. "Shit."

Oh yeah, it was kind of hysterical. Like that time with the cello in the Bermuda Honda trunk. The orange globe of tent was disappearing past the horizon as if it were a setting sun, and all of those electronics were sitting oddly out in the night, exposed and trembling in the wind. But that wasn't what Ben was laughing about.

"Oh, man." He wiped his eyes. "God. *Gavey*." He laughed.

Ash was a good guy. I knew he was. He appeared out of nowhere, helping to lug inside the generator and the controllers and the speakers and the bags of freeze-dried foods in foil pouches. We didn't speak. We all hauled everything up the boardwalk, away from the sand now rising and spinning in the coming storm. Oscar appeared too. He was holding Natalie's hand, and she was smiling shyly. She didn't seem to be minding that chin fluff, not at all.

"I'm confused," Ash said to me finally when he saw them.

"*He's* confused. It was a misunderstanding."

"Not something *else* to sort out?"

"One thing is more than enough for me," I said.

He set a duffel bag of Gavin's on the living room floor. The bottom of the tent, rolled up now, went next to it.

"You know where I am, right?" he said kindly. He grabbed my fingers and gave them a squeeze and then headed out. In the doorway he turned. He had his car keys in his hand, and he tossed them into the air and caught them. "For-ever is a slippery little du-ude . . . ," he sang badly. It felt like someone was crushing my heart.

"Definitely a hit song," I said.

"Later," he said over his shoulder as he went out the door.

All of Gavin and Oscar's crap was in the house now, and they were taking most of it to Hailey's room. It was just in time too, because it started to rain. Pour. You could hear the hard, driving splats against the roof. It wasn't raining cats and dogs, exactly—more like small round gerbils. My mother had found a bottle of wine in the kitchen, and she and Dan and Aunt Hannah were each having a glass, watching the real weather channel out the living room windows.

"Crazy weather. Perfect for a wedding," my mother said. She looked sad.

Dan raised his glass. "To crazy weather, crazy life, crazy parents."

"To crazy parents building crazy golf courses," Mom said. I guess Grandpa had confessed. She and Aunt Hannah clinked.

"To crazy parents in general," I said.

"Never mind," my mother said to me. "Dear God, what next?"

"That's all, Daisy. I promise," Dan said. "There won't be anything else. That's all we can *take*."

Ben appeared. Wiped his sandy hands on his pants. Jupiter was trotting behind him, trying to keep up. Cruiser, who'd been lying there quietly, hopped to attention as if the general had arrived. "Watch," Ben said. "There'll be an earthquake or something."

At that, one of the Goddies playing poker with our lives had a great idea. He set all the money in the world on the earth's green felt poker table. He was looking straight at us.

"What's that noise?" my mother said.

A noise, all right. A vibrating *wha-wha-wha* turning into a *WHUP, WHUP, WHUP*. The sound was so loud now, the windows were rattling.

Dan stood, looked out. "Jesus," he said. He put his arm over his eyes because a bright light, white and blinding, was shining in.

Ted was running down the stairs.

"Oh, my God," I said.

"Where did that come from?" Ben asked.

"Goddamn it," Ted said. "Our stupid-ass neighbor. Randy, he's an ex-marine. I'm so sorry, guys. He's got a helipad on his roof. Louder than hell—it scares the shit out us every time it happens. Sometimes he takes people back and forth from the island."

"Helipad?" I said. I remembered. That helicopter Ben and I saw.

"A landing place for the helicopter," Ted said.

Ben and I looked at each other.

"I tell Rebecca it's like living next to a goddamn airport."

I'll raise you, the Goddie said.

chapter
twenty-four

Janssen—

A List of Things Jupiter Destroyed:

1. Various garden hoses
2. Our old backyard, from digging all those holes
3. Several pairs of shoes
4. One paperback book
5. A rosebush
6. Enough underwear to clothe a small country

7. The heads of those mini Christmas carolers of the mini village we always put under our tree

Actually, I can't even remember everything. No way. When we first got her—man, she was a puppy bent on destruction. But you know, because of all the good things she's done, all that she's given—I don't even care about that underwear. Some of them I really liked too. Some of them were my favorite pairs. Who cares about any of that stuff?

Humans, though, Janssen. It's another thing entirely. We either give forgiveness too easily or we treat it like we're a starving person with the last crust of bread—clutching it, withholding it, hiding it, a basic selfish grasp at self-preservation. If you give it away, you let go of the chance to be safe.

We have more reasons to worry about intentions, though, don't we? Most dogs don't wish ill on people (I think, anyway). I doubt they lie there hoping we'll get ours when we've been mean. I doubt they think about what that other dog has compared to them, or dream about better couches and fancier food that might be theirs if we could only do better. I doubt they are as confused as we are. Things seem pretty simple. Their needs seem pretty clear, except for those times when they stare and stare and you can't for the life of you figure out what they want and you just wish you could *ask*. Mostly they seem just fine. And what a relief that is for a change.

You do them wrong, they move on. They do you wrong, you move on. In the grand scheme of things, what do chewed underwear really matter?

You say this is not about forgiveness. Your last letter: "It's not about you being sorry enough. It's about you being ready enough."

But maybe, Janssen, this is what I'm most sorry for?

Love always,

Cricket

chapter
twenty-five

"It sounds like the air force descending," Dan said. He opened the living room doors. The rain was falling furiously. The full thunderous clatter of *THWUP! THWUP! THWUP!* rushed in.

"All those years in the military for our man, Randy. I think it brings back the good old days," Ted said.

The noise brought everyone downstairs. Gram and Aunt Bailey in their matching robes, and Grandpa and George and Amy and Hailey and Gavin. I didn't know where Oscar and Natalie were—probably making out in Natalie's room. Who cared about a military takeover when you were in love? Jane and John appeared, with a sleepy Baby Boo on Jane's hip. Jupiter began to bay and howl at the noise. Her warning cry. The cry meant for coyotes and mountain lions. Dangerous invaders. I picked her up, tucked her under my arm. She yelped when I picked her up. A cry of pain that surprised me. I must have gotten that tender place under her arm.

"Sorry, sweetie." I kissed her head.

"Are we being attacked?" Gram said. With the door open she almost had to shout. The wind and rain were blowing in. Dan stood on the deck watching now. The wind blew a paper napkin off the table. Cruiser trotted out to the deck and was watching the helicopter too, his chin up toward the sky, eyes fixed. It was the same thing Jupiter did when she tried to catch flies.

"Fool to take a chopper out in this weather," Grandpa said.

"Some idiot didn't think it could wait until tomorrow," Ted said.

"Well, I'm glad that's all it is," Jane said.

Rebecca was there now too. Ted folded his arms when she came in. She stood away from him, looking out those windows. "Good thing there are so many more sane ways to get to Bishop Rock and that Randy's business is generally bad. We don't have to live with this often."

Ben had gone outside to watch, and he stood beside Dan Jax, and Mom did too, and so did I, with Jupiter still tucked safely under my arm. Randy's place was next to Bluff House, and we could see straight across to that flat roof. The helicopter looked like a sci-fi creature with its large glass nose and beaming headlight, its spindly legs wobbling and then alighting on the roof. The blades spun awhile before stopping.

"Cool," Ben said. "Never seen something like that so close before."

"It's freezing out here," Amy said behind me. "We're getting drenched." I didn't know she was there. I didn't know *everyone* was there. We really weren't getting all that wet—the rain had turned to a drizzle—but the wind kept on. The door of the helicopter lifted up when the blades had stilled.

"It is an action movie," George said. "Now the spy from the United States of America will step out with his briefcase of important documents."

"I saw that one," Gram said.

"That's not a spy," Dan said. His voice sounded funny.

"Dan?" my mother said.

"That's not a spy," he said again.

It was a woman. Wearing a big parka and high heels. She was speaking to Randy, and he was gesturing in the direction of Bluff House.

Suddenly Dan was shouting. "Gayle! Goddamn it, Gayle, is that you?"

"Mom?" Amy said.

"What?" my mother whispered. "What! No. You've got to be kidding me. This isn't happening. This. Is. Not. Happening."

"Oh. My. God," Hailey said. "My crazy mother. That's my crazy mother! Gavey, what did I tell you?" She stood at the deck rail and shrieked. "Go home, Ma! Go home! We're fine, see! Fine!"

The voices were lost in the thick tunnel of wind. The woman didn't even look over.

Dan, though—he began to run. Down that boardwalk, down that beach. I had wanted him to do something, and that's what was happening, all right. I've never seen him look like that, so furious. I didn't know he could even get truly angry—it was one of the things I liked about him. But it was there now. Anger, and decisiveness. Needed action.

The waves were crashing white against the dark shoreline. I'd lost all track of time. It had to be quite late now. I watched Dan's determined figure stride across that beach. But it was my mother who made me do what I did next. Her face—crushed, fallen. It looked like defeat. The face of someone who had given up.

"I can't believe this," she said. "This is *nuts*. This is *too much*."

I made my way back through the group. Me, with my dog still under my arm. I needed to get inside. Away. I got the hell out of there. I heard Ben say, "Hey, George. Better than a spy movie, eh?" But I didn't feel like joking. Farthest thing from it. It *was* too much. She was right. I felt the landslide—the ripples building on ripples, the rock pushing against rock, until the cracking, roaring crash became inevitable. The polite image of a balloon tied to the ground with strings—it shattered in natural disaster, the crashing roar of avalanche, and the strings were yanked from the ground with the endless and insistent forces of change. Because the rain keeps falling, and the wind keeps blowing and the sea keeps making small shoves of water against sand, change, change, change, and there was not a thing you could do about it.

I went to my room and slammed the door. I put my face against Jupiter's body. Maybe safety was only a creation of our imagination. I smelled Jupiter's comforting wet-wool-blanket smell. I could feel her heart beating. She looked at me with concern. Her eyes said, *I am worried.*

I found my phone. And then I called my very own Janssen Tucker. I did. There he was. His same, familiar voice. I wept. I could barely talk, I was sobbing so hard. I was filled with sudden, crashing grief. I was saying the most important thing, asking the biggest question. *How,* I cried, *how am I supposed to do this without you?*

I was awakened the next morning by a knock at the door.

"Crick?"

Ben.

"I'm sleeping."

"Do you know where Mom is?"

I sat up. I saw Jupiter over there, looking up at me without lifting her head. She was tired from being up late last night too. "Don't say this. Don't say you can't find her."

"Dan woke up, and she wasn't there. He was wondering if I'd seen her."

I scrambled out of bed, flung open my door. Ben—for all of his easy, let-it-go advice, he looked troubled. He was still wearing the same clothes from the day before. He was unshaven, and his eyes were bleary. "Wedding day," he said.

"Shit, Ben. Shit."

"I know."

"We would have heard that helicopter leave, for one thing," he said.

I pulled a sweatshirt over my head. I clipped Jupiter to her leash. I had the irrational thought—maybe we should look in the same places Charles had hid, the places even small people know to seek for escape.

"She probably just went to get coffee," Ben said.

"I'll be right back," I said.

"Dan was just wondering if I'd seen her. He isn't even concerned. We don't need to get crazy. We don't need another Baby Boo search party."

"I'll be right back," I said again. And then I did something I hardly ever do. I stood on my toes and kissed his cheek, and he crooked one arm around my neck and gave me a hug.

"There's nothing you can do," he said. "She has her own reasons."

"Maybe I just want to see her off," I said.

The house was quiet; only Dan was awake, drinking a cup of coffee and reading the newspaper, innocent about the changes barreling his way. I felt bad for him. Mom's first good guy, and he was about to get his heart broken. I snuck out without going in to see him. I didn't like the feeling of knowing his future when he didn't. I was the doctor with the cancer diagnosis before the patient knows anything is wrong.

Outside, the air felt different. Calm, as if the hard wind had blown something bad away. The fog was jogging past, revealing spots of blue in the sky that meant a sunny day was on its way. The waves twinkled with merry mischief. The storm had brought in all kinds of shit at the part of the beach where wet met dry. I saw a rubber boot and a Coke bottle, the lid of a cooler. It's like the sea had spit out all the garbage and was now feeling better.

I waited for Jupiter to sniff for the right pee spot and squat for what seemed a very long time. Her legs were shaky again. Her little white spot on her back, which always looked so proud, seemed small and unsure. I'd have to tell Mom about her legs. Her old age was catching up, I guessed. It was hard to watch.

I looked over at Randy-the-Ex-Marine's house. I tried to see if the helicopter was still in its place, but the slope of the cliff made it impossible. Ben was right, though—you couldn't have missed the noise of it taking off. Still, I headed toward that house. I could picture the scene—my mother there with her bag and her purse slung over her shoulder. Her wallet would be in her hand, and she'd be taking out the bills to pay for the ride out.

I didn't even know what had happened the night before. I'd forgotten to even ask Ben. Amy and Hailey might be gone already, sleeping soundly in one of Bishop Rock's B and B's with their mother watching over them, preparing to head back to Vancouver.

I walked in the sand, concentrating on our path—I didn't want to lead Jupiter over broken shells or driftwood logs. I was so focused that I didn't even see the figure a short distance away. The figure heading back toward Bluff House.

"Cricket?"

The voice startled me. I was so sure about what was going to happen. But I looked up, and there she was, our mother, bundled up in Dan's sweatshirt, her cheeks rosy from the morning walk.

"Where you headed?" she called.

It was as good a question as any. The best question.

I looked down at her hands. I didn't understand. They were empty except for a whole sand dollar that she must have found on her walk.

Jupiter was pulling at the leash, and I let it go so that she could run to my mother, who scooped her up. It struck me how the ocean had spit out all that junk, but, too, a whole sand dollar. Other treasures, likely, as well. After all this mess, there were no bags in my mother's hands. How do I explain this feeling? It's like my heart opened up and out, and everything I'd been holding released. Relief, sorrow, but joy, too. I had to sit down right there on a big flat sandy rock.

"Ah," I said. It wasn't too different than the cry I heard Ted make in the bathroom. "You're getting married today. Still."

Her face turned concerned. "Cricket, yes. What did you think?"

I put my head down, looked at my sandy shoes. I had gotten this so wrong. It's hard to see clearly when your eyes are squinched tight out of fear.

"What did you think?" she said again, and then she understood. "Oh." She sounded hurt. She set Jupiter down and sat beside me. I scooted over on my rock to make room. Jupiter sniffed happily at a clump of seaweed.

"Cricket, there were reasons before. Really good reasons."

"There are reasons now," I said.

"There's a *problem* now, one that Dan and I can handle. And there are a million more reasons why this is the best decision I've ever made."

"So you're not going to take off to Tahiti by yourself?"

She narrowed her eyes at me like I'd gone mad and she was trying to figure out exactly when that had happened. "Tahiti? Why would I go to Tahiti by myself?"

"To enjoy the blessed isolation."

"Cricket, you lost me," she said. She dug her feet in the sand, buried her toes.

"That pamphlet in your purse."

"What were you doing in my purse?"

"Aspirin."

"I don't know of any pamphlet. I don't know what you're talking about. Wait. Tahiti? Did it have *gum* stuck in it?"

Oh no. Oh, how we could get things wrong.

"Dan and I went to this travel agent to see if we could even afford to take a trip. I was sick of my gum by the time we got out of there. Jesus, Cricket."

I was silent.

"Okay, I know what you thought. I'm sorry you thought that. But, Cricket, I love Dan. I'm committed to Dan. Dan and I are right together."

Wait—last night. "What about Amy? What about the helicopter?"

"Dan told Gayle she needed to leave. Amy decided to go with her mother."

"No." I groaned.

"Cricket, it's okay. It's too bad, but okay. Dan is fine. He's hurt, but he can handle it. Amy will do what she'll do right now, but Dan won't let it get in the way of our life together. He's taking care of it. That's all I can ask for."

"I think it's bratty. And selfish. Yeah, be pissed because your father is actually *happy*. I can see if you were planning to send them away to boarding school, like in the freaking *Sound of Music*—"

"I love when she makes the dresses out of curtains," my mother said. I already knew she loved that part. "Crick, yeah, it's upsetting. But she has some growing up to do."

"It's not like she's seven. She's *fifteen*."

"There are so many different fifteens. And eighteens. And

forty-twos, for that matter. Mature fifteens and young fifteens and wise fifteens and lost fifteens. And angry fifteens." She thought awhile. Then she smiled. Chuckled. "You should have seen Dan last night. Damn. Commando warrior."

I chuckled too. I would have loved to have seen that.

I watched a seagull strolling along the shoreline. He looked like he should be whistling something carefree. Jupiter spotted him too, and started to pull, howling. Mom pulled her close. Wrapped her arms around Jupiter's small black and white chest. "Quit it, monkey," she said.

"How can you be sure?" I asked.

"About Dan?"

"About forever."

Jupiter stopped the howling. Set her front paws up on my mother's knees. Mom put her nose to Jupiter's and Eskimo kissed. Jupiter hopped down and sat nicely.

"Oh, Crick." She sighed. She took my hand. "Experience, maybe? I've had lots of experiences. The bad ones made the good ones pretty clear. I used to think it was so tricky, finding the right person. In some ways it is. But in some ways it's simple. A good man, who you respect and who respects you . . . Of course, 'good'—see, that's a lot of traits right there, though. A lot of things it's *not*."

Janssen was good. Really good. That's where I got confused. What idiot gave up good? "Janssen," I said.

"He's good, all right," Mom said. "But I guess there's

something else. About being sure. Sure about *anything*. Right comes with right timing."

"Right timing?"

"A bunch of things it's *not* again."

I was quiet. Jupiter was digging in the sand with her front paws. She used to do this at our old house, her butt sticking up out of the hole when it got real deep. Mom squeezed my hand. "Crick?" she said.

"Yeah?"

"I need you to stop worrying. I know I've given you reason in the past, and I am so sorry for that. There are so many ways I wish I'd done it different. But I have it handled."

My heart clutched. I felt like I could cry.

"And . . . I know it's a complicated thing to ask. I know it is. But can you ever forgive me for all the ways I got things wrong? I got so many things wrong. My bad decisions hurt you and Ben. I am so sorry for that."

I turned to her on that rock, and we put our arms around each other. You could wish and wish for the big words, love, hope, forever, the most beautiful words, to be only themselves, uncluttered by the things that can cling to them. But always, always, there will be the cracked windshields and the dark nights on some dock somewhere, the raccoon on a roof, the lost children. Love hung in there, that's what it did.

Jupiter popped her head up. She had sand on her nose.

"Of course I forgive you. Of course I do."

• • •

People started arriving that afternoon. Friends of Mom's and Dan's, the girl Ben had been seeing, Taylor. The house filled. Gavin had been put in charge of Cruiser, and he and Hailey were walking him around like he was their love child. Afternoon turned to early evening. The sky had been blue all afternoon, and now there was the sleepy light of a day ending. I got dressed. My blue dress and heels, sparkly earrings. I looked around for Ash but didn't see him. Aunt Bailey was going crazy with the camera, stopping everyone in their tracks for various group photos. She was bossing everyone into poses. Grandpa and George and Ben. Ben and me. More of Ben and me. Gram and Mrs. Jax. Oscar and Gavin and Hailey. Baby Boo in his little suit, with his favorite Goddie, Jupiter, in her one perfect outfit, good for any occasion, black velvet fur with white spot.

The cake was unharmed, but Cruiser had somehow gotten to my mother's shoes. He chewed up one of her white high heels with the seed pearl straps, but that didn't get in the way of her marrying her right one, Dan Jax. Nothing would. When she came down the stairs in her cream-colored dress and stepped out to the back lawn overlooking the ocean where everyone had packed in, she was barefoot. The dog had wrecked the shoes, but it had turned out to be an act of right timing—Mom had always liked being barefoot best.

Ted sat on a stool on the grass, next to a woman with dark hair and a big smile. The minister. She held an open book—a book with the most timeless and complicated stories of all. Ted started to play his guitar. He sang, and Ash was right. A beautiful voice, sweet strumming. *As it was in the beginning is now and till the end . . .*

"I love Peter, Paul and Mary," Gram whispered next to me, but I saw that her eyes were wet.

We had come so far from the days of baby toys and the Bermuda Honda and the U-Haul and the too-big lawn. We all had, and there was so much hope. *There is love,* Ted sang. I took Ben's hand, and he squeezed mine. Gram took my other one, and Aunt Bailey held Gram's. I saw Ash now, standing off to the side next to Rebecca, grinning at his father proudly. Rebecca watched Ted with a sweet smile, set her arm around Ash's shoulders. Mrs. Jax fixed the sweater that was falling off of Mr. Jax's shoulder, and then he put his good arm around her waist. Grandpa blew his nose into a hankie. Hailey stood with her aunt and uncle, holding Baby Boo, who was eating Cheerios out of a Baggie like a little gentleman. The dogs were watching from the living room windows. The sky turned orange off in the distance.

My mother, in her cream dress, and Dan Jax, in his dark suit, both beaming, made promises to each other. The white rose on Dan's collar fell off, and he shrugged and everyone laughed.

He turned and faced us. "All of you . . . My wife." His voice cracked. "I am grateful."

My mother's own voice wobbled. She looked at Ben and me. "This . . . this is how it should look," she said. She was crying, and so was Dan, and then so was I, and even Ben, and then Dan Jax held my mother around her waist and lifted her high up off the ground, her bare feet in the air. She was grabbing him around the neck and laughing, and I could see that those big words . . . They might never be perfect, but they could get very, very close.

The party started back up on the deck. The music came on. We ate great food and we toasted each other and Mom and Dan cut that beautiful cake. And I overheard something that made my heart break. Mr. and Mrs. Jax, standing under one of the hanging lanterns.

"I guess I'll have to watch you die," Mrs. Jax said. "I just didn't want to do that."

He took her bony hand in his. He heard her just fine. "I'm not going anywhere yet," he said.

"Thank you, Cricket," Natalie said. "Thank you for inviting me, and for everything else."

"I'm so glad it worked out for you." I gave her a hug.

"I didn't even know I could feel like this," she said. Her eyes danced. Goofy Oscar was getting her something to drink.

"I am so happy for you."

"Hailey said Gavey's going to Vancouver with her after this. Gavey? Do you think he'll lose his job over at Tech Time?"

I looked over at Gavey and Hailey, feeding each other stuffed mushrooms by the food table. "I don't think he'll mind."

"Hmm. True love?" Natalie said.

"Probably not true or love."

"They're having a great time, though."

Everyone was dancing now. Gram shimmied with Dan, who'd taken his shoes off to match Mom. Poor Ben—Aunt Bailey grabbed him for a spin. He wore the grim sort of dancing smile that meant he was racking up heaven points. Baby Boo was bending his knees, and his mother twirled him in a circle.

I felt a hand on my waist, and there was Ash.

"One dance?" he asked.

"Yes," I said.

"You look beautiful," he said.

"You look pretty great yourself." He did. Dress pants and a button-up shirt, a tie, now loosened.

He held me close, even though the song was tripping along. "A slow dance?" I asked.

"Slow is good," he said.

We understood each other then. He danced me out of the large group, eased us over to the deck rail looking over the sea. I felt his broad shoulders under my hands. Smelled that great smell of his cologne. We moved against the beat, but slow *was* good.

The song ended. He leaned in and kissed my cheek, oh-so-soft. "You get things figured out, and then we'll dance some more," he said.

"All right," I said.

"Good-bye for now."

"Good-bye for now," I said.

I watched his back disappear into the crowd. I felt the weight of loss there in my chest. But I felt rightness, too. One thing *was* enough to sort out.

I looked out toward that sea, wondering what it might bring next—Coke bottles or sand dollars. But then there was my brother beside me. "God," he breathed. "Save me. If Aunt Bailey asks me to dance one more time, I'm out of here."

I smiled. I looked over my shoulder and saw Aunt Bailey dancing with George now. Grandpa Shine just bent poor Taylor backward in a dip.

Now Mom came over, and set an arm around us both.

"Oh, sweeties," she said.

"You're married," I said.

"It's weird," she said. "I feel like we've been married forever, but it also doesn't feel real."

"I'm really happy for you," I said. "For all of us."

"I'm happy for us too," Ben said.

"You babies," she said. "I'm the luckiest mother that ever lived."

"What the hell?" Ben said.

I thought he was being an idiot and ruining the moment. "What is she doing? Do you guys smell that?"

"Is that Rebecca?" My mother couldn't see in the dark to save her life.

I squinted. I couldn't see in the dark either, actually.

"Does she have a bonfire going?" Mom asked.

"She's burning something in that bonfire," Ben said. *"Smell."*

He'd been pretty wrong before, but I sniffed anyway.

"Is that what I think it is?" Mom said.

"She's getting rid of it," Ben said. "She's just tossing it on there!"

Wow, I smelled it now. "Man. How much of that stuff does she have?"

"Goddamn," Ben said. "Enough to get the whole beachfront high."

As the bonfire flames rose and lit up the sky, I could see Rebecca clearly. Her skirts swirled, and there was the glint of her shimmering bracelets as she gave herself back to her true love.

Ted smelled it too. He strode toward that deck rail, furious. But then he understood. He read the smoke signals in the air, or else he saw what we did—Rebecca raising her fingertips to her lips. She lifted her arm high so that Ted could catch her kiss.

Ted cried out again, that same *Ah*, a different realization this time. By the end of the night, a group of high school boys would join the circle around that fire, and so, it seemed, would every aging hippie on the island. Even Randy-the-Ex-Marine himself.

But right then the smoke rose, and the people danced, and we all bore witness to the old story of love, and love's repairs.

chapter
twenty-six

Janssen—

1. A dog disappeared from his home and
    was feared dead, but four months later
    was found by a family who brought him
    to a rescue organization. They wanted to
    check if he had owners who were looking
    for him. He did—a mother and her son,
    who thought they'd never see him again.
    When they were reunited, Frankie the
    dog howled and howled and howled with
    joy and recognition. "You didn't forget,"
    his owner said.

2. Bobbie, a collie who became lost while on vacation with his family in Indiana, went on an incredible journey for months, wandering in circles in the harsh winter, before reaching Des Moines, Iowa. From there, instinctively, the Collie headed straight for his home in Oregon. Writer Charles Alexander did some detective work on the dog's trek and found that he had traveled through Idaho, Wyoming, and Colorado, eventually traveling three thousand miles over six months before coming together with his family again.

3. In another case, a family's dog went missing just before they moved twelve hundred miles away. Nearly a year later the dog appeared at the family's new home.

They never forget, see? I've heard it too—that howl, howl, howl of joy Jupiter gives when we've returned after a long while. Did she know how long we'd been gone? Is a week forever? Did she worry we wouldn't ever return? But we weren't gone forever. No, we weren't.

I know you're right. That night on the dock was
not about graduation and college choices and
needing a solution. I was sad about time passing,
and there is no solution for that.

And you are right about something else. My
mother ran from forever because she was afraid,
and I wanted to stay forever because I was afraid.

I know. It's time for her to stay, and for me to go.

When there is a connection so deep, reunion is
inevitable, isn't it, Janssen? Tell me that it's true. I
hope we will find our way back to each other one
day, Janssen. Even if it takes years. Even if we have
to travel a hundred thousand miles to get back
home.

Love always,

Cricket

chapter
twenty-seven

We all said good-bye. Jane and John and Baby Boo had left early that morning, and so had Aunt Hannah and Mr. and Mrs. Jax. Gavin and Hailey drove off too, waving madly after being properly fueled with coffee and chocolate doughnuts, and then Natalie left with Oscar. Ben would drive me and Jupiter back in his truck, leaving our mother and Dan to head home on their own with Cruiser. I gave him a good scratch good-bye, in that spot that made his hind leg go like a crazy fiddle player. We'd all arrived believing some things and left knowing others.

We hugged out in front of Bluff House.

"Keep it under a hundred, Gram," Ben said, and kissed her cheek.

"We're stopping again at the outlet mall on the way out of

town. You need anything?" Aunt Bailey asked me. "They've got some cute parkas."

I had visions of fur-lined hats, or snowflake patterns. "That's okay," I said. "I'm set for parkas, but thanks."

"We'll follow you," Grandpa said. "That golf store—"

"We just can't get rid of you, can we?" Gram said. Grandpa gave her a hug.

George shook my mother's hand. "You have a beautiful family," he said.

"Oh, George, give me a hug. We've been through enough together."

Ted was slapping everyone on the back happily, and Rebecca was kissing cheeks. I think they were just giddy with relief that we were finally leaving. I looked up at the house, toward the third-story windows. We had said our good-byes, but I said another silent one to Ash. I reminded myself: Bishop Rock was not very far away, if I wanted that. A quick trip by helicopter, ha.

"People. It's not like we don't live a few miles away from each other. We're going to be together in two weeks for my birthday," Ben said. "Let's get a move on. Crick, you ready?"

We got into Ben's truck. I lifted Jupiter up and set her between us. Ben reversed out of the drive, honking his horn. The house got smaller and smaller in the distance. Ben turned the radio on, to his regular station.

I kissed Jupiter's black velvet head and put my arm around her so she wouldn't slide around up there. "You're an idiot," I said to Ben, for no other reason than that change kept coming, like it or not, but, too, there were always the things you could count on.

"I'd rather be an idiot than have a face like an ape," he said.

We settled into my mother and Dan's three-story Craftsman in Seattle. The movers had taken everything from our old place and brought it to the new one. Even though there was nothing left for me to do there now, I went out to our old house. I drove down Cummings Road, past the llama farm and the paragliders. Past that secret shortcut road we'd take on the way to school, where we'd see Bob, Betty, and Louise. Past the Country Store and Johnson's Nursery and the church and the little shed that was mine and Janssen's.

I drove down our own dirt road, careful of the potholes. I turned the corner, and there sat our house, with its peaked Victorian roof and its big porch. I half expected to see Jupiter peering out between the deck railings, barking at the sound of my car. I half expected to see Ben's light on, or Mom out there with the hedge clippers, her Jeep in the driveway. The electronic gate, the Mighty Mule, was shut, so I parked in front. I rolled my window down so I could hear the creek. I just listened to the sounds of home.

I walked up the long drive, past the fruit trees. Tiny apples were beginning to appear. The rooms of the house were empty. They were Christmas rooms and birthday rooms and heartache rooms and joy rooms and plain old everyday rooms. I turned away, and took a last look over that large stretch of grass. I looked toward the road leading to Janssen's house. I wished for it: to see him riding down right then on one of his mother's horses. If that had happened, I would have thrown away everything I knew right then and gone to him. To hell with growing up. To hell with moving on. But that didn't happen. He did not come down the road then, and I did not drive up. It would have been too hard to see his house or to run into his mother or father.

I pulled a blade of grass from our lawn, no longer our lawn. It was stupid, but I put it into my pocket. I wished I could take it all and keep it forever—the blueberries, the lilac tree we had given Mom for Mother's Day, those old rosebushes. All the animals: John Deer and Gauca-mole, and Dan and Marilyn Quail, and those salmon we would hear splashing in the winding water come mid-October. The sound of the creek.

But I would always have one thing no matter what, one thing that time or circumstances would never take from me— the story that happened here. The story of us.

I spent the summer with my mother and Dan and Cruiser and Jupiter, and I decided I did not want to go to school in Los Angeles. I enrolled at the University of Washington. Natalie and I were talking about getting our own place the following year, after we could save up some money. Maybe some people who felt safer than I did could release ropes and suddenly fly up, up, up. But I needed to untie them more slowly. The right time—not yet.

I started classes that fall.

Are you going to cry on the first day of school like you always do? I asked my mother.

I don't cry, she said.

We know you do. Ben and I both know. Every year.

I can't help it. It's always a big day, she said.

I found my way around the large campus lined with cherry trees. The leaves turned orange and then fell. I got a part-time job at the university's bookstore. We had the first snowfall of the year, which made the city go crazy with skidding cars and abandoned ones, and my English 101 class gathered to sled on one of the steep nearby hills. We had Christmas in the new house, a big, high-ceilinged place that was a hundred years old, and which sat on a street not far from the university. Dan's business was nearby, and my mother now had a studio in one of the gabled rooms upstairs. *Monkey M. Monkey Moves to the City.*

Dan called Hailey and Amy a lot, and while Amy still refused to visit, Hailey and Gavin came over once together and we went Christmas shopping with Natalie and Oscar. I went to see my own father, back over the bridge where he lived, him and his new girlfriend. We watched movies together, tried to make the past disappear into the future. Mom got lost over and over again in the city, trying to find the street where we lived.

Ben stayed with us during winter break, and Gram and Aunt Bailey came by and drank eggnog until their cheeks reddened. We all went to a ground-breaking ceremony for Grandpa's golf course.

And Jupiter and Cruiser. They didn't get to choose if they wanted to be together or not, but they made the best of it. Maybe they would have picked different relatives for themselves, but they worked it out. Jupiter, our old girl, she still kept Cruiser in line, but they'd gang up on their humans, sitting together by the treat jar. They'd both go crazy when anyone came to the door, barking and trotting around like teammates defending the same goalpost. The mailman made them nuts. *We've been over this a hundred times,* I'd say, but they had a job to do.

I'd bundle up and walk Jupiter by herself too, on the hilly streets of Seattle, her new home. I could see her funny little breath in the cold. But her gait was slow, and her nose seemed always dry. You can fool yourself into thinking it will never happen, even though you know it has to happen. I knew it was happening for a while, really. Her muzzle had gotten gray. She'd been looking old. Dog years—you could forget what that meant. But then the strange, worrisome things came— how thin she got. The shaky legs. Shivering. No one could say what was wrong with her. She began to yelp in pain even when resting quietly. She couldn't walk down any stairs, and sometimes one leg would give out on her and she would stumble. We tried to give her her dignity, even when she peed in the house, which began to happen a lot. She felt so bad about it. Her stomach was always sick too, and none of the medicines we hid in bits of cheese or bread seemed to help.

She started panting hard. She had nights where she would wander the house, climbing the stairs, pacing. I saw my mother holding her in the middle of the night. She stayed with her and held her on her lap. I laid my head beside Jupiter as she slept on her bed. After years of locating every microscopic bread crumb, stealing candy from purses, and trying to fake us out by stepping back over the door ledge for a second you-came-when-we-called treat, she lost interest in food.

But the worst thing was, her tail stopped wagging. She held it low and still.

I could feel the seasons changing. I knew it was an important time, *that* time, same as you know all big things. Same as you know a person will be important in your life, or know when you've made a choice that will change you. I could feel heartbreak and loss just like that, waiting, getting ready. I wanted it gone. I didn't, don't, understand why this had to be. I didn't, don't, understand that kind of forever.

I went with Mom again to see Dr. Mary, Jupiter's vet. We were there a lot. They shaved the side of her for another test, an ultrasound, and they sent her through X-ray machines again too, more tests, and still no one knew what was the matter. We brought her home. But one night—we heard her. We all did. Suffering, throwing up, so sick. We piled into the car, and Dan Jax drove us to the animal hospital emergency room. We sat in plastic chairs and my mother held Jupiter on her lap in a blanket. The doctor said it was time to think about doing the kindest thing.

It didn't feel like the kindest thing. It felt wrong. You must choose their death because you love them, but loving them makes the choice an impossible one. It was mercy, an act of compassion, a mercy that rips your heart out. Still, we had brought her from her beginning to her end.

A dog—a dog teaches us so much about love. Wordless, imperfect love; love that is constant, love that is simple good-ness, love that forgives not only bad singing and embarrass-ments, but misunderstandings and harsh words. Love that sits and stays and stays and stays, until it finally becomes its own forever. Love, stronger than death. A dog is a four-legged reminder that love comes and time passes and then your heart breaks.

At that hospital, late that night, they taped a plastic vial of morphine to her leg. We brought her home so that we could spend a few hours together. Suddenly it's the last day, and then the last few hours, and then moments, and then moment. You wish for so many things. To do it all over again, but so much better. To have even a little more time. You hope and hope she can understand that you are doing everything you can. You hope and hope she isn't afraid. This time it's terrible not to share language. You try to say it all anyway.

That afternoon Ben came over. Mom and me and Ben— we sat in a circle on the floor, and we set our Jupiter in the middle. Could she have known? Because she came to each of us one by one. We stroked her and told her how much we loved her, and we said thank you to her, and then we snipped a piece of her hair, the white spot on her back, and that's when I knew she would really be gone.

Dan drove us to Dr. Mary's office. He stood respectfully aside, because this was our good-bye. My mother held Jupiter on her lap and told her what a good dog she had been. My mother was crying and so was I, and Ben, too. See, she was one of us. Three and a half. Our little beloved. We had her favorite blankie, and Rabbit. My mother held her and stroked her and spoke softly to her, and Ben looked into her eyes, and we were there by her side as she had always been at ours when Dr. Mary slipped in the needle and when Jupiter left us.

chapter
twenty-eight

Dear Janssen—

The Worst Things About Dogs:

    1. They die.
    2. They die.
    3. They die.

Love always,

Cricket

chapter
twenty-nine

We were heartsick, of course. Some people think sorrow and pain over dogs is silly. But they don't understand what it means to love them deeply, they don't know all the corners of your life that a dog gets in. There's no rightful place for the sadness. Somehow the grief is supposed to be wrong or embarrassing.

But why wouldn't the loss be as true as it feels? Why wouldn't we grieve her? A dog is there, always. Ours was. She was there, for us and with us, when we suffered and when we celebrated. She was there, part of us, when we were just making breakfast or cracking jokes or falling asleep. She joined us just as we were starting a new life together, and she left us just when that particular life was ending. We were family.

"I keep hearing her everywhere," my mother said.

I knew what she meant. We took Jupiter's collar off after

she died. Her jingle. It sat on the mantel next to a picture of her, and if you gave it a shake, it would sound like she was still here, trotting around and checking things out. But you didn't have to shake that collar to hear her. I heard her in my head constantly. I kept seeing her too, trotting around the corner or barging through the bathroom door. I wondered if her sound, and the sight of her, would get further and further away.

"I keep finding her hair. How can her hair be here but not her?" I said. I didn't get *dead*. I didn't understand dead one bit.

"I regret so many things," my mother said. She was sitting at our old kitchen table in our new house, her hands around a mug I had made in the second grade.

"Like what?"

"Back when she was younger, I kept her in the garage at night for a while, remember? Jon Jakes didn't want her getting into trouble. She wouldn't have gotten into trouble. Why did I let that happen? I put a rug out there, her pillow, but still. God, I wish she knew that I was sorry about that."

I put my arms around her shoulders.

"So many things you'd do different, if you really knew it was going to end," she said.

The doorbell rang. Cruiser ran to the door, barking madly as always, skidding on the polished floor. I made him sit. He was a mostly good boy, but, oh, it was hard to see only one crazy dog scrambling toward the door. I asked Cruiser once where Jupiter was. I whispered it into his soft, folded-over ear. Maybe it was another secret super-intelligence they had, some kind of knowing. Maybe he knew those answers but was keeping his little black lips shut on that one. Cruiser lay down, then rolled over on his side to show his butterscotch belly and his willingness to do what I asked.

"Stay," I said, and I answered the door.

And there he was. Right there. My very own Janssen Tucker.

He took me into his arms, and I cried.

"Why, Janssen?" I sobbed.

He tucked my hair behind my ear and kissed my tears. He had something in his hand. A stupid old chewed-up rawhide that had been left on our lawn. One of those long ones, rolled up like a newspaper. She loved those. The ends were gnawed and her teeth marks were embedded in it.

I invited him in. But he only shook his head. *Too hard,* he whispered. Too much love and missing. We stood on the porch of the new house and hugged. Janssen was familiar but new. He smelled the same, but had a shirt on I'd never seen before. After a while he said he'd better go, and I agreed. Cruiser was spying on us out the window.

Janssen was down the sidewalk before I called out to him.

Wait, I said.

He turned to look at me.

A dog traveled three thousand miles to return home again, I said.

Janssen Tucker, he nodded. *That's how the story goes,* he said. *You travel safely, Cricket. And come back soon.*

He left then. His same old car backed out of our new street, and his old, familiar arm waved to me in that new and unfamiliar shirt. He had my stories and I had his, and we both had our story together. Each story, good and bad, short or long, yes—they are each a line or a paragraph in our own life manuscript. At the end, a beautiful whole, where every sentence of every chapter fits. I believe my mother is right about that.

I watched Janssen's car drive off. The sun was shining down, and the day smelled grassy and warm, like summer. I waved good-bye to my very own Janssen Tucker, and then I put my arms around myself and watched the empty street where he once was. Then I went back inside to my family.

Why, Janssen? I had asked. But I think I knew.

The story, our real story is this: doomed, precious, imperfect love. Love, deep and endless and brave in the face of certain loss—through death and leavings and growing up and letting go. Love, *given over.* It's the tender pulse of every word and every line and every chapter. It's our story, and it's the place where our heart, no matter what, always finds home.

Jordan's life is pretty typical . . . until it isn't. Her new boyfriend is turning out to be a major jerk, and her father is seeing a married woman. Both relationships will implode, but only one will go down in a shower of violence.

Ruby's always been The Quiet Girl. Dating gorgeous, rich, thrill-seeking Travis Becker changes all of that. But Ruby is in over her head, and will become a stranger to everyone . . . including herself.

Cassie is in love, but she can't let her stepfather know. He's a beloved public figure, but a private nightmare whose manic phases and paranoia are getting worse. Cassie begins to fear for the safety of her boyfriend . . . and herself.

Jade struggles with panic disorder. Her boyfriend is a calming influence . . . until she learns that he's hiding a terrible secret. A secret that will force Jade to decide between what is right, and what *feels* right.

When a stranger leaves Indigo a 2.5-million-dollar tip, her life as she knew it is transformed. Indigo's sure the money won't change her . . . until the day she looks around and realizes everything that matters—including her boyfriend—is slipping away, and no amount of money can buy it all back.

As if it's not bad enough that Quinn is surrounded by women who have had their hearts broken, she's just been dumped. Tired of being taken for granted, Quinn joins forces with her sisters and sets out to get revenge on the worst heartbreaker of all.

Scarlet spends most of her time worrying about other people. So when her older sister comes home unexpectedly married and pregnant, Scarlet has a new person to worry about. But all of her good intentions are shattered when the unthinkable happens: She falls for her sister's husband.

Clara's relationship with Christian is intense from the start, and like nothing she's ever experienced before. But what starts as devotion quickly becomes obsession, and it's almost too late before Clara realizes how far gone Christian is—and what he's willing to do to make her stay.